DEADLY TRUTHS

Kiss Her Goodbye #3

REBECCA ROYCE

FOREWORD

Dearest Reader,

I asked you to take this trip with me and Everly. Thank you for doing it. I promised you a happy ending. Let's get there... together.

With love,
RR

PREFACE

"These violent delights have violent ends, And in their triumph die; like fire and powder,
   Which, as they kiss, consume:"

— William Shakespeare, Romeo and Juliet

I looked down at my burner phone, hoping it was time for me to get off work, and was utterly disappointed to see it was only five minutes since the last time I'd checked, which meant I had another three hours to go before my shift was over. Fortunately, we weren't too busy tonight. It was officially off-season—not that *Yodel's* was ever overly busy during the so-called on season, either. We were a local bar in a town of college oriented bars. Our clientele didn't wane and wax with the comings and goings of coeds.

I liked it that way. For now, it suited my needs. Gene Yodel paid me in cash and didn't ask me questions. He liked that I showed up on time and made a mean old fashioned. I liked that he never inquired about anything personal and left me the fuck alone.

I'd never frequented dive bars before I'd lost everything and had to figure out what to do with the time I had before some crazy assassin got a hard on for killing me. I used to think I was trendy and therefore had to seek out sex partners and expensive drinks in places where the girls laughed too loud for the sake of attention and the men didn't have to try too hard to get into the women's pants as long as they had a college degree heading their way in the near future. I'd put up with a lot of asshats coming into my bed because they had seemed like the right kind of guy.

The illusion of pedigree. The illusion of safety. All of it was smoke and mirrors. Ants traipsing down sidewalks not knowing they were about to be squished. Eighteen months since I'd woken up in Judson's Vermont-based hunting lodge, and I preferred the humming quiet of a dive bar now.

In movies, they would have called this place rough. The director would have the cinematographer scan the room, focusing on the peeling wood and the stools with the worn material on the seats. Old would have equaled bad. I knew better now. Dive bars had the same clientele all the time. Regulars who came in night after night, drank their drinks, talked their truths, and got the fuck on with it. They didn't like people coming in and messing with the bar staff since they actually wanted to see the same faces over and over.

And the bar staff didn't like to see outsiders coming in to screw with their regulars.

That was how I knew the asshole who'd stumbled in off the street, talking too loud with his Midwestern accent and his wallet hanging out of the back pocket of his jeans, was about to get punched in the face for spending too much time trying to get in Molly Dane's pants. She wasn't interested.

I watched the scene with only a modicum of interest. Scott and Joe Prentis, brothers who owned a local plumbing shop, were going to interfere any second. It was better they did it than me. They'd punch the asshole out. He'd wake up with a headache, maybe in a jail cell if Gene felt like calling the cops.

If I interfered, I was going to take the screwdriver that was under the cash register for those times the register broke and I had to jam it open, and I was going to shove it straight into the Midwestern guy's eye socket. He'd stumble forward before I'd haul him up onto the bar to let him bleed to death, watching as his brain took the last seconds of life to realize he was about to die. In this dive bar. Because the bartender stabbed him in the eye.

That was why it was better that I not do one thing, not even utter a word.

The world spun, but I wasn't normal. Would never be that again. The days of my functioning on all cylinders, of going about my business without needing to constantly control myself from hurting someone, yeah...I'd kissed them goodbye.

My sanity was spread out in multiple places, each location taking a little bit of me and giving nothing back. Vermont. St. Croix. Florida. New Orleans. Boston. Seattle. Montana. San Diego. Ben's basement.

Piece-by-piece, location-by-location, I'd slowly lost my mind. The Alliance took everything from me and didn't even leave me myself in the end. All I had now was this contorted, forever altered, version of me.

"You okay?" Gene asked me as he walked past, heading for the other side of the bar. His eyes were on the same scene I pretended to ignore.

I smiled at him. "Sure. Never better."

I was such a good liar. It was really too bad I couldn't fool myself.

He nodded. "Good. Didn't you graduate last week?"

"I did." The less said about this the better. I wasn't even sure why I'd wasted my time or my money finishing that degree I'd never use. I'd had two requirements left and a paper to write for a class I'd never think about again. That was all I'd needed to be part of the pedigree people, to be part of the phony world. I'd finished it because when I'd come back home after killing my father and leaving the

Letters standing in a hotel room filled with blood to clean up, I hadn't known what the heck else to do.

Finishing my college degree had at least seemed productive while I'd packed up my childhood home and sold it.

It had given me something to do every day before I'd found this place and decided to set myself up to disappear. Small things occurred to me now that hadn't then. Someone filed a death certificate on my father that allowed me to inherit the house, fast, so I could sell it. Things that normally took months and months of paperwork hadn't for me. Plus, the death certificate itself hadn't said "shot to death by daughter" as the cause of death. No, my father had a good old-fashioned heart attack as far as the authorities were concerned. A clean, no fuss no muss heart attack.

No need for anyone to investigate my role in it. His body had come home to my house—in ashes—the day after the death certificate arrived by mail, tucked inside a nondescript black urn with his initials carved on the outside.

I kept him now in the back of my closet, between my brown boots and a pair of sneakers I needed to replace. The fact my clothes arrived the day after told me that the Alliance boys... my Letters... were taking care of closing up my unfinished business with them. I'd told them to leave me alone and they were.

No one arrived to beg me back. I wasn't hiding. Not yet. They could have found me if they wanted me. No, they'd respected my wishes to leave me alone. I only regretted that every fourth or fifth day and in the scheme of things, I still thought I'd been right.

It was lonely to not have anyone I could tell the truth to, ever.

"Everly, if you want to go full time while you look for work, I can do that for you." Gene patted me on the back.

"But you'll have to go on the books. I can't pay you that much in cash every week."

That was kind of him, which threw me for a loop. It took a beat, but I recovered my center. Why was he being nice to me? That wasn't normal and therefore was suspect. My whole life was like that. Anyone could be Alliance, and I might encounter them anywhere. These people were the definition of scary. Gene absolutely could have been Alliance this whole time, just waiting for an order to kill me.

I'd ended Ben, my father, several other Alliance members who'd come after me in the hotel and Derrick's hospital room. There would be revenge for that. I was certain of it. Even if they served it to me cold.

I might have to move up my plans and leave sooner. A change in behavior might have meant Gene was coming after me, lulling me into a sense of security to take me out.

Or it might have meant he just wanted to fuck me.

Or it might have meant nothing at all.

That was the problem with life and why I had to get off the grid and simplify. If I didn't see people, they couldn't turn around and betray me.

"Everly?" Gene still waited for my response.

I smiled. I could fool them all with my grin; I could slaughter them all in my sleep and keep smiling about it. These were new truths for my life. "Let me think about it?"

He nodded. "Sure. Tell me whenever. Bob wants another beer."

I poured Bob his beer. While we made the standard drinks here, the classic old fashioneds and martinis, this wasn't a place to find an IPA. The beers were simple. I liked that about it. I didn't have to think too hard to function here which left me time to consider the motives of every person around me, all the time.

The TV blared in the corner and our local stock broker cried out, putting his head down on his hands. I didn't have to look to know what the problem was. The financial markets were in chaos. Things were up and down from one second to another. Savings were made and lost before people could get their money out. I'd never seen anything like it and neither had the television commentators who were on twenty-four-seven talking about it.

Our bar had been a little more filled than usual with everyone needing a drink. I had an account Warden managed, where I'd stuck the money from the sale of my house when it had closed. I never looked in there.

It didn't feel like mine. I hadn't earned any of it, and the portion from the sale of my house constituted blood money as far as I was concerned. I'd killed my father to get that money. I rubbed my arms. There were certain images I could never get out of my head. My father, lying dead on the floor, sent there by me, that was one of them.

The door to the bar opened and closed. No one called out greetings so I lifted my head to see who it was. The regulars tended to say hello to their crew of nightly visitors.

My heart skipped a beat, and I tried to steel my face but likely failed considering how seeing the newest patron enter threw me into an internal tailspin.

Warden White walked to the bar and sat at the end of it. He'd met my gaze the second I'd looked up and continued to hold it. He hadn't said a word, no greeting of hello, he simply waited on the worn stool to be recognized by either me or Gene—whoever got to him first.

I made myself breathe.

The markets were crashing and Warden White wandered into my dive bar. That couldn't be coincidence.

I touched Gene's arm. "The new guy is an old friend of mine. I'll get him."

Gene nodded. "First one of those to come in here for you."

"I guess I don't have that many friends."

I walked to Warden. "What can I get you?"

He tilted his head slightly. "Jack Daniels. Neat."

I nodded. This was strange. Had we really just interacted like that? I poured his drink and tried to pretend that hearing the low cadence of his voice didn't make me go mushy inside. I'd had some incredibly intimate, sexual experiences with that man. At first, I hadn't thought him handsome but that was before I'd really started to look at him. There was nothing about Warden that wasn't intense. His nose was slightly too big, his eyes were such dark brown they were nearly black, and his hair was the same color. He always had a beard. His clothes were expensive, always perfectly tailored, and his watch probably cost more than the gross national income of some small, developing nations.

The world markets were in upheaval and Warden ordered whiskey in my dive bar.

I handed him the glass and waited. He took a long pull and then another. I watched his lips on the glass. Fuck. He was so sexy.

I'd always liked sex—needed it—since I'd discovered the joys of it as a teenager. Most of it was pretty mediocre, but the Letters had all been able to make me come. W once in tandem with K on W's expensive couch in his mega mansion in San Diego.

Warden took a second long sip of the amber liquid.

It had been too long since I'd had sex. I'd not engaged in any since my time with Judson in Warden's guestroom. I'd thought about going home with one of my classmates who'd propositioned me two months before. But when I'd come out of the bathroom, he'd been gone, and he'd never spoken to me again except to say he'd changed his mind and decided in that moment to get back with his ex. I'd actually been hugely relieved. The time it had taken me to pee had made me rethink the whole thing. I'd been coming out to tell him I needed to not have sex with him. I wasn't over my exes either.

Clearly, I should have looked for another partner if I was this obsessed.

He finished his drink and slid it to me. "Another one, please."

I took the glass, giving him a generous pour, and placed it in front of him again. We hadn't said a word that mattered yet and maybe he wasn't going to. Maybe this was some kind of sick game where he'd come in, drink, and leave without doing anything other than throwing my equilibrium into a tailspin.

I turned back to my other customers, making conversation with them and deliberately not looking at Warden. I left him alone for ten minutes. If he wanted my attention, he could ask for it.

Finally, I returned to him and his empty glass. He pushed it forward again. "Another one."

I lifted my eyebrows. "Are you driving?"

I didn't ask my customers questions like that, not usually. I would sometimes order someone a cab or help them use their phones to get a rideshare. Most of the time, I existed in a mind-my-own-business mentality. Gene was always here. He could handle the patrons of his bar and their sobriety issues.

Or not.

Warden shook his head. "No."

I poured him another drink as my temper flared. Life was too short for this kind of crap. "What are you doing here, Warden?"

His lips quirked like he might smile, and then he rethought the idea. "You graduated last week."

That explained nothing. "Yes. And?"

He sipped his drink. "I watched four and a half hours of a feed of that graduation and you never walked across the stage." Warden swallowed the rest of his whiskey and set the glass down on the bar with a loud clank. "Why didn't you go to your graduation?"

Was he serious? This was how he was going to answer me when I asked him what he was doing here? I didn't have to answer. I walked away, serving others, counting the cash in the register and answering the phone for Gene once.

My fingers tingled and my jaw clenched. He hadn't moved, left, or done anything but sit there and wait. I finally stormed over to him, leaning onto the bar so that our faces were close. "I didn't go because I don't like the idea of being exposed, walking across a stage like that where anyone could take a shot at me, and because I don't have a single person in the world who would have been in the audience to watch me do that walk, so why bother? They mail you your diploma if you don't go."

I poured him another drink. If he didn't want it, I'd take it, and I never drank when I worked. "What are you doing here? And why were you watching my college graduation?"

He sipped for a minute before he answered me. "I'm here because I wanted to know why you didn't walk." He slurred a little bit. The whiskey must have finally hit. Four drinks... maybe more like five considering how much I'd poured him... was his limit. I wasn't going to pour him anymore. "And to congratulate you. And to give you your gift. I watched because I wanted to."

Damn him. I looked away. "Warden, you can't give me a gift. You shouldn't be here at all."

"Screw that." He set a bill on the counter, much more than the drinks cost, before he pulled a small black box out of his pocket and placed it on the bar next to the hundred.

"Throw it out if you don't want it. I'll leave."

He'd told me he wasn't going to drive. "Where are you going and how are you getting there?"

Warden didn't answer me as he stumbled out the door.

I sucked in a long breath. It physically pained me to see him, but it wrecked me to watch him leave. I grabbed the black box, still not sure what was inside, and swung around to Gene. "I have to go."

He waved his hand. "I can see that. Go. Make it up to me tomorrow."

I rushed after my W. That was what he was. I didn't forgive him, could probably not get over all the things that had happened, but that didn't make him any less mine. I couldn't watch him stumble out the door to who knew where.

"Warden." I reached him before he turned the corner. "Where are you going?" He stared at me for a long second, and it was instinct that had me grabbing him around the waist before he fell. "You had a lot more to drink than what I gave you, didn't you? Come on. I'll get you wherever you're staying. My car is over there."

"No, it's not." He shook his head. "Your car is in front of the bar."

Did he not think I knew where I parked? I managed to get him into my father's four-door sedan. The only thing I'd kept from him as it was useful and I'd needed a car. I would leave it here when I left. I didn't intend to ever find out what happened to it.

Warden got in the passenger side, and in the thirty seconds it took me to get around the other side of the car, he was snoring with his head against the window. I laughed, couldn't help myself. This was lunacy.

"Warden." I shook his arm gently. "I don't know where you're staying."

His eyes opened to slits. "A house, gorgeous." Having

delivered that nothing statement, his head flapped back down to the window and he snored again.

I sighed. Okay. Surely somewhere there would be written down the address of his hotel or the house he rented. I felt around in his jacket for his wallet, but I didn't find anything, and I wasn't going into his pants to check. That would have been too much. I didn't have permission to touch him there and drunk guy was the same as drunk girl as far as I was concerned. The answer needed to be an assumed no.

We could stay in this car until he sobered enough to tell me or we could go to my apartment. I didn't feel like sitting in a parked car until possibly tomorrow at lunchtime, depending on how long this took for him to sleep off.

Fortunately, I lived in a ground floor apartment. Much as I might have liked the safety of an apartment on an upper floor, I liked the idea of being able to run out and escape any time I wanted even better. I'd only looked at ground floor options.

Warden managed to rouse himself enough to walk with me inside. I didn't own a couch. Everything here was disposable. All would be left behind when I vanished. It hadn't seemed like a good idea to waste money on something I wouldn't use.

It looked like Warden was sleeping in my bed.

He lay back, his eyes still the glossy, unfocused gaze of a man truly out of it. W lifted his hand and managed to touch the side of my face as I took off his shoes. "You took them away."

"Took what away?" I didn't know if he'd answer me, if he'd even know we were having a conversation or if he was basically dreaming.

"Your eyes. You took them away from me. They haunt me."

In the seconds it took me to think of something to say, he

was out cold again. I sighed. Warden White was in my bed six months after I'd told him and the other Letters to leave me alone and let me go.

I turned him onto his side and grabbed the garbage can, just in case he needed it. When I finally fussed over him enough, I climbed in next to him. I thought I'd probably not be able to get to sleep because he was in my bed but that wasn't the case at all. Instead, it was the morning rays and the sounds of his deep breathing that roused me. I hadn't even dreamed as far as I could remember.

I'd sprawled out over his chest in my sleep and he now rested on his back, one arm over his head. One or both of us kicked the covers off, which didn't surprise me at all. It was hot in my apartment. The whole building was old and the small window AC units weren't great for a Louisiana summer. The two of us sleeping so close to each other would have only added to the problem.

I climbed out of the bed and made my way into the bathroom to shower, half expecting him to be gone when I came out. He'd floated back into my life, not making any sense, and he might disappear like that, too. But Warden was still out of it when I left the bathroom showered, and fresh, which meant it might be lunchtime before he roused.

That was okay. I had plans to make. I'd stepped into my small closet when he let out a long sigh and I heard the bed creak. The sigh was followed by more of a moan and then a groan. Yeah... I bet his head hurt. Badly.

Still in my pink bathrobe, I regarded him from the closet.

He looked around, confusion coloring his features, before he spotted me and must have realized where he was. "Hi."

"Hi, yourself." I marched over and sat next to him on the bed so I could get the painkillers out of my bedside drawer. He was going to need them. "How much had you drunk before you got into the bar?"

"It wasn't booze that was my undoing last night." He sighed. "Let me take these and I'll... explain."

I cleared my throat. "That sounds ominous."

He held his head in his hands. "I just need a minute."

"I'll go make us something to eat." I wasn't running from the room. I refused to consider the idea. Things were different for me than they were six months ago. Just because Warden busted his way into my bar didn't mean I had to fall back into my old ways of constantly doing things on their timetable. I was hungry so I would eat. *Now*.

If I walked a little fast, I just hoped he didn't notice.

2

Plato once said that necessity was the mother of invention. For me, that had proven to be true for cooking. Wanting to live off my cash, and not the money the Letters helped me with or my father's hidden millions, meant I cooked a lot more than I ate out. I didn't have expensive food in the house, but I did have enough eggs to feed us.

I scrambled them up. It was the only way I could cook an egg. I'd destroyed too many good ones trying to learn how to do it over easy one day. Simplicity was the only way I could function. Warden walked out of my bedroom, shirtless.

I almost spilled the eggs all over the floor. At first, I couldn't see anything but the fact that he was shirtless and beautiful. But that quickly faded as my gaze zeroed in to the massive wound on his right shoulder.

That hadn't been there before.

"What happened to you?" I strode over to him and almost touched it before I thought better of it. Scars hurt. I knew better than most. "Warden?"

He held up a bottle of pills. "I'm going to take these

instead of the ones you gave me. They work a bit better but only a little bit."

"Warden?" He wasn't going to deflect this.

"I got shot. About three weeks ago. It really sucked."

My body went cold. I touched his arm, right below where he'd been hurt. "You got shot? Who shot you?"

"I decided I was out. When you were done I was done. I walked away. You wanted space. I gave it to you. I had a date in mind for when I would reach out and see if you were ready to see me again. To let me... well, there's no way to make it up to you, Everly. But to see me again. To let me try to make you happy. They didn't want me to leave. If I hadn't happened to be armed right at that moment I'd have been dead. They got a shot in but so did I."

I hugged him to me tightly. "Warden." I didn't know why I kept saying his name, but I did. He'd been hurt, could have died, and I'd have had no idea. "Who ordered this hit on you? Judson?"

"No. Judson hates me but he's gone as missing as the rest of us. This is the new Alliance. It's not the gentler, friendlier Alliance Judson dreamed of. They want me dead because I know where Marcus Petrone hides all of his money. The good news is he thinks I'm dead. He's the only one from the original crew still alive. I let him think I was dead."

I squeezed him tighter. "Warden." I really had to come up with something else to say. "Are you okay?"

"Yes and no. Things could have been a lot worse. I could be dead. But right now the feeling in the tips of my fingers are coming and going. They still work, obviously." He stretched his hand to show me. "But I keep losing feeling in some of my fingers. When it comes back on, it feels like a rat has bitten me. It's weird. And I shouldn't have been drinking at all on the meds. But poor choice."

I touched his hand. "Can you feel that?"

"Right now I can." He brought my hand to his lips, and he kissed it. "I know you said stay away, but the achievement had to be recognized. You graduated. That's huge. You did have someone watching."

His body slightly shook. Okay, Warden was not okay. "What do the doctors say?"

"I haven't really been able to see the right ones. I'm dead, remember?" That would be a problem and I didn't like it. "You're not at risk. They're not looking for me on satellite anymore. I'm dead."

I had to think but I also had to hug him. He'd been shot. I pulled him against me, and I held on for a second as I tried to still my racing heart. If one of the Letters were dead, I'd really have no idea. Going off the grid would mean even less contact.

"I'm going to be okay." Warden spoke to the top of my head, his mouth pressing down on my hair. "Did you like the car?"

Car? I lifted my head. "What car?"

He blinked rapidly. "The car I gave you for your graduation. I did give it to you, right?"

I stepped away. "You handed me a box. I didn't open it. You bought me a car?" I'd left the box on the counter and opened it now. Two sets of car keys and a picture of a black SUV were inside the box. It was beautiful, but it was way too much. "Warden, this was not... necessary. Why did you do this?"

"Because I love you, too."

I set down the box and stared up at him. "What?"

"Before you left, you told us in the hotel room that you loved us. None of us answered. There was so much going on and... I should have told you that I loved you, too. I do. I love you, too. You graduated from college. I wanted to get you something you could use on your going off the grid plan."

How did he know that? "What gave me away?"

"The working for cash, the not having stuff things. You haven't looked in your bank account since you deposited your inheritance and paid tuition. Not a glance. It tells me you're doing something else." He looked around. "You're in a small one bedroom with no furniture and you're a multi-millionaire. You're getting ready to go. Take that car." He cleared his throat. "And me."

If he were Trace, I'd think he was manipulating me. But this was Warden. He only dealt in serious. "You came to me because you're hurt and you wanted to be with someone you loved who loves you, too. I'm so angry at you Warden, at all of you, but I do love you. That was real. Fucked up but real." I pressed my forehead against his chest. "You didn't have to bring me a car to get me to take care of you, to be here for you. How did you even pay for it? You're dead."

He winced. "I have bail out money all over the place."

"And you used some of that to buy me a car?" I shook my head. "Thank you. But you could have shown up and said, Everly, I'm hurt, and I love you."

He visibly swallowed. "It's not easy for me to be needy."

I actually understood that perfectly. "Go sit down." I nodded toward my tiny table. "I'm going to feed you and then we're going to figure some things out."

He nodded but he didn't move. I leaned up and kissed him. It was instinct, and I didn't overthink it. Warden had clearly been through hell. My back was straight and anger made me clench my jaw. I didn't want to be around the Alliance. I didn't want anything to do with that. But how dare anyone come after what was mine?

I wasn't sure I one hundred percent understood my own feelings. I could work it out later.

Warden kissed me back. His lips were the same. I recognized him, the feel of him, the way he tasted. I pulled back to look at him, both of us panting, and it was just from a kiss. My nipples hardened. I could have lost my head right now and push him down on the floor, fucking him until we were both somewhere in oblivion. I wasn't going to do that.

Somehow.

I stepped back. "Go sit down. Eggs."

He nodded. "Okay."

I spooned eggs on to the plate and tried to make myself think. I had to... function. Warden's presence was a giant elephant in the room and taking up all the space in my brain. I brought him the eggs and set them down in front of him. "They're not going to be wonderful, but they're not awful either."

He furrowed his brow. "Are you going to eat?"

"What? Oh. Yes. I am." I jumped up before I grabbed myself a plate and returned to the table. I sat back down and Warden picked up his fork.

He smiled as he ate the eggs. "That was an apt description of them. Thanks for the pretty good eggs."

I laughed, nearly choking. "You're welcome. Warden, why can't you go to Judson? I think he would help you."

He shook his head. "Somewhere along the lines in the years we plotted together, the five of us stopped trusting each other. When you spend all your time with other people showing just how awful, just how completely untrustworthy you can be to the rest of the world, there comes a threshold upon which you can't go back. They know I'm an accomplished liar, a ruthless person, and I know they would sell me to the highest bidder if it reached some kind of agenda for them."

I touched his hand, squeezing it. "Would you do that to them?"

He seemed to consider my question for a long moment. Sweat had broken out on his brow so he either was in a lot of pain or the medicine he was taking had that effect on him. Of course, he might have been hot because the apartment was and I'd just sort of adjusted during the day when I wasn't trying to sleep.

Finally, he spoke. "I wouldn't. I know that the others had plans in place, but I always sort of took it for granted that to save myself I could take them out financially. I never wanted to do that. I wouldn't have, unless they struck first."

"So maybe they feel that way, too. Maybe there's an assumption of mistrust that isn't real?" I really didn't know. This was one of the things that had exhausted me when I hung out with them all in a large group. Where was their loyalty, and if they couldn't be loyal to each other was there any chance of them having that sort of feeling for me?

He set down his fork. "I really don't know, gorgeous. You know if I was up to par, I'd be all over you right now."

I linked my foot with his under the table. "Judson is loyal to me."

As I spoke the words, I realized they were true. He absolutely was. His feelings might not be the same as Warden's. He might have been pissed and never wanted to see me again. I wouldn't blame him for that. I'd announced I was done with all of them. He was entitled to be done with me.

But he wouldn't hurt me. I was sure of that. Judson had his own morality, his own ethics. They didn't necessarily match the rest of the worlds. Even knowing that, I was sure Judson would help me if I asked him to.

If for no other reason than he was sorry I'd ended up in that basement.

"I need to go for a run." I could think better after I exercised. I'd started doing it again a month after I'd returned here. If I ever had clarity, it was after I'd moved my body to the point of exhaustion. "I'll run to work." That would be a good five-mile exertion. "And get the car you bought me. Where did you park it?"

He pointed to the box. "That's why I left you the picture. So you'd know which one it was. Right in front of the bar. I wasn't sure if I was going to just walk in, hand you the box, and leave."

"Instead you stayed and drank on pain meds that then made you stumble around so you might have hurt yourself more? Or left yourself vulnerable if there was someone looking for you?"

Warden shrugged and then winced. "Not my smartest move."

It turned out Warden White didn't do pain or neediness very well. I kissed his chin. "Maybe take a nap. You're three weeks from taking a bullet."

"I'm trying really hard to not insist I drive you in your car to the new car and we both drive back together. I want to protect you, Everly. I'm always going to want that."

I sighed. "I'm not a child. I don't need protection. I did when I first got out of Ben's basement, but I've lived on my own for six months now. I'm fine to run. You'll just have to get used to it if you're staying here."

He tilted his head. "I'm not leaving unless you kick me out."

"Then don't do anything to piss me off, I guess." I winked at him. I was really only half kidding. I could love a person and also want them to leave me alone. These were all gifts from Ben and his basement. I wasn't sure I could love exactly the right way for most people anymore. Maybe that was how W could love, too. We cared about each other but we were really pretty fucked up, too.

Halfway through my run, I'd decided we had to get in touch with Judson. There was no question about it. He'd know someone Warden could see and still be safe. The problem was how to do that. I didn't have my phone anymore. I'd use Warden's and hopefully Jud wouldn't let me down.

By the time I'd gotten to the car, I'd changed my mind. We weren't going to call, we were going to show up in Boston. It would be a lot harder for Jud to decide to not help Warden in person than it would be over the phone.

Why was I even worrying about this? It would never have occurred to me that Judson wouldn't help until Warden put that idea in my head. So much for my mental clarity.

"Ms. Marrs." A man I'd never seen before said my name. He came out of nowhere, and I wondered if he'd been standing in the shadows waiting for me. I had a knife taped to my back, I never went anywhere without it. I didn't like carrying a gun. I'd shot my father without meaning to. With a knife, I had to look before I struck.

I put my hands on my hips. "Who are you?"

"That doesn't matter."

I shook my head. "Listen, buddy. I don't talk to nameless assholes who come out of nowhere on the street. You're going to want to back off."

The knife right into his eye. Lately, I did seem to be obsessed with eye sockets, but I could get him before he'd be able to stop me. He'd be down before he could touch me.

"Ms. Marrs, I'm here to give you a warning."

That was nice. I wasn't going to give him a warning before I took him down on the sidewalk. All I needed was a reason. I ignored the fact that I was pretty much wishing he would.

"So give it then."

"We have left you alone and will continue to do so as long as you don't interfere with Alliance business. There has been some movement lately and Marcus feels you may need a reminder that you..."

A motorcycle screeched to a stop in front of us, and we both jumped. I backed up, fast. A man jumped off the bike and strode toward us. I ran toward the car, my new keys in hand, but the rider wasn't interested in me. Instead, he pulled a bat off his back and swung once at the man delivering the warning. A strong hit to his side took him to the ground.

"Tell Marcus he should know better than to send anyone to speak to Everly. I thought I made myself clear."

Before he'd even spoken, I knew who the newcomer was. Derrick Norris. My D.

Derrick pounded on him again, this time in the gut. "I'm not going to kill you. You can't deliver my message if you're dead. Tell Marcus if he comes near Everly again, I'll serve his brains in a cocktail sauce to his girlfriend. I don't like having to repeat myself."

The man cried now; he screamed. For an Alliance member who presumably had been through the same training as everyone else, he was pretty wimpy.

I stormed forward, grabbing Derrick by the arm. "You can't do this on the street. There might be cameras."

He shook his head. "There aren't."

I pulled him with me to the car. "Come on. Let's get out of here in case someone sees. Can you leave the bike?"

"Sure." He jumped in the car with me. "Where did you get this car?"

"Warden gave it to me. It's really nice to see you, Derrick." Even if it was strangely normal to see him beating someone on the street with a baseball bat.

He grinned at me before he gaped. "Everly, Warden is dead."

"He's not. He's in my apartment. Injured, badly. Didn't get

the right help. I'm trying to figure out exactly what to do. But not dead."

Derrick shook his head. "When did he come to you? How did I miss it?"

"Hold on." I pulled the car onto the not busy street. I didn't know this car, I'd never had a new one since my father thought used cars were a better deal, and I wasn't entirely sure I knew all the ins and outs of driving it. Still, it was pretty much turn on and go with most cars, so I did just that until I'd traveled far enough to pull over.

I put my finger right in Derrick's gorgeous face. "You've been spying on me."

I didn't phrase it as a question; it wasn't one. Probably because of this, he didn't answer me. We sat there like that, me with my finger pointed right in Derrick's face and him saying nothing. Finally, I spoke again. "Even after I told you to leave me alone?"

"I was never going to leave you alone." He smirked at me. "What's more is you knew that, too. And don't act like you didn't. You wanted to pretend you were all on your own? Fine, go for it. But in your soul you knew better."

I hated being called on my bullshit. "Then you were clearly not very good at your spying if you missed Warden last night since he made a pretty big scene on the street when we were leaving."

"Last night, I did get caught up tracking Marcus. And you're right. I'm much better at striking and leaving than stealthily watching."

I shook my head. "I should be throwing your ass out of the car."

"You would be if you weren't happy to see me. You admitted as much. Can't take it back now." He sat back in the seat. "Fuck Warden for getting you this car. I could have bought you a car. Makes my gift seem like nothing."

I couldn't believe any of this. "You didn't have to buy me a gift."

He pulled a box out of his pocket. It was wrapped in silver wrapping paper. "I'm going to make you wait until we get back to your place to open it."

I narrowed my eyes. "Just to torture me."

"Yes."

A disturbing thought dawned on me. "Derrick, did you bug my apartment?"

"I didn't. That doesn't mean someone else didn't. I have no need for that kind of surveillance but I'd be happy to look when we get there. Warden's probably already checked it out."

"No." I pulled the car back onto the street. "He's very injured. Got shot three weeks ago. He's in bad shape. He needs a doctor we can trust not to out him. That's why he's here, really. He needed me." And I hated the part inside of me that longed for just that kind of relationship. It was nice to be needed, particularly when I'd thought I was alone and wanted it that way. I was such a constant lesson in stark contrasts, and I didn't know that I could ever be fixed, not really.

I didn't know if I wanted to be, which was more important. I'd gotten very comfortable in my constant level of fucked up.

"I've been shot. That's no fun. I'll go check him out. And... even though he's vanished and not involving himself in anything... Judson would be the person to ask. I don't think he'd betray Warden."

I drummed my fingers on the steering wheel. "He wouldn't betray me. I'd decided on my run over that I'd contact him."

"You're right on that. But let's just go to him. Let's not

give him the chance to not pick up or be passive aggressive. We'll take my plane, and we'll go to him with Warden."

It was nice to have someone to talk to about this. "Thank you, Derrick."

"I need you, too. Just so you know. Warden might be in crisis but don't ever think he was the only one who needed you. I do. Every day. To function."

Sometimes it was scary how easily Derrick seemed to be able to read my most private thoughts. It must have been that his crazy matched my crazy.

He smirked, and I knew he was going to say something on the verge of being shitty. "Besides, you told me you loved me. Can't take that back."

I barely remembered throwing that out there to all of them the day I killed my father. It seemed none of them were suffering from the same slight lapses in memory.

As we pulled into my complex and I parked the car, I turned on him one more time. "That time with the guy I was going to go to bed with? Did you get involved in that?"

Derrick lifted his lids slightly. It was so ridiculously sexy, and I hated him a little bit for it. "You're lucky you didn't get that boy killed, Everly. There are four people in the world I share you with. You told us to go away. We didn't. That's the problem with having Alliance men in your life. We don't take directions really well. It's okay. I forgive you."

I jumped out of the car, and he did the same. "You forgive me? I'm not asking for your forgiveness. Are you telling me you've been monogamous?"

"Since the moment I saw you. Can't speak for the others but I can almost guarantee it. I just helped you to stay that way, too."

I poked him in the chest. "You're a famous baseball player. You can't go around threatening people and beating people on the street. You're going to get caught."

He took my finger and brought it to his lips before he bit down on it—not gently. I yelped but didn't pull back. I liked it. "Haven't so far."

"Don't be smug. That's not sexy."

His smile was ridiculously cute. "You don't really think that."

I finally pulled my hand back. "Unless you suddenly picked up a career in reading people's minds you can knock it off pretending you know what I'm thinking."

The trouble was that it was apparent he really did. Derrick was always astute and he'd had months to watch me, and I'd let him, not even considering he might be, not allowing myself to do that. I shouldn't have liked how stalkery he could be; I shouldn't have desired him after he'd kidnapped me, spied on me. The trouble with Derrick—with all of them, actually—was that they were exactly what I shouldn't want and absolutely did.

That was just another example of how screwed up I'd let them make me. And I had no doubt I'd done just that.

3

Warden was awake when I got back with Derrick. Lying across my bed, shirtless, his scar on display for view, he lifted his head, seeing Derrick for the first time.

"Look who I found." I motioned toward Derrick. "Apparently he's on a long-term visit and never dropped in to say hello."

Warden rose slowly. "Derrick."

"Warden. That doesn't look good." He pointed to the red, raw scar that was barely covered by a bandage that had started to fall off. "And I've been shot. Someone didn't do right by you. Glad to see you're not dead."

They had an awkward exchange of nodding heads. I walked over to Warden, placing my arm around his waist. "So you see what I mean about needing help?"

"I do." He held up his phone. "Getting my plane."

Warden winced. "Must be nice to still have one of those. We're settled on going to Judson, then? I'm fairly certain he washed his hands of us all."

"Jud doesn't get to write me off. I'm family." The grin

Derrick gave Warden was almost shark-like. "What do we need to pack for you?"

Warden sighed. "I have the clothes on my back. I rented a house near here, but I left only a shirt and pants in it. I had to take off, go dark the second I left the underground hospital. I didn't know how long I'd have until the doctor there sold me out to the highest bidder."

"It doesn't seem he did. I thought you were dead. We'll leave the clothes. Get you some more in Boston. Everly was just approached by one of Marcus' men. I want out of here. Get your bail out bag, babe."

I stared at him. "Did you call me babe?"

"Not good?"

I shook my head slowly. "Not good."

"Right, well, get your bag anyway."

I touched his arm. "You're assuming I have one?"

"You've been plotting to go off the grid for six months. Yes, you have a bail out bag. I'm certain of it. Don't get it if you don't want to. I can buy you whatever you need and…"

"No," I interrupted him. I was abso-fucking-lutely not going back to having to buy clothes wherever I landed. I did have a bail out bag. It included almost all the cash I'd earned. I supposed I was leaving Gene in a bind, but he'd be okay. Some other girl would come through the door needing a job and be glad for the full-time work.

Warden put on a shirt, wincing when the material touched his skin. He reached out, rubbing the back of my neck. "How did you like the car?"

"It's gorgeous. Funny to say about a vehicle, but it is so pretty. Seriously." A thought dawned on me. "I'm leaving it here."

Derrick rolled his eyes. "That's what parking places are for. It'll be here when you get back, or I'll have it brought to you wherever we are. Go get your bag."

He was really being pushy which could only mean he was concerned. He'd beaten that man up on the street but left him alive. That could mean retaliation. I went to grab the bag I kept under my kitchen sink and returned with it a second later.

"I'm ready to go."

"Beautiful and ready in under two minutes." Warden grinned. "Everly puts all other women to shame."

I patted him on his good shoulder. "Yeah. Yeah. Yeah. Flattery will get you everywhere."

He threw back his head to laugh but then groaned. The movements must have hurt. I winced on his behalf.

Derrick handed me the gift box. "You can take mine with you."

Warden side-eyed him. "Dude, I bought her a car. I don't care what's in that box. Unless you stole her the crown jewels, you're not winning this."

"I'm not a competition." I took the box from him. "I'm overwhelmed that either of you thought to do this at all. Thank you. I was feeling very alone in the world since I shot my father and left."

I spoke the words, and yet they moved through me like someone else had said them, as though I was hearing them instead of speaking them. My body went cold.

Warden put his hand on my back, rubbing in small circles. "You don't say that aloud very much, do you? Maybe you don't say it at all. Who would you say it to?"

Derrick leaned over and kissed my cheek. "I'd like to talk to you about that. Sometime. Not now. Because we have to go. But maybe on the plane."

I shook my head, opening the gift. I didn't want to talk to him about it. What was there to say? I hadn't looked. I'd pointed and fired. Boom. I'd been cocky because once I'd been lucky to take two assassins by surprise because I wasn't totally incompetent as they must have expected me to be, and the second time because I'd had Derrick there to help me.

The end was because I was a jackass. I'd killed my father. He was a bad man who had my mother killed and yet living with the idea of patricide wasn't something I could imagine anyone wanted to face, even when their father sucked.

I gasped. Derrick had bought me a diamond necklace. I stared at it. I'd never seen anything like it, and I'd certainly never imagined holding in my fingers anything as expensive. I opened and closed my mouth.

"Note to self, the woman likes diamonds." Warden shook his head. "Nice one, Derrick. It's classic. How many diamonds are on that thing?"

Derrick didn't take his gaze off me. "One hundred and five."

I almost dropped it. "What?"

Warden grinned. "Sweet. You win. This time. But as soon as I'm not dead I'm going to consider it a challenge."

Derrick's whole face brightened up. "Oh, it's on."

"Boys." I was finding it hard to breathe. "I can't have this. I can't even look at this. I'm not a diamond girl or a fancy car girl. I'm more like... I like expensive dinners, that's my one indulgence, and I can even do without that. I'm not this person."

Derrick kissed my lips gently. "Happy graduation, Everly. Let's put it on."

"I'm in my running pants and my t-shirt. I'm sweating. This doesn't go with that."

"Evs." He was back to using that nickname. I seriously preferred it to babe. "A diamond like this? It goes with everything."

That was how I ended up wearing one hundred and five diamonds as I carried my bail out bag out of my little apartment, helping Warden keep steady as we headed toward Derrick's private jet.

I was back. In under a day, these Alliance men had sucked me back in, and I hadn't even resisted. They'd returned me to this world with a visit to a bar, a beat down on the street, a black SUV, and a diamond necklace. Not to mention their sultry gazes, their sweet smiles, and how much I'd missed their presence.

I had to get control of myself before I accidentally killed someone else or ended up in Marcus' basement.

We were at thirty thousand feet, heading for Boston, when I finally decided what I wanted to say to these two. And if Kade, Trace, and Judson wanted back in my life—and I didn't know that they did—I'd say it to them, too.

"I am in love with you. All of you. That is bound to be fucked up." I held each of their gazes, not letting them look away. "I don't even know if it can be. I said no more and yet months later, I'm sitting here with you two on a private jet once again caught up in Alliance business."

Warden nodded. "It's going to be fucked up, as you say. Everything about us is. But you're not afraid. You're the only woman I can imagine who isn't. You needed space, you got that, and yet rather than fall apart you only rose further. How did you do that, Everly?"

"I don't want to talk about me and what I did and didn't do. I want to talk about what happens now." I sat forward, feeling the slight presence of the diamonds tugging on my neck. "I don't know what Judson will want. He may very well set Warden up to get better and never want to speak to me again. I may never see Trace and Kade again."

Derrick shook his head. "You're saying that, but you don't really believe that."

I pointed at him. "The acting like you know what I think and feel all the time is getting old, and I've only been back with you a few hours. The diamonds don't give you the right to decide you know everything about me. You can take the necklace back if you think it does."

He held up his hands. "Apologies."

"You're saying that, but you don't really mean it." I twisted his words a bit, throwing them back at him, and Derrick nodded. We did seem to understand one another.

I stared at both of them for a long moment. "If we're going to do this, if we're going to proceed like there is any chance I could be with both of you, then I can't have it that you two would ever consider hurting one another." I held up my hand before they could answer me. "That was a deal breaker for me before when I didn't know there were deals to be made. I recognize there are things I can't have any control over. Like men threatening me on the street and death plots, but I won't compromise on that. If you're on my side, you're on my side. And that means you never—and I mean *never*—even consider hurting the other one."

Warden swallowed. "As I told you before, I'll tell you again: I never had those intentions. I can't speak for Derrick."

Derrick nodded. "I can do that. I don't often offer loyalty. But I will give it to Warden if that means I get to share you with him. I'm not going anywhere, Everly. Even if you kick me out, I'm hanging around to protect you. I'd rather be on the inside."

I rose. The plane was relatively smooth in the sky, and I didn't know what made me act the way I did. Instinct, maybe. I walked to Warden. He'd been the first to answer me. I bent over, placing my mouth close to his. So close I could see the pulse in his neck, hear his soft breathing, and practically taste his lips against my own.

"Promise me you'll never betray Derrick or any of the others if we find our way back to each other. Promise me. Swear it like you mean it, in a way that can never be taken back. Knowing if you do, we'll never be together again."

He sucked in his breath. My nipples were hard; they pressed against his chest. He had to have been able to feel them. Warden nodded before he spoke. "I promise it, beautiful. I swear it. Whatever you need. I'm in love with you. I'll never betray Derrick or anyone you love. I'll do that because of how I love you. How I've continued to love you despite not being able to see you. Living on parcels of news, tidbits. How when I thought I was going to die, not seeing your face was the only thing I couldn't stand about it." He touched the side of my face and shivered from the need I saw in his eyes. "Yes, I promise you, Everly. I swear it."

I kissed him. Hard. Warden ran his good hand up my back, and I stayed like that against him for a long second. I wasn't done so I couldn't linger, couldn't really take this where I wanted anyway since Warden was injured.

Still, even though, it was fast, when I pulled back, his eyes were glazed.

I stepped back, turning my attention to Derrick. I expected a smirk. I didn't get one.

"My turn?"

I walked over to him. The plane shook in the air now a little bit so that when I got to him Derrick, he put his hand on my waist to steady me. I hated flying but I was too distracted to care right now. "Derrick, I can say to you what I said to him. Being loyal to me means being loyal to him and anyone else who comes back to this odd relationship we all keep choosing to twist ourselves up into. I can't be worrying about my loves hurting each other. I won't do it. I'd rather call the whole thing off."

He squeezed my waist. "I can do that, Evs. I've waited my whole life for you. I didn't know having you was even possible. This loyalty you're talking about? It never existed for me. I was willing to settle for the superficial look of it. Yes, I'll be loyal to Warden. To Judson. Kade. Trace. If they come back. But that's it. You can't decide you're in love with some guy named George down the street and expect him to count, too. This is closed. That is the caveat I have."

I nodded. "Only you guys. How could I possibly add to this? Who would want to come play in this fucked up playground with us?"

"Anyone who spent half a second looking in your brown eyes." His voice was low. "You don't know it, somehow. You don't understand what it is that you do to a man's soul."

I smoothed my thumb over the side of his face, feeling the slight bite of stubble under the pad of my finger. "Why Derrick, you're suddenly a poet. Swear it."

He smiled at me. "I swear it."

I kissed him, pressing my already heated body right up against his. He moaned against my mouth, and for just a second, I let us stay like that. Then I pulled back. This wasn't the time we would have sex, this was just the time I would use it to get what I wanted from them.

Yes, I could admit that to myself.

I walked back to my seat and strapped in, feeling their gazes on me the whole time.

I'd made them swear to me what I needed to hear for this to continue, and I'd absolutely pressed my breasts against their chests and reminded them what we hadn't been doing for months in order to get that assurance. My grandmother would have said that well-bred girls didn't use their bodies to get what they wanted.

I'd been locked in a basement and the woman who emerged knew that sometimes life required us to use whatever means necessary to achieve our goals. They wanted me, I wanted them, too. We could all eventually have what we desired.

The Alliance was back in my life but this time it wouldn't control me. I'd see to it.

Derrick jumped to his feet. "We've made a huge miscalculation."

Warden tilted his head. "What?"

"They're watching me. That means they've now seen you, Warden." Derrick's eyes darted around in their sockets. "Marcus will know you're not dead. Do you know why he wanted you that way?"

Warden shook his head. "More than the rest of you? No. I really don't. I've speculated it's because I know where his accounts are."

"With Warden it has to be financial, right? He doesn't want you to find something money wise," I added. That seemed pretty obvious to me. They all had things they were good at, but Warden could hurt them where they kept their wallets and that was damned serious.

Derrick rubbed his face. "You managed to get away. That's good. They won't make that mistake a second time. I have to protect you like I have to take care of Everly."

I would have objected if he'd been wrong, but he wasn't. When it came to this kind of stuff, I absolutely wanted Derrick to take care of me. I didn't want to accidentally kill the wrong person again. The right people? Fine. I was game.

Warden shook his head. "Look..."

"We're landing early. I have this worked out." He rushed

toward the cockpit. Warden and I exchanged a look. If I was reading it right, he didn't know what Derrick had planned either. He came back fast. "Warden, give me your clothes."

"Your plan requires me to get naked?"

I laughed, this wasn't funny and yet that was hysterical. Derrick rolled his eyes. "No. You're going to put on the co-pilot's clothes, and then when it's time to land for you, you're going to get in the luggage."

I rose and the plane shook, hard. I groaned. Some smooth flying would be nice for a change. "Let me get this straight. Warden is going to give the copilot his clothes and the copilot is going to get off in this first unscheduled stop wearing Warden's clothes."

Derrick tapped the end of his nose. "Exactly."

"Does he know there's a hit on Warden? That he's putting his life in danger?" I was crazy but not willing to sacrifice strangers. Not yet, anyway.

"For a million dollars." He grabbed his phone and pressed a button. "Transferred. He's risking it for a million, and he's willing to do so for that money. Even said, I'm going to try to keep him alive because it has to look like it's Warden."

I pointed at the floor. "And he has to get in the luggage?"

"It has to look like only you get off this plane. Trust me, just do as I said. All will be well, and I'll meet you at Judson's tonight."

The plane shook harder, and I buckled myself in. Warden stripped and Derrick took out his phone, seeming to ignore the other man getting naked. I didn't let the smile that wanted to come out happen. I'd told them to be loyal to each other and suddenly Derrick had a plan. I wasn't wrong. We needed this. Fuck the Alliance and any other secret societies that wanted to come crawling out of the woodwork. They could keep their secrets. We would be loyal to each other and outlive them all.

I would see to it.

And then if we were lucky, maybe we'd get to love each other, too. In the weird, screwed up way that we did. However that worked.

Derrick took out his phone. "I'm on my way to you. My plane is landing in an hour and a half. Long story. Just do it. I need a black, untraceable van, I need them to be very careful with the luggage, and I need you—only you—to come onto the plane when it lands. No, it's not a fucking bomb. Why would I have you collect a bomb? Just do it, Jud. You'll understand soon."

He hung up the phone.

"Why are you being so secretive with him?" I tried not to notice just how rough the skies had gotten. "Why not tell him?"

"I don't want him trying to alter the plan, and I think it will be good for Judson to be surprised seeing you. That part... that's just me having some fun."

Warden handed Derrick his clothes. "You have some for me to change into?"

"Nope. Lied about that. You're going in the luggage when you land in Boston in your boxers. Sorry, brother. I had to get you to give them to me. There's no point in dressing you like the pilot. I mean... unless you want to for some kind of kinky thing."

Derrick threw a gray blanket from one of the overhead compartments to Warden. My currently injured boyfriend groaned but took it. When Warden was back to full form, Derrick was going to suffer for that. I unlocked my seatbelt and made my way over to Warden. I locked myself in next to him and cuddled against his good arm. "This is almost over."

"I am going to find ways to torture him. Not betray him. But between the diamonds and the clothes, he is due some serious revenge. Like maybe I'm going to... have his driver's license revoked. Something small and not going to kill him."

I kissed his shoulder before I wrapped him in the blanket better. "I'm pretty sure he just saved your life."

"I recognize that. I'm more annoyed about the diamonds than the clothes."

Derrick sat down across from us as my ears indicated we were descending. "I love my car, and I am just in awe that you thought to do that at all." I kissed his cheek. "Thank you."

"You got to drive it for two minutes. I could do diamonds." He closed his eyes, his whole face scrunching up like he was in pain.

Derrick nudged Warden in the shin, and Warden lifted his lids. "You could never have gotten the diamonds while you were on the run. How did you get that car?"

"Paid cash. Fake IDs. It's nothing you couldn't have done. I just wanted my girl to know I remembered."

Derrick nodded. "That's what I wanted, too, which is funny since if either of us had respected her wishes we wouldn't have known she was even back in school. How did you find out?"

I watched the exchange, joy filling me again. Derrick was distracting Warden. I winked at Derrick, which he saw and indicated only because the corner of his mouth lifted into a slight smile.

Warden shifted slightly in his seat. "I hacked into her account and saw when she paid for school. After that, I hacked into the school's account and watched how she was doing based on her grades. Sorry, Everly, I'm totally a stalker. Derrick's not the only one."

I sighed. "All of you could regularly be arrested for something. It's creepy. But I'm screwed in the head so we'll just go with it. Maybe I'll stalk you sometime and we can call it even."

"Would you? I'd love that." Warden laughed. "Stalk me, Everly. Have at it."

We'd landed in Maryland where Derrick and the co-pilot got off the plane. I grabbed Derrick's hand. "Don't die or get hurt. And try not to let that random man who is now a millionaire get killed, too."

Derrick pressed his lips to mine, kissing me hard. "See you tonight. I love you." He kissed me again. "I want to see you in those diamonds. Totally naked. Just the diamonds on your body."

Warden groaned as he unlocked his seatbelt. "I want you naked in the car. I am going to have sex with you in the back of that car. In public somewhere. When I'm not in pain."

Derrick exited the plane, and I grabbed Warden to kiss him softly. He sighed against me. "Sit down, Warden. We're not getting off here."

He blinked. "That's right. Sorry. I'm getting distracted. Not good. Might need another pain pill."

It hadn't been that long since he'd taken the last one. "Not yet. I want you to have a liver and kidneys when we're done with this. Can you hold on a little longer?"

"I can." He sat back down. "I'm just going to think of you naked in that car not wearing Derrick's diamonds. And by the way, Judson is going to freak out when he sees them. I mean downright silently lose it. Just so you know. He won't say anything, but he will."

As the pilot readied the plane for our departure to Boston, I thought about what Warden said. "I don't know if Judson will want back into this. I don't know if Kade and Trace will. They might all be done."

Warden kissed my temple. "Trust me, love. That is not what they want."

I hoped he was right. I loved having Warden and Derrick back, more than I could have imagined I would feel. But it did feel like there were holes in this crazy thing we were doing. We needed to be all together, for many, many reasons.

Safety and love were intertwined this time.

4

After landing, the pilot came back and opened a compartment toward the back of the plane that I hadn't even known existed. Warden managed to climb down, and with some help from me leaning over into the compartment, we managed to get him into a duffle bag.

He looked up at me before I zipped it. "This is really going to suck if Judson doesn't show up."

"He doesn't let Derrick down. Maybe it's leftover as some sort of post mortem favor to Alyssa or because he feels bad about what Alyssa did. In any case, he'll be here, and he'll know who can help you."

He nodded. "I believe you, but you and I both know that things have a way of getting really fucked up."

I pretended to consider this for a second. "True, but we both know I can't kill my father today so that's always a bonus."

He groaned. "I love you."

They were so easily saying that to me. I wouldn't pretend it didn't make me warm inside. What human being didn't want to feel alone? Maybe I was justifying. Maybe I just missed this, missed something about being in the center of this.

Maybe I didn't have to figure it all out lying on my stomach on this plane.

"I love you, too. I hope this is fast. Don't make a sound until we get you out of this duffel bag, okay?"

He nodded. "There are words I bet you never thought you'd say in your life."

"Look at you, W." I winked at him. "Thinking like the common folk. See you in a minute."

"That god damned letter."

I smiled at him one more time before I closed the compartment. I stood up. Now what? It was hard to follow Derrick's directions when there were so many variables and I had no ability to manipulate any of this if it went wrong.

"Ma'am?" The pilot caught my attention. He stood by the exit, ready to open the door. I'd forgotten he was still there. I had to do better with details. If I was going to live this life, at least for the present, I had to remember that lives depended on focus and not accidentally shooting my father in the stomach because I didn't look before I shot.

I rubbed my arms. "Hi. Thanks for getting us here, safely."

He nodded. "You're welcome. I'm glad Derrick called me. I've worked with him a lot in the past. I'm hoping now that you're back, he'll call on me more again. We're all hoping the group he's usually associated with comes back in power."

My body went cold. I needed to be smart right now. Judson's sister, Alyssa, who was also Derrick's late wife, died because she'd tried to insert herself into the Alliance. Just because this man was loyal to Derrick didn't mean he wouldn't turn around and hand me to Marcus for acknowledging that I even knew what he was talking about. Warden was so weak he'd allowed a plan that involved him to be put in a duffel bag. My weapon was five feet away from me. How fast could I get to it? My hands itched to grab my knife. It should have been strapped to my back, but I hadn't wanted to prick Derrick or Warden with it accidentally.

"I don't know what you're talking about." I smiled and inched forward. "Derrick's group? Is it a baseball thing? A sports network thing?"

The pilot sighed. "That's the right answer, but I am harmless to you. I'm a nothing in the Alliance, and I prefer it that way. I have three sons. I don't want this life for them. I'm sorry your father was killed in the crossfire of Ben's madness. Now Marcus?" He shook his head. "He was the least in control of all the leadership. What is he doing now? I can't fathom any of this."

I scratched my head. Two more feet and I could have my knife. Ten more seconds and it would be in his eye socket. "I don't know who any of those people are. My father had a heart attack."

"Right. Well, have a good day. Take care of yourself. I'm... hopeful I've just played a small role in setting things right. You might not know anything," his tone indicated he didn't believe me, "but we all know you. And whether you want to be or not, the fact that you are here with Derrick and Warden, that inspires me to hope things can get back to how they were when my grandfather was Alliance."

I really wanted to ask him what that meant but that would acknowledge I had a clue what the Alliance was. This was dumb. Everyone knew I'd been at the Alliance meeting in Boston. I had to know what he meant. But if playing stupid kept me, alive then so be it. I wasn't going to be the girl in the horror movie who went up the stairs instead of out the front door.

"What's your name?" I should know it in case there came a time I had to take my knife and stick it somewhere to kill him. I tried not to picture it. These things were coming easier and easier to me. Before too long I'd be as apt to accidentally stab as I had been to shoot.

He smiled at me. "What name?"

I supposed two could play at that game. Derrick knew him. I'd get it from him later if it became important.

He opened the door and exited the plane via the steps that dropped down. I sank into a chair. I had to wait for Judson. If he didn't come, I'd release Warden from the luggage container and we'd go somewhere safe until we could reconnect with Derrick and get some help. I had my burner phone and Derrick's number stored in it. He'd done that without asking me at some point when I'd been busy.

I shook my head. I was glad he was on my side.

"All right." Judson's voice echoed into the plane as he must have been climbing the stairs. "What the fuck is going on, Derrick?"

I jumped to my feet as he came through the door. Whatever he would have said died on his lips just like the words didn't come out of mine. I let my eyes drink him in. I wouldn't even pretend at this point that I hadn't missed these guys. They'd come and screwed up my life beyond recognition. Somehow, at the same time, they'd managed to shove themselves deep in my soul where I couldn't kick them out.

Beauty was subjective, but there was nothing questionable about how good-looking Judson was. He was the prettiest of all of them, although I'd place on money on his hating that description, so I'd never use it. His brown hair looked like it had gotten sun kissed which told me he'd been spending a lot of time outside, his skin was tanned to follow up that look. He might have been on vacation except that his greenish, blueish eyes were haunted, tired. Dark circles were visible even through the deep tan.

He moved before he said anything. It wasn't until his arms were around me that he spoke again. "Everly."

Judson pulled me so close up against him that it would have been hard to breathe if I'd cared at all about oxygen right then. He smelled like coffee and cinnamon.

"Everly." He said my name again, sort of choking on it. "How are you here? What's going on?"

His arms shook as he embraced me, and I held on as tightly as I could. "Hi, Judson."

He pulled back to look at me, his hands traveling up my body until they cupped my cheeks. He breathed hard. "Hi, Everly. You're okay? I've been really, really worried about you."

"I'm okay." I brushed his hair out of his eyes. He needed a haircut. For Jud, he was downright disheveled. "Are you?"

"The last time I saw you... fuck. There is so much to say. Not here. Not on this plane. You came home. I'm so glad you came home. Where have you been?"

We did need to talk about all of what he'd just said, including the home comment. And it seemed he hadn't been following me through the art of stalking like the others. "Jud, before we do any of this, and there is a lot to say, we need to help Warden."

He ran his thumbs over my cheeks as his face got tight. "We can't help him, Everly." He kept saying my name, and I didn't mind hearing it spoken from his voice. "He's dead."

I shook my head. "He's not. He got away. He came to me. That's how we're here. Derrick appeared. It's a long story but Warden needs help. He didn't get the proper care when he got shot. He can't feel his hand sometimes. He needs help. Derrick said to come to you, that you'd help if he asked. Will you? Please."

His face softened. "You're serious about this? Warden is alive? Where is he? Where is Derrick?" I watched as clarity came back into his gaze. The shock of seeing me was wearing off, and the doctor was taking over his mind again, but he still didn't let go of me.

I grabbed onto his shirt. "Derrick got off in Maryland to lead them away. Warden is in the luggage compartment in a duffle bag."

"He's in a duffle bag?" He looked around like he might see it. "They're loading him into the van. Fuck. Okay. Yes, I can help. Not me particularly. It's not the kind of medicine I practice. But there's an underground hospital network. Most of the doctors left the Alliance with me. We're trying to do what we can to rebuild, and we have each other's backs. If it's not simple, there are techniques we haven't released to the general public."

I nodded. "Like my face. Like how they fixed my face when I was little."

"Yes, how they fixed your beautiful face." He kissed my cheek where the scar should have been but never was because of a procedure most people would never have. A huge number of my problems in life could be traced to that day I decided to pet a dog I should have left alone. Funny how one decision could so concretely lead to so many others.

I trembled as his mouth touched my cheek. "There are so many things to say, but we need to check on Warden."

"Yes. Come." He dropped his fingers only to link them with mine. "I hope they listened and didn't drop the bag too hard into the van." He sighed. "I really did think he was bringing me a bomb."

"Well, it is Derrick." I couldn't deny he might bring a bomb.

Judson stopped abruptly. "What is that?" He pointed at my neck, and my free hand went straight to the necklace I'd all but forgotten was there.

"Oh." I let it go. "My graduation present from Derrick."

Judson tugged me closer, and I went, following him down the stairs. "What graduation?" he called over his shoulder.

We got to the bottom of the stairs before I answered. "I finished school. Not a big deal."

We both climbed into the back of the van. Like a limo, there was a barrier between the driver and us. I couldn't see who it was. We sat in a row of seats, and I was relieved to find Warden had let himself out of the duffle and was in one of them himself. Still, he was bent over, and I could see sweat on his forehead. I didn't think it was there because of the duffle bag being hot.

Judson stared at him for a second before he put a hand on Warden's good arm. "I thought you were fucking dead."

"That was the idea." He nodded. "Sorry about that."

"I'm really relieved to see you're not. And that however it happened, you got here. Plus, you brought Everly with you so that's a bonus."

Warden grinned. "I thought it might endear me to you. Did she give you the speech yet?"

"Speech?" Judson looked over at me, nodding toward the seatbelt he clearly wanted me to put on. I strapped myself in, and he did the same. "What speech?"

"I didn't." I kissed Warden's cheek. "I will. I promise it won't just be you and Derrick who get it."

Judson knocked on the divider, and it opened slightly. "To the warehouse."

The divider closed, and I had to ask an obvious question. "Do you not trust the driver?"

"We trust each other as much as we need to. I think that's true for all of the Alliance."

I sighed, and Warden shook his head. "Have the talk with him."

Judson shifted slightly to look at me full on. "What talk? And can I pause that for just a second? Warden, did you see what Derrick did here? It's half a million dollars' worth of diamonds. Would have been nice for him to have maybe alerted the rest of us that he was going to do this so we could all have known it was graduation, and I could have bought her something, too."

My whole body froze. "How much money?"

Oh, I had to get this off my neck just as soon as I could find a safe place to store them. I was not a person who walked around with half a million dollars of anything. What if I ended up having to hide in the dirt somewhere? I couldn't have half a million dollars of something I had to take care of.

"You just panicked her." Warden put his hand on the back of my head. "I actually bought her a gift. She likes it although she only got to use it once since I'm so fucked up right now." He grabbed his head. "I'll get it wherever we end up staying, beautiful."

"You bought her a gift?" This time Judson raised his voice. "I don't love you less than they do. I just didn't know. You said stay away. You'd been through hell, so I respected your wishes. For now. I was coming back. After enough time for you to decide you didn't hate me. Fuck, now I'm the only one who didn't buy you a gift? What did you get your degree in? I'm two steps behind. No, I don't accept this."

Warden side-eyed me. "I told you he was going to hate those diamonds."

Judson hated them, and I was practically afraid to move lest something happen to them. "First of all, this isn't a competition. I don't need gifts. I'm overwhelmed with them, and I... please don't buy me anything. We need to talk about things. What Warden keeps talking about. This isn't ideal."

Warden shook his head. "Don't mind me. I'm going to close my eyes. I'm really wishing you would let me have another pain pill."

I winced. "Judson is the doctor. I just suggested it had been very little time."

"You probably have the wrong one." Judson sighed. "We're ten minutes. Can you hold on? I'm not carrying any. Derrick didn't tell me to bring my medical bag. I expected more to be defusing a bomb."

I tilted my head. "Is that something you can do?"

"If I have to. But not as well as Kade."

Hearing his name panged my heart. I missed him. And Trace. This really was only going to work if they all wanted to be with me. Otherwise, it was just me being some sort of psycho that couldn't be satisfied with what she had—what she shouldn't want to begin with.

"Judson, I don't know if you want to pick things back up with me or not. Derrick and Warden seem to want to do that. I'm not pressuring you. The thing is, I've had a lot of time to consider what happened. A lot of time to think."

He met my gaze. "I have, too. Believe me. I have a lot of things to say to you. I'm deeply, profoundly sorry. Maybe the most I've ever been in my whole life."

That was saying a lot because Jud had been through a lot of huge life events that he carried guilt for. I squeezed his knee. I'd worked Warden and Derrick over sexually when I'd done this, but they'd both made overtures that way. Judson had been affectionate but made no moves on me.

"Everly." He started to speak, and I interrupted him.

"I need to finish. Please. I've changed a lot. I'm really dark inside."

Warden's eyes flew open, so the idea that he wasn't paying attention really was bullshit. I'd not thought otherwise. He opened and closed his mouth, maybe rethinking whatever he was going to say.

"But if you do, what I told Derrick and Warden, is there's just one thing I cannot live with from before. I need you to swear, to mean it, that you won't betray each other. I can't be in whatever this relationship is with the five of you if I think you have any plots or plans behind each other's backs. I can't. It's a non-negotiable thing to me, and I have to have your oath on it. I have to know you mean it. I need you to all be as good to each other as you are to me."

It was hard to read Judson when he had his guard up, but he didn't right then. He tilted my chin until I looked him straight in the eyes. "I can do that, Everly Marrs. I can be that guy. I can do that. For you."

He kissed me, square on the lips, softly at first and then harder. I moaned against him, and he dragged me closer, hindered only by the seatbelt he'd silently ordered me to put on. Warden stroked my back, and for those quiet seconds, I felt as adored as I ever had in my entire life.

When Judson finally pulled back, it was Warden who spoke. "You're not dark inside, Everly."

I leaned back, taking deep breaths to try to calm my heart. "I am, Warden. Know that up front. I'm very dark inside now. Or maybe I always was and it's just less hidden. I don't know."

Warden winced but managed to kiss me on my shoulder where my shirt had moved down to expose part of my skin. "We like all your messy parts."

Judson pushed our foreheads together. "For sure we do."

"I wanted to stay away. To be done with all of this, all of you. And then I was so lonely for you and I didn't know what to do about it. I was going to run farther away."

"We would have found you," Jud whispered. "I can promise you that. I might not have been invading your privacy yet, but I would have. Shortly."

Warden laughed. "I have no patience."

The car slowed and Judson nodded. "Time to go, Warden. We'll get you fixed up. I promise you. It's a day for that."

The warehouse was just that from the outside. On the inside, it was a hospital like any other I'd ever seen. Doctors and nurses, all male, ran around treating patients. It seemed like there were a lot of injured. Things must have been really bad. Maybe my pilot was right. My guys needed to get back in charge.

"Kade." I was alone, and I spoke to no one unless Kade happened to be monitoring me. I hoped he was. "I miss you. Come and find me. Please. Unless you don't want to. In which case, I'll respect that. The trouble is that I don't know if you can hear this so I may bother you one more time. This is crazy."

Trace was probably not listening. That wasn't really his style. He was more of an in the room guy. I missed him, too.

Judson rounded the corner, meeting me in the waiting room. He drew me to him like he had on the plane. We hadn't really done this before. Touching was tricky with him, but he seemed to really like it now, need it almost.

"He's going back. The right surgeon is here. They just botched the whole thing. There is this technique... it has to do with nerves. Do you want to hear the science?"

I shook my head. "No, not ever. I don't do medical all that well."

"I'll spare you." He laughed. "Everly, you needed me, and I was giving a fucking speech to a room full of psychopaths and assholes."

I laughed, the description striking me as so funny I almost cackled from hearing it. "It was a little bit like you were there. You were over the speaker from the television. You were talking the whole time, actually."

"Fuck. Really?" He shuddered. "I'm sorry that happened. How are you doing with it?"

I leaned back. "Not well. But I'm sleeping. That's a plus. I'm functioning. I finished school, held down a job. Managed to get back to running. I'm... making do. And now I'm back here which should feed my need to do evil things. A very real problem for me. Every person has become a person I might potentially stab in the eye."

He blinked. "Marcus is doing a lot of destruction. I've all but stepped away entirely. I don't understand it. He was a non-entity on the council, nothing to the leadership. Now he's sending people to try to kill Warden, destroy the financial markets, and leave death and destruction everywhere? I don't get it. All of this to say, you may get your chance to stab people in the eyes."

I kissed his chin. "How long will Warden be out?"

"Couple of hours. Then he's going to stay here mostly out of it for two days. Then we can bring him home. Come on, you can see him before they put him under."

He took my hand and led me back. It really did seem like a working hospital and no one blinked about me being there. "Jud, is this okay? This is Alliance stuff."

"Everyone on our side knows you're with us. The other side might act like you can't know. I don't know. I can't understand them."

Warden turned his head when I entered. He had an IV in his arm, and his eyes were cloudy. They'd clearly already given him something. "Hey there, beautiful."

I leaned over and kissed him on the lips. "Hey, handsome. I'll see you soon. And you might not feel better but you will again."

"I'm kind of floating right now. I'll see you soon. Don't come back here. I'll come home. This is no place for you. Okay? Judson, keep her home."

Judson stood over my shoulder. "I'll do that. Thanks for bringing her back, Warden."

These were some of the kindest things I'd ever heard them say to each other.

I watched as they wheeled Warden away and tried not to panic. The last time I'd been in a hospital setting I'd ended up killing assassins. Judson drew me back against him again.

My little apartment and my job at the bar already felt really far away, and I couldn't say I minded. That was just how fucked up I was.

5

Judson's house was a wreck. That was my first thought as I walked through his door. He was such a fastidious person it really struck me as wrong. "Where is Marco?"

"I asked him to stay in my property in France. I'm worried about things here. I don't want him in the crosshairs." He looked around. "Pretty obvious I've let things go, huh?" His eyes twinkled. "Spoiled kid grew into an entitled adult who can't clean up after himself."

I reached up to kiss him on his cheek. His breath caught, and I whispered in his ear. "Maybe. And I'm not cleaning up after you. Wrong girl. I'm more likely to drop my clothes on top of your clothes and call it a day."

"When it's safer, I'll get a maid service in." He smiled at me. "I do have food. Hungry?"

My stomach grumbled right on cue. "I'm always hungry."

"Then I'm going to feed you." He put his forehead down on my shoulder. "What would you like?"

I didn't know if I'd ever seen Judson so tired. "How about if you go sit in your living room and I'll make us grilled cheese sandwiches?"

He lifted his head. "Will you do something else for me?"

"Sure, what do you need?"

He cupped my cheek. "Take off the diamonds. Put them in my safe."

I laughed, throwing my head back. "They're really bugging you that much? I swear by the universe that I am not looking for gifts. This is not a competition."

He ignored my statement. "The safe is in the kitchen. It's next to the back door. Code is 8 numbers 19864905."

"I'll take if off because I'm uncomfortable with the idea of wearing such an expensive gift. Although Derrick may ask me to put it back on when he gets here. He wants to see me in it."

Judson groaned, but didn't say anything else. I left him to go sit in his living room. The kitchen didn't look like anyone had cooked in it in a long time. There was a slight bit of dust over the chairs but despite that there was food in the fridge. Someone was keeping him stocked. I doubted he went to the grocery store. This was probably food delivery.

I took off my necklace and placed it in his safe. There wasn't anything else in there, which told me Judson didn't really use this safe for keeping his valuables and secret stuff. There was probably a basement somewhere holding all of that. Maybe he'd even buried it. I smiled at the thought. Judson with a shovel...

Fortunately, he had cheese, bread, and butter. I was able to cook up some grilled cheese sandwiches—a favorite when I'd had a long day—fast. There were pretzels in an unopened bag in the cupboard that I added to the plates. Judson and I both loved food. It was one of the things we had in common. I didn't know that we'd ever done this kind of eating together. He tended to take me to expensive places where we drank slightly too much.

I poured us both water and managed not to spill anything

on my way to his living room. Halfway there I wondered if he'd be asleep when I walked in. I'd seen Jud conk out on that couch before, and he was tired, strikingly so.

However, when I got in there, the television was on and he was awake, staring at the news. He got up and took the plates out of my hand, setting them down on the coffee table.

"Good news on Warden. He's done. They did have to use the secret technique. I won't get into it, but it's pretty cool stuff. He'll be home in two days."

I let out a long breath. "That's great news." I sat down next to Jud on the couch, the world feeling lighter since Warden was okay.

"How do you feel about graduating?" He took a bite of his sandwich and grinned at me. "This is really good. I haven't had one in years."

I smiled. It was good. "I feel mixed. Glad I did it. Foolish that I bothered. What am I going to do with a degree in social work now? I'm mixed up in all this craziness, and it's not going away. Even if it would... I've already told you I missed all of you. I was planning on going off the grid, but that would probably have meant I showed up on one of your doorsteps eventually because I was only going to be able to resist doing so for so long." I shrugged. "Nothing has been simple in my life. Not before I killed my father and not after."

He set down his plate. "Everly, from the way Derrick described what happened, it was a totally understandable accident. Not that I expect that to matter much. But it's not like you set out to kill him."

"I shot without looking. That's on me no one else." I bit down on my lip. "It's hard for me to talk about. I obsess about it and never speak about it. I've said more on it in the last two days than I have since it happened."

He sighed. "Well, that's not good."

"Who was I going to tell?"

We sat in silence for a while, watching the news on the financial markets as it struggled through another day of making no sense and being a hot mess. Jud set down his plate. "It'll be good to have Warden focused on them again. Not that he was before he was shot. He'd given up on this. We all basically have. If people weren't dying, I'd say let Marcus have it and run with it."

I didn't want to talk about the economy or death. I put my own plate next to his. With a steadying breath, I got on my knees on the couch to face him. "Do you have your tie?"

He blinked, realization coming into his gaze. "You're sure? There's no rush."

I laughed. "We might both be dead tomorrow."

"That's true." He got up on his knees, too. "Everly, no tie this time. Thinking about it, yes, makes me hard. I definitely want to get back there with you, but I've spent all these months without you, thinking of your hands on me. I used to be able to have sex both with and without it. That changed and I only wanted with. Today, no. Without. That's what I want. Unless that's not what you want."

I kneed my way over to him, almost falling off the couch because I wasn't graceful and I never had been. Judson tugged me to him. "I missed you. Stayed away so you could see that I could listen. I've never wanted anyone like I want you, and if that means that Warden, Derrick, Trace and Kade get you, too, then so be it. I want it however you want it, and I can't say that's been true ever before in my life."

"I haven't talked to Trace and Kade. I don't know what they want. I don't know how to find them. Right now, it's you and me. We're going to figure this out day by day. That's it. That's all I can promise."

I tugged at his shirt, and he swung it over his head. Judson had gotten stronger and leaner. I ran my hands over his chest, dropping them down to feel his abs. His muscles jumped under my touch, and his breathing kicked up.

"This okay?" I lifted my gaze. "I can stop and you can say tie and I will be game. You don't have to force yourself into some kind of touching torture for me. I want you, Jud. Whatever package you come in."

He smiled. "Everly, if you think I'm jumping because I don't like what you're doing, you're misreading the situation. I like it, too much."

His words were amazing, but the slight tremble when I smoothed my hands over him told me my J was not as comfortable as he wanted me to believe.

"Lie back," I whispered in his ear, and he did what I requested. "Let me... love on you for a while."

That word was out there. I'd used it. I couldn't be afraid of it anymore. He nodded, but he narrowed his eyes. None of us were good at this. Judson and I were defunct at love. That didn't mean we didn't need it, didn't crave it.

I just had to figure this out. Somehow.

I kissed his chin and made my way down, stopping to tongue his nipple. He sucked in his breath. "Shit. Everly, I didn't think we'd be here again. I wanted it. I was going to... figure out how to convince you that you wanted this. I... I can't believe..."

"Sshh." I lifted my gaze to meet his. "We can do that later. Let's just feel now."

He grabbed onto the back of my hair, massaging my head as I kissed him. I loved how he responded to each caress of my mouth like it was the best thing he'd ever felt. The sounds he made, they were small, almost a plea in the back of his throat. Judson was starved for me. And it was a heady feeling to know that.

I undid the button of his pants, pulling them down and

finally discarding them onto the floor. Judson squirmed beneath me. "I want to touch you, too."

"Soon." I winked at him. "I promise."

I bit down on the top of his boxers, admiring how hard he was, how his cock pushed out against the fabric. He moaned as I pulled his boxers off of him, exposing him to my eyes.

"I haven't," he cleared his throat like he couldn't quite make his voice work, "been with anyone since you."

I nodded. "Me neither. You can actually thank Derrick for that."

"I don't want to know."

I was so hot from wanting this, so turned on that I was wet and I hadn't let him touch me yet. My nipples ached. I pulled my shirt over my head and threw it aside. Judson flared his nostrils as he stared at my breasts. He reached forward, unhooking the front latch of my bra. I pulled it down, my breasts bouncing against my chest as they were freed.

It was possible to be adored by someone's gaze alone. I scooted backward, and then pushed forward with just my chest, caressing his cock with my breasts. His hips jerked as my breasts came around his erection.

"Fuck." He grabbed onto the couch.

Clearly, he liked it, so I did it again. I was going to breast fuck him until he begged me to stop so he could get inside of me. Heat surged through me. If he touched me, he'd see I was already dripping, and I hadn't taken off my pants yet.

I'd get to it. Right now what I wanted was to keep rubbing my breasts against him. I liked how it felt, and I loved how he responded. I'd never get enough of this.

He tugged me forward, the act startling me so much I almost fell off the couch, again. His mouth was on mine before he spun me over. Judson kissed me like he was possessed, like he couldn't do anything else. I wrapped my arms around his neck and held on. He stopped as abruptly as he started. I gasped, suddenly cold.

Jud traveled down the couch until he was in position to pull off my pants. He threw them away and my undies were next.

"You're so beautiful."

I never got to answer him. How could I think when his mouth came down on my pussy? I grabbed onto the edge of the couch, holding on for dear life. Right then I wouldn't have minded the tie to give my arms somewhere secure to hold onto.

Judson stroked my clit with his tongue. I closed my eyes. Pleasure rode through me. It wasn't going to be hard to come tonight. It had been too long since I'd had any pleasure except from my own fingers. I hadn't even bought any toys.

A surge of pleasure startled me and my hips came off the couch. Judson must have liked this because he moaned against me.

"I'm going to come, and it isn't going to take long."

He laughed, which was a funny, sort of hysterical sound. Weird and sexy coming from Judson, somehow both at the same time. "I would love for you to come. Come, my love. Please."

Judson went back to what he was doing and it didn't take long. I worked at keeping my hands where they were like he'd told me to do so even though he hadn't.

I exploded, my body needing the release more than I could have imagined. I shook against him as his mouth continued to draw pleasure from me even when I was sure I had to be done. He pulled back, finally, and we stared at each other.

This was so different than the last time Judson and I had been together. This was raw. We'd both been beat up. I didn't know what had happened in the time we'd been apart, but I could see it on his face, could feel it in my soul. The truth kept coming back to the ways we were alike. I was dark inside and so was he. But we could feel each other. If there was some kind of light left in us at all, we could see it in each other.

Maybe I was overthinking this. Maybe I just wanted Judson more than I wanted to breathe. Or maybe that was the darkness playing its ugly games in me again.

He kissed me hard, almost punishing as he pressed against me. My lips were going to hurt later. I didn't mind.

Then, he was on me fast. Our mouths fused together while he pushed me down on the couch, all of his weight coming down on me for a second before he readjusted, holding himself slightly off of me when he did. I missed the feel of his bigger weight on top of me. It was an odd feeling. For a second, it had almost been like he'd shut out the world.

But I could hardly dwell on that, not when he pushed a finger inside of me and smiled against my mouth. "Just wanted to make sure you were still wet."

I smirked back at him. "I'd say it was a pretty good guess that I was still wet. You just wanted evidence of what you did to me."

"Pretty much."

He inched his way inside of me. I was tight. It had been a long time for me, and Judson wasn't small. When he was finally seated deep, he pushed my bangs off my forehead, the two of us staring at each other. I was lost in this moment. I'd never thought to be here again. He moved slowly at first, inching out the way he had come in. I closed my eyes, reveling in the sensation.

"Everly," he whispered my name. "Give me your eyes."

I lifted my lids. Judson breathed heavily. He seemed to be searching my gaze for something, and when he saw it, he nodded. I didn't want to ask him what he sought; fear that he could see me all too well kept me silent. I wrapped my legs around him, urging him deeper.

He flared his nostrils before he pressed in and out of me. I cried out, arching my back, meeting his movements with my own.

"Fuck. You feel so good." Judson clenched his jaw, strain evident in the muscles in his neck. He was holding back. That wasn't what I wanted. I needed to go under to this pleasure and I wanted him right there with me.

We'd go there together.

"I need just a little more." I could hear the begging in my voice, and I hoped he understood.

He nodded, shifting his hips just a little to change the angle that he entered me. Yes, he brushed my clit. Once. Twice. That was just what I needed, the friction was perfect, and I shattered around him. He cried out my name, his body jerking as he emptied inside of me.

I closed my eyes and hung on. I couldn't breathe. Couldn't think. The good thing was I didn't need to. Not for a few minutes. I could bathe in the happy, pleasure-filled nothingness that took up all the space in my mind.

Judson always had whatever was needed nearby. He rolled slightly and opened the coffee table and pulled out a large blanket. He shifted me again until I was on top of him and covered us both with the blanket.

Remotely, in my pleasure filled haze, I tracked him doing all of these things.

I lifted my head. He couldn't be comfortable like this. I wasn't tiny. "Are you okay?"

"Hmm." He took my face in his hands and kissed me. Once, then twice again. "Are you?"

That was sweet, but I hadn't meant because of the sex. "With me lying on you. Are you okay?"

He breathed out. "I'm good. Are you not comfortable?"

I wasn't the only one in pleasure-ville. Judson was also obviously not feeling things like weight and discomfort at this moment. I snuggled down. I'd just go with it for now. When we had to readjust, we'd do just that.

I kissed his chest, right over his heart, and he ran his hands through my hair. "It grew in."

"My hair? Not completely. But closer, yes." The fact that he'd noticed made me grin. It was all part of this happy thing I had going on. Everything was the most wonderful whatever in the whole world.

"Are you still on the pill?"

I grinned against his skin. "I am. But you know, the time to ask me that would have been before we went skin-to-skin with you deep inside of me. That's a do we need a condom question."

When he didn't answer, I lifted my head. Judson was out cold. I stared at him. The light and the television were both on. There was no way we were spending the whole night on this couch. I should have woken him and made him go upstairs to his bedroom to sleep.

But there was no rule in the universe we couldn't take an early evening nap. I wasn't tired, but Judson clearly was. That had been obvious before he'd conked out before hearing whether or not we'd left ourselves open to an unplanned pregnancy. I turned my head just slightly enough to be able to watch his television.

I liked listening to his heartbeat more than I did the newscasters going on about the economy. The only person I knew who could fix it was healing in a hospital-disguised-as-a-warehouse. I hoped he was okay. He didn't want me to come, and I knew that was because he didn't like to seem weak.

He'd already exposed himself to more vulnerability than he probably had ever before in his life.

Judson breathed deeply. This wasn't a little light sleep for him. He was out of it. The good news was his face was relaxed. It seemed like he was having pleasant dreams.

The minutes passed by, and I lulled into a passive, happy sort of mild awareness. I wasn't sleeping, but I probably couldn't have recited my social security number if someone asked me to.

Maybe I should have just gone to sleep. If Judson woke up and needed to move, he could just wake me and we'd go from there. Maybe a second round.

And in today's news, the sad passing of billionaire James Robert Michaels. Michaels, a charitable giver, was found murdered in his home in the Caribbean this evening. Officials say he was shot to death while taking a meeting with an unknown male.

I darted upward, falling off the couch.

"What?" I shouted at the TV like it could answer me. I knew the picture they showed. That was Jim-Bob, the man Trace manipulated in his going-to-Mars plan.

Judson sat, rubbing his eyes. "Beautiful? What's wrong?"

I pointed at the TV. I needed the remote. I needed it to back up, to rewind, so I could see it again. Unknown male. Was that Trace? Had he been shot? What were the chances it was Trace? Fuck, this was Alliance. It was too damned high.

"Everly?" Judson was next to me on the ground. "What's going on? What am I missing?"

I saw the remote on the edge of the coffee table, and I used it. Thank the universe to whoever invented the ability to rewind live TV. I was young but old enough to remember when I couldn't do that unless we recorded it.

The screen backed up, and I pointed to it as the newscaster spoke the same words again. "That's Jim-Bob. The asshole Trace was scamming to get money for the Mars trip.

He's... he's an asshole. Was an asshole. Hit on me. Trace hates him but meets with him a lot because of the money. Do you think it could be Trace? Could he be the unknown male?"

Judson got to his feet, grabbing his boxers before he shoved them on.

He hadn't answered me. "Jud?"

"I don't know, beautiful." He grabbed my arm. "I wish I could say no. But James Robert was mixed up in Alliance business without knowing anything about the Alliance. That's mostly on Trace. Yes, it could be him. Particularly because he's not named. Is he dead? Did they say that? Rewind it again."

I did, and we stood there, putting on our clothes as we listened to it again. They absolutely didn't say if the other man was dead.

Judson's phone lit up, and he grabbed it. "Someone is here. My security camera shows movement approaching the front door. Everly, I want you to..." His voice trailed off. "Never mind. It's Kade."

I jumped. "Kade?"

"Go let him in. I'm going to try to reach Derrick. He might know how we can find out about Trace."

I stared at the clock. It was almost nine. "He said he'd be here tonight. Should he be already?"

"Don't panic." Judson kissed my cheek. "We know nothing yet. If he's leading Marcus on a chase, it might be a great deal more time before he gets here. I trust Derrick. He'll still be standing when it's just him and the cockroaches alive."

I didn't love that imagery, but his point was made. I rushed to the door and flung it open. Without saying a word, I threw my arms around Kade. He caught me and held me close. I shook and couldn't do anything about it. I was so glad he was here. Ridiculously, stupidly, glad.

He carried me and closed the door behind us. "I heard you, Evy. I heard you so I came. I was in Canada. That's why it took so long to get here. But I came. Thank you for missing me. I missed you, too."

"You were watching?" I'd never been so glad Kade spied on everyone as I was right then.

"I had it set to tell me when you moved around. I started paying close attention when Warden appeared—I thought he was dead until then—and I was able to delete you guys from view. I know Derrick is off running around, trying to lure the eyes away from here, but he didn't have to do that. I've sent him a message, and he's on his way here. I... I heard what you made the others promise, and I figured if you were making them, you'd make me. Since you missed me and wanted me to come."

I kissed him, and he startled before he kissed me back. Kade dropped his bag with a clunk, all of his attention going to kissing me. "Do you swear it?"

"I do. I swear it, Evy. Let me be with you. No more separations. And I have a gift for you."

"Of course you do." Judson stormed into the room. "I'm going to be the only asshole without one. What did you buy her?"

Kade grinned. "Hey, Judson."

"Kade. We're worried about Trace."

Kade set me down, turning his attention to Judson fully. "Why? He's in the Caribbean. I have you all on movement algorithm."

"Fuck." I grabbed onto Kade, needing to feel him right there. I would not give in to terror. Trace was alive. He just was. That was all there was to it.

6

"We never unpacked you. We'll just go, somewhere more off the grid, and figure out how to get to Trace, to find out if he's alive." Judson strode past me into the kitchen. "I need coffee. I can't think yet. This is why I don't sleep. It makes me... sluggish."

Judson knew better than that. He was a doctor. I wasn't, however, going to argue with him while it would be like poking a bear. I'd probably roused him right from REM. Instead, I spoke to Kade who was on his computer running through searches to see if he could get a reading on what happened. So far, whoever had done this had left a big old black hole right where we needed to see. He'd been muttering about Marcus. "We can't just go. Warden is in the hospital."

"We'll get him," Jud yelled from the kitchen. "I'll do his care, which will be minimal, wherever we go. I have some thoughts on that."

"Actually..." Kade walked away from his computer, but the screen still ran through the search pattern. He must have set it up to run continuously. "I know where we can go." He tugged me against him. "You missed me," he whispered in my ear. "I was afraid you didn't. That you... that you wouldn't be able to forgive me for what happened."

I turned all my focus to him. "You aren't to blame for that."

"Fuck, yes, I am. My system failed. That's how they got up. I couldn't break into their system to get up to you. It's all on me."

I sighed. "Kade." I kissed his chin. "This is not on you. This is on Ben. On the Alliance. Not on you. Unless we want to chase this back to you guys deciding to kidnap me to begin with, and I'm over that. Really done. That is over with."

He rubbed his eyes. Like Judson, he was sporting dark circles under them. "I... I'm not accepting that."

"Okay, well you said something about where we should go, so let's focus on this and I'll alleviate you of guilt for the fact that I, not you, killed my father later." I patted him on his arm.

"Am I making this about me?" He lifted his eyebrows. "I'm just recognizing my role."

I sighed. "Look, I'm in love with you. I told you I was."

He liked that. A red hue lit up his cheeks. It was adorable. "I love you, too."

"That's good. But we're all narcissists. You are. I am. That might be why this works or why this falls apart. I don't know. I can't predict the future. But yeah, you're making this about you, and I'm making this about me. This is what we do." I kissed him again. "Let's shelve this until later."

He sighed. "Kiss me again, and I'll think about it."

I did that because I wanted to, not because of his statement. Or at least I'd pretend as much. I was good at deluding myself. I couldn't do this too much. The loop of my "what am I" thoughts tended to screw me up for days.

He ran his thumb under my eye. "I bought you a house. I think that's the right place for us to go."

"You bought her a house?" Judson shouted from the hall, holding his coffee. "Shit. Tell me did you do that before or after you saw the necklace."

Kade met him by the doorway before he patted him on the shoulder. "Before. Absolutely before."

"Like you'd admit otherwise."

They could go ahead and do this song and dance. In the meantime my head spun. I gripped the wall. "A house? Where did you buy me a house?"

He grinned. "Destin. Florida."

I gaped at him. "I love Destin. Happiest family vacation of my youth."

Kade nodded toward me. "I know, Evy. That's why I did it. You could go off the grid there without going off the grid. It's not in your name, and it can't be traced to any of us. I worked on this for a while. It's a hole in the satellites because I made it one, but I cut out like a thousand other places too. We'll be safe because it doesn't look like a hole. I made it a loop."

I put my hands on my hips. "You bought it for me?"

"I started to realize you were going to go off the grid. I didn't want... you really off the grid. I'm sorry. But how am I supposed to keep you safe if I were to somehow lose you?"

That was so sweet it almost pushed out of my head how much money he must have spent. "So you bought me a small place in Destin. That is very sweet."

"Oh, I bet it's not small." Judson laughed. "Is it on the beach, Kade?"

The word yes banged around in my head. I thought I might have passed out with my eyes open. I had a car. A diamond necklace. A house. And Judson had given me an orgasm I'd never forget in getting-reacquainted sex. All I needed was Trace to be alive. I needed that more than anything.

Judson's phone blared to life. "It's Derrick. He's outside."

I grabbed the door and flung it open. Derrick walked in like he'd gone out for bagels instead of distracting bad guys.

"Hey." He looked around the room. "Warden okay?"

I nodded. "He is. Trace may not be."

Derrick sighed. "Fill me in and where are your diamonds, Evs? You can't be bored with them already."

Judson groaned. This was almost perfect. If only I didn't have one love in pain, just out of surgery, and one who knew where, not dead—I couldn't let him be dead, even in my head. Not now, not ever.

"We have to get to St. Croix. If Trace is there, he's in hiding. Or if they've taken him, we need evidence of that. We have to go look. If Kade can't see from the satellites, that either means that Trace is being really careful or Marcus has him. And at some point, can one of you give me a rundown on Marcus?"

Kade sighed. "I'm shocked it's him. I thought he'd go into hiding. He was Mr. Uninteresting on the council. Sort of stupid. I can't believe he's running things."

"I feel the same." Derrick sighed. "He's a fucking idiot. A good shot but that was about it."

I walked over to Jud, leaning my head against his arm. "We can't leave Warden, and we can't take him with us just yet."

"I know." Judson kissed the top of my head. "I'll stay here with him until he's ready and then we'll travel to Destin. Assuming Kade will give me the address?"

Kade grinned. "I'm all in on this new let's-not-betray-each-other thing that Evy wants. Yes, I'll give you the address. Keep in mind, the way we keep it secure and offline from the satellites is by not drawing attention to it. So no guards. Show up in an expensive looking car but not flashy. The people there have money. They'll expect whoever is there to have it as well, but a red sports car with Dr. Nose on the license plate will catch attention we don't need."

I looked up at Judson, amusement flashing through me. "Do you have a car with that license plate?"

"No. I'm not cheesy. I'm old money. That goes against my cellular makeup. Nondescript car. Anything else. Presumably I need a key to get in this place? How are you keeping it from being attached to Everly?"

Kade lifted his eyebrows. "The bills are being taken care of through over a thousand different companies located all over the world. It's impossible to trace. Take my word on it, I'll never let her down again."

I sighed. "Kade, seriously."

"Evy." He winked at me. "I get to feel how I want to feel. The whole narcissist thing."

He was so going to keep using that now that I'd introduced the topic. I grinned. It was absolutely ridiculous that I liked this so much.

Judson shook his head. "So no noticeable car. I bring Warden in. We hang out and wait for you guys. Ever going to tell me how I get in?"

"I have a code," Kade answered. "Texting it to you now. Go in through the garage."

"Got it." Jud stared at his phone before shoving it in his back pocket. "I'll go to the grocery store."

I stared at him. "You will?"

He rolled his eyes but smirked at me at the same time. "Yes. I can do that. Sometimes. What I can't believe is that I just got you back and now you're leaving. Everly, it is everything I can do to do not wrap you up in a warm blanket and figure out where to put you that you can be safe. We can all take turns being with you and keeping you that way." He held up his hand to stave off any argument I'd have made. "But Warden's been shot. Trace might be dead. And if he's not, he needs you guys, so go." He pointed at Kade and Derrick. "Take care of our girl. We're all sharing her. It's not conventional, but it's the only way this works. We're loyal to her, and she wants us loyal to each other. We'll make it work."

Derrick disappeared to the kitchen without a word. Maybe he wanted some coffee. Kade responded to Judson. "Well, since not one of us is going to give her up, I guess we all have to figure out how this is our normal. For me, I never expected to want or love anyone past a night. I'm keeping Everly. If you guys fuck it up, she's still mine."

I sighed. This really wasn't going to be simple, but I'd never expected it to be.

Derrick came back out, holding the diamond necklace. Judson gaped at him. "Did you break into my safe?"

"I didn't have to break in. You and Alyssa used the same code. I knew hers, I know yours. Come on. I'll keep this, Evs. You can wear it in the Caribbean if we're not running for our lives. I like you draped in diamonds."

Judson put out his hand, and I took it. He drew his lips to mine. "Be careful. I haven't slept in months without you. I don't want to know what a lifetime without you would feel like. We can all be done with the Alliance. Get Trace and we'll walk away."

Marcus had shot at Warden and now maybe killed Trace. I didn't think that was exactly going to be possible, not the way he'd had me threatened on the street. Still, it was a beautiful sentiment, and I wouldn't spoil it with reality. I leaned up to whisper in his ear. "Bring the black tie to Destin. Tonight was incredible, but I want my wrists tied up again by you sometime."

He jolted before he kissed me hard. My bruised mouth hurt, but I loved it. I stepped back. "See you soon, Jud."

"Love you."

The plane was quiet. Derrick and Kade were both asleep, stretched out in chairs on either side of me. I remained upright in mine. I scanned through the pictures of my house on Kade's tablet. It was bizarre that it was mine. If it was technically mine. I wasn't really clear on who legally owned it, if anyone at all.

When I'd tried to tell Kade it was too large a gift, he'd lowered his chair, placed his hand on my side where it remained, stretched out, and fallen asleep. Derrick had been out before takeoff. His hand remained staunchly right below my left breast so that every time the plane jolted at all, I got a little thrill. I was half convinced he'd done that on purpose while the kinder side of me thought he'd wanted to feel my heart beat.

The house was beautiful. I wondered if Judson knew it was unfurnished or if he was going to arrive and be shocked that there was nowhere to sit. I needed to ask Derrick to text him about that. Warden was going to need somewhere to lie down. Judson could order furniture. The man had the ability to get things done fast.

Derrick moved his leg, which caught my attention. I stared over at him. He was quiet and peaceful in sleep. I hadn't shared a room with him since his surgery. He didn't snore anymore, air making its way in and out of him almost silently. I reached out to touch his face, running my finger down his nose. He didn't stir. He was beautiful.

In my need to admire the men in my life, I turned my attention to Kade. He frowned in his sleep and shifted slightly. Whatever he dreamed, it wasn't pleasant. I ran my hand through his dark hair, and he shifted.

"Evy?" His voice was light. He didn't open his eyes, and

his face relaxed. Maybe I'd disrupted the dream long enough for it to move on.

I needed to sleep. We were going to get there, and I wasn't going to be any good to anyone.

Why wasn't I tired? I should have been. It had been a long time since I'd rested. Warden asleep in my bed had been my last bit of shut eye. I hadn't even knocked out after the incredible sex with Judson. It was like my mind wouldn't shut down now that I'd returned to this life.

Fear wasn't playing a role, at least not for me. Worry about Trace and Warden did make me squirm. But I wasn't afraid of things suddenly happening to me. Other than death, I'd already pretty much been through everything.

Like they could sense it, or maybe because I'd disrupted their sleep, both Derrick and Kade lifted their lids.

"Evs." Derrick pushed at my chair. "Lie back. You need to sleep."

"Come on." Kade reached over me and hit the button for the chair to lie flat. "He's right. Sleep. It's very late. Lots of stuff to do when we land. Just a couple more hours. Not enough. Take a nap."

Kade's speech was stilted, like he wasn't really awake. He never slept much as it was, and I was immediately sorry I'd disrupted him. "I don't think I can guys. Can't seem to calm down."

"Yes, you can." Derrick was more alert. "Here." He opened a drawer under the seat, pulling out a blanket. All of their planes were very different, and this one had a lot of storage. We were officially on Kade's now. Maybe Derrick had been on it before. He tucked me in before he scooted to the edge of his seat to put his arm entirely around me. Kade did the same. We weren't pressed against each other, but it did feel like I was in bed with them.

"It's just a few hours or so," Kade whispered. "Not enough. But just rest your brain. Shut it off. We've got you."

I closed my eyes, although I didn't expect to sleep.

Except I did.

I walked toward my father, running down the stairs in my childhood home. He held out his hand, which I didn't think he'd ever done in his life, but I put out my own to grab it. Just as we would have linked fingers, he vanished. I stumbled forward, barely avoiding hitting the floor.

I spun around. What happened? Where had he gone? Then the floor was gone. I was falling. I screamed for my father, but he never came.

With a splat, I hit the floor. Unable to move, I watched in horror as the room changed. I was back in Ben's basement. He walked toward me, a sick, twisted smile on his face. "You killed us." My father stepped up next to him, and they both leaned over, staring at me. "But we're never really going to go away."

I sat up, my heart racing loudly in my ears.

"Hey." Kade tugged me to him, reaching over to pull off my seatbelt in a swift motion, so that I ended up in his lounge chair with him. Derrick had been asleep and didn't move until I was all the way up against Kade.

"What's wrong?" Derrick took off his own seatbelt and came over to sit on the edge of Kade's lounge. "What happened?"

I pushed my head into Kade's chest. He'd held me through another bad nightmare once. He did seem to know when I was having a freak out.

"Bad dream." He held me tighter before he kissed me on top of the head. "She gets them sometimes."

Derrick rubbed my back. "I'm sorry that's still happening, Evs."

I lifted my head. "Just dreams. I thought they had

stopped. I'd been doing really well lately but now—I guess with seeing you guys and being thrust back into this—they're back. I'll get it under control. I'm sorry I woke you."

My ears clogged, indicating that we'd started our descent. I tried to sit up but couldn't because Kade didn't let me go. The lounge chair was not made for three people to sprawl across and yet that was just what we did. Kade lay on his side and so did Derrick. I was squished between them. We were clearly not in the right position for landing, but they didn't say anything and neither did I.

"Do we have any idea where we're going to start looking for Trace?"

Kade ran his hand through my hair. "We'll go to James Robert's house. From there, we'll see if we can get in. Get some sense about whether the second person was killed. That might take some maneuvering. If he is... and it's Trace..."

I clenched my jaw. I hated this, but I had to hear it. "Then what? If it's Trace?"

"We get his body, and we go home. We don't let him be identified or taken," Derrick answered, as he ran a hand through his hair. It was loose and soft looking. I reached out to touch it, and he smiled at me.

"If Trace isn't dead?" This was the best case scenario, and even though I was not a glass half full woman anymore, I would hold onto this until the idea was physically forced from my head.

Kade sighed. "Then we figure out where he went from there. The man's house was sort of a dead zone in the satellites. Trace wanted it that way so the council didn't figure out that Trace was still working with him after he was told not to. I did that for him, so consequently, I don't know what went on there. We have to go look physically and then maybe ask ourselves, hey, if I was on the run for my life, where would I go?"

Derrick nodded. "And you have the search engines going so if he appears on satellite somewhere else, like he's left the island, we'll be notified."

"Immediately."

Most people dreamed of going to the Caribbean; they looked forward to these kinds of trips. So far I'd been twice and both times had been hell. I might become a skier to avoid doing this again. Or just give up travel altogether.

"All right. Sounds like a plan."

We remained in silence, and I didn't try to predict their thoughts. My own were difficult enough to manage. If Trace were dead... Marcus and his crew were going to wish they'd never been born. They might end up feeling that way anyway, but if Trace were dead, they were going to hurt, badly.

I'd needed space from my guys after I'd killed my father. Everything had been too much. Yet, somehow the world was supposed to understand that these were my guys. They weren't to be touched, they weren't to be bothered. They were to be left alone while I sorted things out. Warden had been shot. Trace was missing. Kade and Judson both looked like they'd been through hell. And Derrick... he held his secrets to himself, but it didn't mean he wasn't suffering.

I wanted to cause the Alliance nothing but pain.

Derrick stroked a finger down my cheek. "You're having dark thoughts."

"Deadly ones." There was no point in hiding it. "I don't carry a gun anymore, Derrick. I can't be trusted not to shoot the wrong people. But I'm armed with knives, and I know how to use them. I will take out anyone who comes near us the wrong way."

Kade touched his foot to mine, like he wanted to play footsie on the lounge with me. "Just think, if you hadn't met us, you could have gone your whole life without saying something like that."

I grinned. "What a sad life that would have been."

Derrick ignored our exchange, bringing back up what I'd just said. "I'm giving you a gun. You need one in this scenario. You made a mistake. You shot your father under extraordinary circumstances. That is on me, actually, not you. I'm deeply experienced, and I should have been guiding you better in that moment. I should have shouted don't shoot. The blame belongs on me, not you."

"I pulled the trigger. I killed him."

Kade shook his head. "Is no one going to say that your father was doing bad shit? That he was most likely not in that elevator to go negotiate a ceasefire? Are we all going to pretend it wasn't possible, particularly because he was armed beyond belief, that he wasn't going there to hurt Ben? Only Ben's people had access to the elevators in that moment. I couldn't get on. How did your father get to the room to begin with? Did he know that Ben was coming there to kill his daughter?"

My ears rang. I'd had these thoughts myself, particularly in the beginning, but there were no answers for them, no way to know, and so it left one resounding truth. I'd killed my father. I didn't get to automatically assume it was self-defense because I'd never know. Anyone who could have told me was dead.

"Should I not have said it? Are we all going to be silent and not speak the truth?" Kade sounded tired.

I took his hand in mine. "I actually think you're trying to make me feel better. For that, I thank you, Kade. But I get to live with my own guilt and not one of you fuckers is going to talk me out of it."

He kissed my fingers. "We'll see."

The plane touched down, jolting us all and reminding me that landing really went better when I wore a seatbelt.

I had my knife strapped to my back, where it usually was. I'd even gotten used to ignoring the way the tape that held it in place irritated me. I'd had it off since the plane with Derrick and Warden, not strapping it back on with Judson, but now it was back. My first weeks of wearing it when I'd gone back home had driven me crazy. I'd wanted to scratch all the time. Now, I could tune it out if I got busy doing something else. But the gun I had in my pocketbook, making it just slightly heavier than I was used to, seemed to make me crazier by comparison.

Derrick insisted I have the damn thing, and as much as he was all about me having what I wanted, whenever I wanted it, it turned out that when he put his foot down, he was unmovable. We were, apparently, not getting off the plane if I didn't take the gun. Only my concern for Trace had allowed me to abandon my own intractability.

I tried not to notice how Kade smirked through the whole exchange.

We'd pulled over a block away from the late James Robert Michael's home.

I was in the front passenger seat while Kade drove. Derrick sat forward, his body tense, alert, in the back. I could feel them like they were somehow inside of me. I was that attuned to them in that moment.

"What do you think, Derrick?" Kade's eyes stared straight ahead. "Just bust through the door?"

Kade held up his phone. He'd installed an app he invented that allowed the zoom function on the camera to be as far reaching as a sniper rifle. He could actually see the door. I hadn't looked yet, but even as he passed it to Derrick, I knew bust through the door wasn't the right move.

"Are there guards?" I asked both of them. Whoever wanted to answer could go right ahead.

Derrick nodded. "One. They have one police officer stationed outside the door."

"Is he young?"

Kade blinked at the question. "Ah, I'd guess mid-twenties. Why?"

He'd catch on fast. Kade didn't need me to hold his hand through this. "Run a quick facial recognition on him. Is he gay or straight?"

"Give me half a minute. Ah... Okay. Jeremiah Green. Back living here after going to school in Texas and working there for two years. He's relatively new to this job. Oh, and very, very straight. His online presence..." He stopped speaking for a second before piping up again. "He'd like to be a player, but he isn't one. Straight. Twenty-six years old."

I nodded. "Great. Then I'm getting inside. You two, hide in the back. Get down. I'll drive up and go have a look. You can watch from my phone. Or sneak in behind me if you can be quiet enough. No needs to go busting in anywhere."

Kade groaned. "Are you going to sleep with him?"

I laughed. "No. But I'm going to let him think that I might."

"And what would you have done if he was gay?" Derrick lifted his eyebrows.

"Then I guess it's such a good thing you and Kade are so cute, D."

He groaned, and I laughed. This shouldn't have been so amusing, considering the seriousness of the situation. Kade narrowed his gaze at me. "What if he were married?"

"How many people do you know who wouldn't cheat if given the chance by a willing person and the assurance of never getting caught?"

Kade took my hand. "Me. I wouldn't. Not on you."

My amusement died. He was dead serious, and from the look Derrick was shooting me from the back, so was he. It was time for some truth. "I'd never cheat on you either, but let's face it. I don't really get to say that, right? I have five boyfriends, and I'm dating all of you in front of each other after having basically broken up with all of you in a group shout. Well, four of you. I don't actually know if Trace is going to want back yet."

"He will." Derrick shifted in his seat. "We're all good, and as far as I'm concerned, this is our version of monogamy. Maybe single guy over there would be the same or maybe Evs is right and people are generally pieces of shit. I don't know. I don't spend a lot of time thinking about human nature. I just kill whoever gets in my way or threatens someone I care about. In any case, we're lucky today. If he'd been taken and loyal, we'd have had to run over him to get in there, and if he'd pulled his gun, I'd have had to kill him. So, yes, go flirt with him. If he doesn't take the bait, we still have that option."

Kade dug in his pocket. "Forget your phone. This is a live stream. Put it right there on your shirt. He'll never see it unless his last job was as a spy. Even then, this is a new design. Looks more like a water stain."

He pushed the camera onto my shirt before he got out of the driver's side to crawl in the back with Derrick. One step closer to Trace. I had to keep my eye on the goal.

He needed me. I just knew it.

"Oh my god." I got out of the car and headed toward Jeremiah Green. His eyes widened at my approach. I was a girl in shorts and a tank top. It helped that I'd deepened my southern accent. I'd always possessed a light weight drawl, but I knew how to do my best *Steel Magnolia* version of Louisiana in my voice. I always had.

I used it on police officers when they pulled me over. That and my breasts tended to get me out of tickets. I was counting on both of those things to get me in that door.

"Is this where that old guy died?" I pointed at the door. "The rich dude who was gunned down days ago?"

"You don't belong here." Jeremiah had a stern voice, but his gaze was on my breasts.

"I know." I shrugged. "I'm here on vacation. Staying with my great-aunt Bessie. She retired here from Boston. Couldn't do winters anymore. You know how it is. Or maybe you don't. Anyway, I'm visiting, and I've just been thinking for days of getting in there. I have... a thing... about murder. Oh, I can't believe I just said that aloud." I laughed, throwing my head back. "Don't you find it really exciting?"

As I spoke, I moved closer and closer to him until I had completely invaded his personal space. This was a police officer. He should never have let me this close. Part of me wanted him to reject me, just to prove to me that my breasts and my pretty accent couldn't get me what I wanted. The other part, however, didn't want him to get shot. I hoped that Jeremiah Green wanted to fuck me. Really, really badly.

"You like... murder?"

"Well, I've only ever seen those documentaries on Netflix. They show the dead bodies. It's just so... exciting." My breasts were officially hitting his shirt right now. It was hot outside, and I fanned at myself. "You can show me, can't you? I should have introduced myself. My name is Julia." *Steel Magnolias* was really on my mind. "What's your name?"

He stammered. "Jeremiah. You don't belong here. I should ask you to leave."

"You should." I grinned at him. "But you won't. I know it. You're going to show it to me." I tugged on his shirt. "You look very handsome in your uniform. Ours back home are different. They're kind of blue, the ones the police officers wear, and..."

He cleared his throat. "How long are you here on the island, Julia?"

I had him. I knew it. Trace had feelings like this. When the person he was playing gave him or herself over to him. There was something ridiculously on point with this. I was using Trace's tricks—the ones I'd learned on this island—to rescue him.

"I'll be here till September. I'm finding myself." I touched his chin. "Maybe you could help me with that."

He backed up fast, nearly falling in his haste, but he opened up the door to James Robert's home. I'd thought of the man in pretty derogatory ways while he was alive, most of which he earned for being a total douche bag. Now that he was dead I was thinking of him in a kinder manner. He didn't deserve the shift, but maybe that was just what people did for the dead, making them nicer than they were in life, sometimes.

Or not. I'd never think highly of Ben. He could rot like the scumbag he was. I followed Jeremiah inside.

There was tape and chalk all over the house, but otherwise the place looked exactly the same. "He was killed here?"

I spun around like this was the first time I'd seen the place. It felt like yesterday I'd been inside pretending to be Trace's assistant. "Someone just came inside and shot him?"

"It was a sniper rifle. He and another person were hit. We're not sure what happened to the second person. We have evidence there was someone else here, but they seem to have vanished. Ran out the back door and then we can't find any trace of him."

I almost choked on his choice of phrasing. I stared at him for a long second, trying to judge if that had been purposeful. Was he being sneaky and showing me he knew? No. I didn't get that reading. He was still going on and on about the gruesome murder and blood.

The other person had run out the backdoor and disappeared. My mind was already off Jeremiah.

I needed him gone so I could get going and...

His phone rang. He paled before he put it to his ear. "Sir? Oh, sir. No, I'm not inside the house. I..."

Kade had done this. He'd known what I needed without me saying anything. I rushed past Jeremiah and out to my car. When I got into it, the vehicle was empty. Derrick and Kade had moved on to the back of the house. I'd put money on it. I had to ditch this thing where Jeremiah wouldn't see it.

My phone pinged, and I looked down at the text Derrick sent. *Half a mile down the road behind the big rock. Leave it there. Then come back around to the house.*

That was just what I did. My heart rate kicked up, and by the time I got to where Kade and Derrick waited, I bristled with excitement. Trace wasn't dead when he left the house, and if anyone could disappear, it would have been one of my guys. The questions were: could we find him and had he managed to get help, still undetected, since.

Kade fiddled with his phone holding it in the air like he searched for a signal. I wrapped my arm around his waist. "Anything?"

"Not yet." He shook his head. "Fuck. I did this too well. I always seem to be defeating myself."

"Okay." Derrick nodded at me. "That was gross to watch, but good work. Don't do that thing with your voice again. I don't like it."

I rolled at my eyes at him. "Like you've never played on how good looking you are to get what you want."

He winked at me. "What's good for the gander in this case is not good for the goose."

"Ugh." I waved my hand on him. "Talk about gross. Nice comparison. What now?"

He squared his shoulders. "I am asking myself what I'd do. I'm Trace. Being shot at is not something that happens regularly. I'm hit. James Robert is dead, and I've run for it. I'm bleeding but not enough to leave a trail. We don't know where I'm hit. I have to hide; I have to get help. I have a phone, but I haven't used it, not to call to any of us anyway. Why is that? Where do I go?" He spun around. "I'm acting on instinct, but I'm a genius. I've had training. I got the shit beat out of me learning this crap in the Alliance the same as everyone else. I'm not in pain yet."

The fact Derrick knew that caught my attention. "How many times have you been shot, Derrick?"

He chewed on his lip and didn't answer me. Kade held up three fingers and pointed to Derrick. That many? Well, fuck that. We were all done getting shot at. When this was over we were somehow going to live a bullet free life.

I rolled my eyes at my own thought. That was never happening. If we managed to have an after-this part of our life, it was going to be as blood soaked and dangerous as this one was.

"This way." Derrick nodded toward the ocean. "He's going to think that the beach is the best way to go. It was sunset. He'll think he can follow the sand to wherever he's comfortable going. Also, if he's thinking at all, he'll know that the fact that the sniper hit them through the kitchen side window means it'll be hard to see him down here. Now, I just need to figure out how long Trace would go before the pain would take him down."

I chased after Derrick who, now that he'd picked up an idea, was running pretty quickly. Kade caught up to me and together we trailed after Derrick. "Does it matter where he was shot?"

"It does," Kade answered, looking left and right when he did. "But we have to go with the idea that if it were an automatically fatal thing, he'd have been found when he dropped dead. Unless the Alliance picked him up. Then I think we'd also know. They'd parade around his body through the dark net so I'd see it and know. Marcus doesn't seem to be pulling any punches."

"Why is that? Was he so devoted to Ben and the others he has to get revenge? Or is he scared you can take it from him?"

Kade shook his head. "We need Trace and Jud for this. I'm just the dude who can hide us from the satellites."

"You're a lot more than that. And you know it." I kissed him on the cheek. "But it's seriously cool you can hide us from the satellites."

His smile was genuine and adoring. "Everly Marrs. I let you go once. I won't again. Leave and I'm going to pull a Derrick and follow you."

We ran down the beach and Derrick stopped. "Wherever he was shot by now he's feeling it."

I looked all around. The beach was lined here with small huts. I sighed. Would he go into one of them and look for help? That didn't sound like Trace but maybe he didn't have a choice.

"What do you think?" I needed Derrick to tell me what to do here. "Where would you go?"

He took my hand. "We'll go look, Everly. We'll…"

A woman who sat by the water's edge turned and looked at us. Her movement was so abrupt that it caught my attention, and I stopped Derrick from talking. I held up my hand.

"Pretend like you're moving on. Don't go far."

Kade nodded. "You're still on feed. Come on Derrick."

They continued to walk on, and I paused. "You go on. I need a minute to collect myself. I'm so worried about him."

I'd not been letting myself really feel any of this. How could I and still do what had to be done? Emotions were to be put away when they got in the way of things. Or so my grandmother used to say. A lady didn't make a scene in public. Everything I felt and thought didn't have to be at the front of my mind. That didn't, however, mean I couldn't dredge them to the top when I needed them as I did now.

Trace had been shot days ago. No one had heard from him. He was probably dead. I let my tears flow down my cheeks. They were real, even if my manipulation of them wasn't. Funny how that could be, how something could be both real and not real at the same time.

The Caribbean was beautiful, but I'd hardly gotten to enjoy it the last time I was here, and the bright pinkness of the sky seemed startling mean to me tonight. Nothing should be beautiful while I was this worried.

I didn't wipe my tears away. Somehow I had to not overplay this. There could be a million reasons the woman reacted to my name. One of them might have been that she'd heard Trace say it. It wasn't like saying a name that people heard all the time. I'd never run into another Everly.

"Oh, Trace, where are you?" I stared up at the sky. "I will find you, my love. I will."

I could practically hear Kade roll his eyes from the distance down the beach. The woman approached me. She was what my grandmother would have said was an example of a person who had spent too much time out in the sun. If I had to guess her age, I would have put her at forty, but the lines and the sunspots made her look older. She'd clearly spent some time working on her body. I would have killed for her arm muscles.

I wiped at my eyes. "Can I help you?"

"I'm sorry, but I heard your friend call you Everly. Is that your name?"

I put surprise on my face and in my eyes. "It is. How can I help you?"

"It's a very unusual name, and one I've been hearing a lot lately." She had the slightest accent. Her English was flawless, but there was a touch of something... maybe Eastern European. I'd been listening to a lot of podcasts in my runs. One of the commentators on the state of the world was from Armenia. She sounded similar. I wasn't good at this. I bet Trace would know.

I narrowed my gaze at her. "Oh? That's interesting." I was going to play dumb. "Sorry, I'm looking for my boyfriend. Funny to call him that since he's a little bit older than me. Boyfriend makes him sound... I don't know. I'm looking for my love. He's missing. He had a business meeting and things went wrong. I don't know. I'm afraid he's dead. I mean, I'm not sure how he could be okay or why I thought I could find him." I pointed down the beach. "His two best friends are trying to help me. I can't let him just be... gone."

I hoped I hadn't overdone it. She kept her cards close to her chest. I really couldn't read her that well. I spoke again, trying to finish it off. "Sorry to dump this on you. I guess you have one of those faces that people just talk to you."

"Your friend. He is a good looking man, brown, blondish hair, and he wears all black?"

My mouth fell open. I had two choices. I could continue to play this ruse, or I could grab the gun in my bag, hold it to her fucking head, and demand that she tell me where he was right that second. I forced myself to smile. This was working. I didn't need to blow up the world, yet.

"Yes, that sounds just like him. Have you heard something? Do you know? Please. Could you help me?"

She leaned forward. "What's it worth to you?"

"Everly," Derrick called down the beach. "We're going to keep looking. Stay here. We'll come back."

Okay. They were making it look like they were disappearing, but they'd heard that, too. They knew what was going to happen here. That was also Derrick telling me not to attack her. He'd never have even pretended to leave if that was going to happen.

"How much is it worth to me?" I hated this dumb person I was playing. "Oh, everything. He is the love of my life. And... I'm pregnant." Yes, I'd gone there. I needed to seem desperate. There it was.

She liked that. I saw a gleam of happiness in her eyes. She thought she had me right where she wanted me. "Five hundred thousand dollars U.S."

"You want five hundred thousand dollars to tell me where Trace is?" I widened my eyes. "How do I know he's okay? I'm not just going to give you that money for nothing..."

She smirked. "He says your name in his sleep. He calls out for you in pain. That is how I knew you, Everly. Fine. You come with me. I'll show you where he is. You transfer me the money, and I'll give him to you. Tell your friends or the police and I'll kill him. Well, my husband will. He's very good at causing pain. We knew when we found him that this would be a payday. That's why I haven't given him to the police. I could still do that."

"Oh," I cried. "Please show me. I'll do anything. Anything." I followed her, whimpering the whole time. "Is he okay?" Not a hard act, I wanted to know.

She shrugged. "I have some experience treating wounds. He might be fine. Right now he has a slight fever."

I'd love to ask anyone if that was normal. Instead, I just cried louder. At this point it was all pretend. Anger was the predominant emotion rushing through me. And it was everything I could do not to lose my shit. I followed her into her shack. If I'd actually been alone, and not at all certain that the guys were right behind me I might have been legitimately nervous.

I should have been scared. A sane person would have been anxious.

I wasn't any of that.

Her shack was on the beach. I did a quick calculation. It was small, maybe two bedrooms. No. One bedroom, with a center living room if I was guessing correctly. I needed to practice my ability to read a room.

The woman's husband rose when we came in. He was huge, maybe as tall as Derrick. I'd put him at three hundred pounds, and it wasn't muscle. His arms were inked up, and he belched loudly. "What do you have here?"

"I think she knows our guest. I am proving his alive, and then she will pay us."

Trace was here? I shuddered for effect. "Please. Is he okay? What is going on?"

The husband rolled his eyes. And I let this bitch of a woman lead me into the second bedroom. Trace was on the bed. He was out cold. I rushed over to him. His face was covered in sweat and a bandage covered his side. He was shirtless. The thoughts all seemed to hit at once.

"Trace?" I said his name, and he didn't respond. But his heart beat and that was the point. For now, that was enough.

"I think we are going to ask you for more than half a million." The woman said. "Take her picture, darling. Let's see what we can get for her. If we have both of them maybe her family will pay for both of them."

I sighed, rising from the bed. "Part of me sort of hoped I wasn't going to have to kill you. And part of me sort of hoped I would. I'm in a constant conflict. Which Everly wins? Day in and day out. Today, you made it easy."

"You think to hurt me?" The older woman lurched forward, and I ducked out of the way, my only concern not to let Trace get more hurt than he already was. These people weren't going to take me out.

The door banged open, and she whirled around. Derrick and Kade were suddenly in the room with us. Trace's captor-slash-rescuer screamed out. "Get them, Archie."

Well, now we had a name. I didn't know what Archie would have done, but he never got the chance. He hadn't realized he was in the presence of Derrick and his incredibly lethal skillset. I heard a bang, but I didn't turn to look at it. I knew the noise and so did my nameless enemy.

"You kept him alive but only so you could extort him or me once you found me." I stepped toward her. My gun was in my purse, but I didn't need it. In fact, I preferred not to. I didn't want to accidentally shoot Kade. "I am grateful to you for keeping him alive. It looks like you performed some basic first aid on him. Do you hear me?" I stepped toward her. "This is me saying thank you? Was he ever coherent? Did he ask for help? He said my name. I bet he said other things.

That makes you a liability. A stupid liability. Guess what, cookie? If you want to imprison and extort? You need to do better than you did. We're not stupid tourists. Take my word for it. We've been held hostage by the best. We've been beaten. Tortured. Only because you didn't let him bleed to death on the beach, I am going to make this fast."

I ripped the knife off my back, feeling the sting of the tape tearing off my skin. She hit the wall behind her. Ben had taught me that intimidation came as much from intent as anything else. I meant to frighten her. I wanted her to know fear before she died. She'd held Trace here. He was my love. I didn't have a lot of room for those sorts of feelings anymore, and she wouldn't take what was mine. I wasn't losing him to this piece of shit.

My knife was controlled. I couldn't accidentally hurt anyone I didn't want to. And I really did want to cause this woman pain.

I'd never again wonder what it felt like to jab my knife into someone's eye. I'd always know.

It wasn't as exciting as I'd thought it would be.

I cleaned up in the bathroom. There was nothing I could do about the blood on my shirt, but I scrubbed down my skin where the woman had bled on me before she'd dropped dead. I'd save the big shower for later. With no choice, I discarded my gray t-shirt into the bathroom and changed into my white one.

Feeling a little more like myself and less like something from a horror movie, I came out to see what was happening in the main cabin of Kade's plane. Whatever the pilot thought about the scene when we boarded, he didn't remark. Maybe, like Derrick's pilot, he wanted them back in charge enough to pretend he didn't see a gravely wounded Trace being carried over Derrick's shoulder and me covered in all things grossness.

Trace twitched and muttered to himself on the airplane. Derrick worked on him, rebandaging his wound. "It doesn't look infected."

I walked over to his side. "Then what is wrong with him? Did it hurt an internal organ?"

He shook his head. "I don't think so. Jud or another doctor will know better. My best guess? He got shot. That fucking sucks, and he needs real medical care. He'll have it soon. He's tough." Derrick turned to me. "How are you?"

"Fine. That might make me a sociopath. I know. I'm just not sure there's anything I can or want to do about it."

Kade laughed, throwing his head back. "No. You're not a sociopath. You're just not sorry. You said it yourself, we're all narcissists. She had what was yours, and she was threatening the safety of it. You took it back. You didn't want to hurt that cop. You don't want accidental deaths or needless ones. You feel remorse. Just not about this. Don't sweat it, my love. It's just Alliance. This is what we all are."

Trace said my name. "Everly." His eyes were still glued shut.

I walked over and stroked his hair off his forehead. He was warm to the touch. "I'm here. You're on your way home. I love you."

If he heard me, I had no indication. Derrick kissed my cheek. "It was hard to do what you did. If you miss, it hits the forehead and that is hard. The whole skull is a problem. You have to aim just right. And that was well done."

"No one has seen us or spotted us. I'm watching all the cameras. I took care of it all. We're free. So is Trace. We managed to pull this off. I have an email from Jud. He's mad. There's no furniture in the house."

I whirled around. "Fuck. I meant to mention that."

"Judson's fixed that. Whoops. And the markets seem to be leveling off for the moment. You know what that means?"

I grinned. "Warden is up and alert enough to be playing on his computer."

Kade touched his nose. "Bingo."

Derrick had managed to get an IV into Trace's hand, not something I'd known he knew how to do, but it seemed my D had some skills I hadn't known anything about. He yawned. "I gave him some pain meds, and I'm hoping he sleeps until we get to Florida. I'm going to nap. You should sleep, Evs."

"Honestly, I'm kind of up right now. Not sure I can."

Kade touched the chair next to him. "Come on. Let's watch shows together."

The plane shook just enough to make me nervous, and curling up with Kade sounded nice. We weren't going to be in the air more than two hours. I'd sleep when we got to Destin. Maybe I'd even have Judson give me something to knock me out. There were things that had to happen now. Once Trace was okay, we needed to know what happened with James Robert.

There were plans to be made.

And they had to be right. I wasn't going to spend my life worried about this Marcus person. He had to be killed and his people dealt with. No one else I cared about was getting a bullet in their body.

Kade switched the screen from the news to an episode of *Doctor Who*. I knew this one well from my nighttime television watching. People were using a drug to lose weight and the fat coming off of them was turning into living creatures. It was bizarre, kind of funny, and memorable. Derrick slept across the plane, and I giggled, my body pressed against Kade's.

"This is like a dream of mine," he whispered to me. "You

and me, watching this show together. I'm hard. It's very...
sensual for me. You doing this with me."

"That so?" I lifted my head. "Keep your eyes on the screen
and don't make too much noise?"

I saw the question in his gaze disappear the second I
slipped my hands through the waist of his shorts. He flared
his nostrils. "Evy..."

"Sshh. Watch the show." I slipped my hand deeper inside,
fitting it through the waist of his boxers until I could rub his
cock in my hand. Kade adjusted how he sat just slightly,
spreading his legs so I'd have slightly easier access, but he
otherwise did as he was told and watched the screen.

I stroked him, watching the show progress as I did. At
first, it was an easy rub. I'd hold his head for a long moment
before I'd stroke the length of him, ending up on his balls. I'd
repeat the motion the opposite way. Long, unrushed movements. Just touching him, he hardened in my hand. I kissed
his cheek, lingering on the side of his mouth. With my free
hand, I ran my fingers through his hair.

As the minutes passed, I increased the pressure and
speed, just slightly. He moaned in my ear, the smallest of
sounds. "Let me touch you, too."

I shook my head. "Maybe later."

If he did, he'd find out I was so wet I'd soaked my panties
just touching him like this. Then we'd never have been able to
control ourselves. I didn't want to be naked on this plane with
Derrick asleep in the corner and Trace injured in the center. I
wanted to make Kade come while we watched this show
together, and that was all the enjoyment I required right
then.

When we got somewhere with a bed, if he wanted to
climb in with me, I'd not say no. As it was, I didn't think even
as turned on as I was that I could relax enough to get to
completion right now. He pressed his head down on my

shoulder. His warm breath touched my neck as he tried to stay quiet. I sped up my strokes and held him harder. It was difficult as he was still in his pants but that seemed to only add to the pressure.

"Kade," I whispered back to him. "I want you to come."

He nodded, his head stroking against my neck. "Yes. I'm going to."

"I love you, and it will make me feel so good to know I gave you pleasure like this."

I didn't know it my words helped or if it was just time, but on a sigh, Kade gave himself over to the moment, spilling in my hand. I held him while he pulsed. His body trembled. This was a man who could destroy empires if he wanted by shutting down their entire electronic infrastructure. He built homes underground that he could then turn around and explode with a push of button. He could be mean, dismissive, and yet he was mine. Kade held me when I shook in his bed, he made me coffee because he knew that I needed it, and he blamed himself for the pain I caused myself.

I loved all his rough parts, and maybe he'd needed to hear me say it.

He lifted his head to kiss me even as he still shook in my arms. I needed to go wash my hand, and so I let go of him only to do that. Kissing him once more, I smiled against his lips. "Next time in my mouth."

Kade shook his head. "Next time in your pussy."

"Maybe if you're lucky."

He laughed, a low sound. "Careful with the turbulence."

"I'm getting better at managing the bumps." There would have been a time I wouldn't have believed I'd be up and moving on a plane while it bounced in the air. But then there were lots of things I never would have imagined doing that were no big deal now.

I cleaned up and came back out, carrying a towel for

Kade. He took it, wiping himself down, although I guessed we were going to have to get him some new shorts before he got off the plane. He tucked me in next to him, and we continued to watch *Doctor Who* together.

All the way until we landed.

"What do you think?" I must have asked Judson ten times in the last fifteen minutes.

He turned to me, giving me the same version of the answer he'd been saying since I started asking. "I think it doesn't seem to have done any internal damage. I'm not sure because I can't take him to a hospital and do a scan. I need to figure out the underground Alliance medical facility in Florida. I've put some calls in. I'll know soon. In the meantime, what I know about gunshot wounds, and it's way too much considering that I'm a plastic surgeon, but people in my life keep getting shot, is that they can be tricky. It was a through and through. That is good news."

I sighed. "Judson? What does that mean?"

He put his arm around me, drawing me close. "It means I don't know. Derrick was right. I don't see an infection. So I'm giving him antibiotics just in case and painkillers. We'll wait and see. I'll be able to take him somewhere soon to get more answers if he doesn't get better. The good news is that it hit soft tissue so... that is excellent. You saved him. I'm sure of it."

"Everly," Trace said my name again before he shook his head back and forth on the pillow. I walked over to him and pushed his hair off his forehead.

I met Jud's gaze when I looked up. "Whatever he's dreaming about me, it isn't good. He says it seconds before he seems to get into terrible pain."

"He hasn't seen you." Judson rubbed my back. "Or even if he was watching from afar, he doesn't really know that you're doing okay. He's probably harboring the same guilt as the rest of us, the same worry. He loves you. But he'll be up and wake and that will stop." He motioned to the other bed. Warden slumbered peacefully, apparently with the help of pharmaceuticals that had knocked him out. "I'm keeping them both in here. I'll watch them closely. Warden is going to be fine. He's already being grumpy about having to follow a healing protocol. I caught him on the computer adjusting the financial markets. He yelled at me about letting you go after Trace. He's fine."

I walked over to him. He breathed deeply: a low sound that I'd never thought of as snoring but was definitely loud enough that I'd been conscious of it when I'd slept with him. It was a comforting sound now. "His color is better." By the time we'd gotten to Boston, he'd been pale.

"He's tough." Judson nodded. "Now how about you? Derrick says you aren't sleeping."

"That's not entirely true." I walked toward him. "And you're one to talk. You're not sleeping either."

He held up his hands. "Lower your weapons. I'm not armed."

I sighed. "Sorry. Yes, I'm not sleeping much. I fell asleep on the way to the Caribbean for half an hour. Had a nightmare. That's pretty much it. I haven't slept in days."

Judson pulled out a pill bottle and handed me one of the tablets. "Take that. It'll knock you out. Get some of your adrenaline down. I'll take one myself once Trace is safe. I'm exhausted, and I've slept more than you."

I stared at the medicine in my hand. "The only downside would be this is going to knock me on my ass and every time I go to sleep I have nightmares right now."

He ran a hand through my hair. "I'm going to send Derrick in to sleep with you. I'd say Kade because he's a lighter sleeper, but he's already face down on the couch in the living room. Derrick can wake you if you start to act like you're having bad dreams. I'd gladly do it, but I'm going to stay in here. It'll be okay, Everly. You might not have nightmares, or if you do, you might not remember them. You're all hyped up. Take a breather."

I knew he was right. I'd thought that myself, but now the idea of sleep seemed less appealing. I sighed. It wasn't one of those things I could put off doing, not if I wanted to function tomorrow.

I had to face the darkness. The trouble was sleep seemed to be when my personal monsters came out to torment me. I guessed I didn't have any choice but to let them.

I took a long hot shower, and when I came out, clean and smelling less like sweat and blood, I walked into a scene I hadn't anticipated. Derrick and Kade were both on the bed, looking at their phones.

I leaned in the doorway. "I thought you were passed out, Kade. That spot in the middle for me?"

Derrick patted it. "He woke up right on time to come intrude on my night."

"I'm supposed to take a pill. I don't think you were getting lucky tonight."

Derrick grinned. "Don't get me wrong, Evs. I want you more than anything, but one of the things I missed in all the months of watching you was just getting to wake up next to you."

Kade scowled at him. "Fuck. Fine. I'll leave."

"No." Derrick sighed. "Better if you're here. You wake up faster to small noises. I've had to train myself to ignore certain things or I can't sleep at all. Two of us are better tonight than one. Although you already got to have some alone time with her on the plane."

My mouth fell open. "I thought you were sleeping."

"I gathered that. No, I wasn't. Come on. This place in the middle is waiting for you."

I needed to swallow my pill first, and I did so before I could talk myself out of it. I grabbed a bottle next to the bed that was presumably Derrick's. I didn't usually like to share drinks, but we were sharing all kinds of bodily fluids. I couldn't really be a hypocrite about it.

I climbed into the bed. Judson had furnished the bedrooms so they all looked the same except the room where Warden and Trace were sleeping. Most of the rooms had California king beds. Night stands. Dressers. Curtains on the windows. But he hadn't thought about televisions or maybe that was just something he hadn't been able to get installed fast enough.

Kade hit the switch to turn off the light and we were all bathed in darkness. I might have liked the distraction of something like television to doze off to. Sometimes, I couldn't even deal with my own grumpiness.

I was safe, warm, and I had Derrick and Kade in the bed with me. I just needed to get over my bad mood.

Kade rolled onto his side and a second later Derrick did the same. It was just like the plane, only we had enough room to be together.

"I love my house, Kade."

I couldn't see him smile, but I felt it in the upbeat sound of his voice. "You're welcome."

"And I love my diamonds, Derrick." Even if I was afraid to wear them. "Thank you for them."

He tugged on the end of my hair. "You're welcome, Evs.

No nightmares. You can sleep soundly, thoroughly. Tell your demons to go somewhere else for the night."

We lay in the darkness. They were both awake. I could feel their alertness on me but the pill Judson gave me started to weigh on me like it wanted to force my eyes closed.

"Thanks for being here. Babysitting me through nightmares couldn't be your idea of a great night with me."

Kade splayed his fingers over my stomach. "Derrick wasn't speaking just for him when he said part of what he wanted was to just be with you. That is a relationship, right? I've never had one, never wanted one, but I do want to be with you. Even if it just means sleeping. You smell good."

Derrick kissed my head. "Stop fighting the sleep. I've had that pill. Practically lived on it for a month after Alyssa died. You should be in dreamland right now."

Maybe because he'd given me permission, I let my eyes close. Safe between the two of them, I decided not to worry, at least for the night, about what would happen next.

"Say yes." Derrick's voice was a whisper in my ear. He stroked his hand down the front of my body and awareness floated into my consciousness along with the bright light of daylight beating through the curtains on the window. "Say yes, Evs, and I'll wake you up this way."

He stopped right outside of my pajama pants, pressing his finger against me but not pushing into my pussy. I opened my eyes even though they wanted to stay closed. The light coming in was hard and intense like it wasn't early. I reached next to me and Kade was gone.

"Say yes."

I smiled and let my lids close. "Yes."

He tugged down my pants, and a second later, his fingers

glided along the edge of my pussy. He was behind me, one arm keeping me against his chest. He petted the outside, running his fingers just over me there. I spread my legs wider. This was an absolutely fantastic way to start the day.

"I should leave you alone, but it's been like fifteen hours since I saw those eyes open. You missed breakfast and it's lunch. I'm selfish and needy. And I am going to make you feel so good so you'll forgive me."

I stretched against him, and he pushed a finger inside of me. As it made contact with my clit, I cried out. Wow, this wasn't going to take much. He laughed in my ear. "Maybe I'm not the only one who is needy."

I squirmed and finally opened my eyes again. "Are you teasing me or didn't you just make me a promise if I said yes?"

His breathing changed, the sounds intensified against my ear. "I'd never tease you."

Derrick stroked my clit, finding my rhythm fast as though he remembered it exactly from the last time we'd done this. This was Derrick, he probably did. I pushed my back against him. This was heaven, but it wasn't enough.

"Other side. Not your fingers." I fumbled; my limbs weren't quite as fast at waking as my mind was at the moment. Still, I managed to cup his cock on the outside of his pants. "Unless you're not interest—"

I didn't get to finish that word. He flipped me over. "I was going to just make you come until you scream my name and then feed you lunch."

I smiled at him. Derrick. The former professional baseball player and secret assassin who had the sweetest heart that he kept hidden away under his usually on display level of crazy.

"Fuck me and then feed me lunch."

"That I can do." He tugged off his pants. We both had our shirts still on. This wasn't the most romantic or intense level of foreplay we'd ever performed. Still, I knew I was going to come fast and hard. I wanted it to be around his cock.

When he was free of his clothing, I stroked his length once. He was already fully erect. This was a man who, according to the media, didn't go very long between lovers since his wife died. "Have you been with anyone else since me?"

"No, the second you pulled that gun out of my hands and pointed it at me, other women ceased to exist. It's just been me and my hand thinking of you all these long months."

I was fucking five men and yet that filled me with tremendous satisfaction. I wanted to be the only one he did this with.

I pushed him down until I could climb on top of him. This hard, it would hurt to try to get him in any other way, or at least it would take too much time. This was about instant gratification, and I wasn't embarrassed to admit it.

I settled atop him and, without pause, pushed myself down, taking him all the way inside of me. It hurt, burned as my muscles stretched to accommodate him, and I didn't care. This was being alive. I'd woken up and he was here. There was light in the room. We'd both made it through the night. What a gift this morning was.

I lifted my hips, squeezing him around me as I dragged myself up over his cock before I pressed back down. He shouted out, a loud noise for Derrick, who was a quiet lover, and I realized I'd done something right. I wondered if it had hurt just slightly and that was why he liked it.

The friction. I did it again, and he bucked his hips, moaning loudly. Oh yes. I loved seeing him get out of control so quickly. I changed my direction just slightly so that each movement also stroked him right across my clit. The next pass I cried out with him.

With each rut of my body, up and down with him, we cried out together. Goosebumps broke out on my body. I took his hands in mine and squeezed them while I rode him.

I wanted to bite him, and I didn't overthink it. If he didn't like it, he could tell me not to do it again.

I brought his hand to my mouth, and I bit his finger. He must have liked it because he emptied inside of me right there. Derrick threw his head back. "Fuck," he bellowed all the way to the moon. Or at least it felt that way.

I grinned. I'd done that. I hadn't come yet but that was okay. He was beautiful in his passion, totally unrestrained, and I so rarely got to see Derrick when he wasn't planning his next step, even if it was in some kind of mania.

He grabbed onto my hips and rolled me over. "Derrick?"

Without uttering a word, he pulled out and a second later his mouth was on me. I gasped at the suddenness of his movement. His tongue made broad strokes over my clit before moving to my pussy. He kept his head steady, using only his tongue, and soon I rocked against him. I'd been close, and it wasn't taking much. Still, the end eluded me, and I couldn't figure out why. It was close, I could practically taste the orgasm. But it wouldn't come. I squirmed, pressing against his mouth.

Derrick put his hand on my knee, stopping me, as though he wanted me to be still, to not move. I did as he told me. I closed my eyes, just feeling his tongue moving over me. The pressure built, and without moving, it was almost too much—an edge of pain to it I wasn't sure I could handle. I certainly couldn't control it. And it was so nice that I didn't have to.

I didn't so much as orgasm as I erupted. My body exploded, pleasure surging through every cell, every piece of existence, that was me. I trembled as I called out his name, knowing I'd needed this more than I ever could have imagined.

It was a new day—in so many ways.

I sprawled next to Derrick. He'd woken me up, and now I wondered if he was going to go down for a cat nap. He smiled at me, a lazy indulgence of a man who knew he'd made me come using his tongue, like I'd never been fucked that way before.

"How were your dreams?

I ran my finger down the slope of his nose. "Fine. How were yours?"

"I don't think I had any last night. When I woke up this morning, Kade and Judson were gone. They took Trace to the underground hospital. I slept through all of that so clearly I was in a deep sleep. I do feel secure having you in the bed with me."

I kissed him. "You're so quiet now in sleep. It's like being wrapped in the warm blanket that is you without any disturbances at all."

He held my gaze. "Good. I love that. You bit me."

I grinned. "Yes. And you loved it."

"I really, really did. But I'll never leave my girl unfinished. If you're going to make me come like I'm a teenager, be prepared for me to flip you over and make you come any way possible."

I laughed and my stomach growled. "It's a deal. I guess I'm hungry."

"Come on." He got out of bed and helped me up. There were much worse ways to start mornings than this.

Warden one-handed typed on his computer. He sat on the couch in what looked like an awkward position. I rushed over to him immediately, wanting to make it easier on him. All it took was adjusting one pillow to get that done. He looked up at my arrival and grabbed onto my arm, nearly dropping his computer as I got him settled.

"Everly. You're awake." His smile lit up the room. Or maybe it just felt that way. "I wanted to stay up to wait for you guys to get back, but Judson drugged me. He's like a prison guard, having to have things exactly his way."

I touched the side of his cheek. "He's taking care of you."

"I like how you do it better."

I didn't know that I'd actually taken care of Warden. "I just got you on a plane."

He pulled me down on his lap. "Putting my eyes on you was the therapy I needed."

I kissed him. "Your color is good. Can you feel your hand?"

He nodded slowly. "I can, and it doesn't feel wonderful but that is fine. Real healing can happen now. You look beautiful. Judson said you had dark circles showing exhaustion under your eyes, but you don't now. That pill he gave you worked. I missed you."

For Warden, he was a little rambling. "Are you on pain meds?"

He nodded. "I am. They did the Alliance surgery on me. So probably just a week or so."

I smiled. "And, my love, are you messing with the world markets while you are a little bit out of it?"

His smile was slow. "Well, I couldn't make it worse."

That was probably true, unfortunately. I brushed his hair off his forehead. "It's really good to see you, Warden. I missed you."

"Derrick was raving this morning about your aim with your knife. Seems you're a natural at it. You shoved it right in her eye socket?"

I kissed his cheek. "I'd been daydreaming about having a reason to do that. I've got to be honest, I'm over it now. I'll have to figure out a new way to contemplate killing someone."

"I'd say that we broke you except you're so damned sexy like this."

I kissed his lips. "I only feel broken sometimes."

"I think that is true for most of us." He tapped his lips. "Look at me confessing I have feelings?"

I laughed. Warden on painkillers really was a trip. When he was stoned on weed he was mostly interested in sex. This version of him was chatty. "Are you hungry?"

"No." He yawned. "But come back and eat whatever you're going to have so I can sit with you."

Derrick entered the room carrying a plate. "She is going to eat eggs. They work all day, don't they? Breakfast, lunch, and dinner food all wrapped into one."

He set it down in front of me along with a glass of water. He was right. Eggs did work for me all day. I grabbed Warden's computer, changing from the financial screen he'd been playing on to a movie app instead. I left it on *The Hobbit*. He liked Tolkien. The fact that he didn't even comment told me it was a good idea to have taken away his ability to play with the finances of small countries or whatever he was doing.

Derrick winked at me. "Eat them before they get cold."

As I chewed and swallowed, I had to consider our situation here. We had some time while two of my guys healed to consider what to do. I didn't want to move forward without their input, and we still didn't know what had happened to Trace. Or at least I didn't. They might have all talked about it.

Why tell me I can be fine if I stay out of the way while at the same time shooting Trace and Warden? They weren't the obvious ones to mess with. Derrick had outright threatened Marcus, and he was still perfectly fine. Judson was much more likely to assume leadership, and Kade disrupted their systems. None of this made any sense to me. I didn't need to understand every small detail of the Alliance, but it had to at least make a semblance of sense. Dots needed to connect.

"Tell me about Marcus. What does he do when he's not trying to have the people I love killed?"

Derrick rubbed his face. "Marcus has kept a very low profile. He mostly stuck to himself all these years. I don't even think he has people working for him, which is weird for the council. He's a dentist. He wasn't particularly Ben's biggest fan, but he never got in his way. I fully expected him to just step aside. But now he has assassins—albeit ones who can't seem to properly hit the broad side of a barn, considering both Trace and Warden are still alive. I don't know, Evs. It's making me a little bit twitchy."

Warden blinked. "What are we talking about?"

"Marcus."

I waited for Warden to answer, and he finally did. "I always thought he was a non-entity. A player on the council just because they wanted someone who wasn't going to get in their way."

"We need a plan to take him out." I cracked my knuckles. "And it needs to be a good one. We'll likely get one shot at this. It needs to work. If we lose, we're all dead. So let's take some time, get schematics on wherever he's staying, and see to it that we know more than he does about everything. Figure out how to take him down without any of us getting hurt. I'm not losing any of you."

Derrick tugged on my hair. "Maybe we can buy our way out."

"Is that possible?" Trying to navigate the Alliance was exhausting. "I thought it was a 'til death do us part kind of a thing."

Warden blinked. "Is someone getting married?" He

pointed at me. "You can't marry Derrick. Not until after you marry me."

I grinned. "Take a nap, Warden." I set my plate fully on the table and patted my lap. "Head here."

Derrick lifted his lids. "Why does she have to marry me after you? I can go first if I want to. In fact, I'm going to. Evs, you have to marry me before you marry Warden."

This was the most ridiculous conversation ever, made even stranger by the fact Derrick did not seem to be kidding. I waited for him to wink, and he didn't. Warden settled in my lap and I closed his computer.

I ran my hands through his hair, while I thought about things. "How would that even work, Derrick? We've never really considered any of this, never figured out how it would play out. You guys wanted me to bounce around following you, and I told you that was not happening. How it might happen has never been sorted out."

He tilted his head. "How do you want it to work?"

"I want to be with all of you. I should just say that. I know it makes me selfish. Maybe everyone is good with that in the short term, maybe you're okay with it long term. With the exception of Trace who is injured too much right now, you've all promised to be loyal to each other. I want all of you, and I want Marcus to leave us alone." I waved my hand to indicate the room. "Do we all stay here in this gorgeous home in paradise Kade found and just play house like it's not totally off kilter that we're doing this?"

Warden sighed. "It's not so off kilter. People have multiple loves all the time. And I don't give a shit what anyone thinks. I'll stay here. Where you are is where I am. When I'm not all drugged up, I can work anywhere."

Was it that easy? Trace and Judson both had jobs that would make that tricky. There was a time I had wanted a husband and children. A big family. It came from being an only child left mostly alone in the world after my mother died. I was certainly not cut out to be anyone's mother anymore. I'd just shoved a knife into a woman's eye socket and watched her bleed to death.

"What happens to the Alliance after we end Marcus?"

Derrick shook his head. "The Alliance can go fuck itself."

That wasn't really an answer. "Derrick, there is always going to be an Alliance, right? Cut off the head, another one grows back. Does this ever end or are we locked up forever in hiding?"

"You're one day into the hiding, don't get stir crazy yet." Warden looked up at me with slitted eyes. "There has been a lot of bloodshed lately. But that wasn't always the case. When our grandfathers were Alliance members, there was none. Alliance isn't supposed to hurt Alliance. I have to believe we can get back from this and return to that. People raised families and benefited from our power structure. My grandfather never had to go into hiding."

I stroked his hair. "This from the man with his head in my lap because he got shot weeks ago and is only going to be okay because of surgery not available to the general public? You think we can do without bloodshed?"

Warden adored me with his eyes. "Maybe I'm just taking advantage of having been hurt to stick my head in your lap and let you baby me."

Derrick laughed, it was a low sound before he stretched out, putting his head on my shoulder. "It's nice to sit here with you just like this."

It was really nice. I turned my head to kiss the top of his hair. Somehow, Derrick always managed to look fantastically put together and smell like sandalwood scented shampoo. I was in a constant state of disarray. I ran my hands through Warden's hair. "I really like it, too."

"To answer your question more seriously," Warden sighed.

"Yes, I think we can get back to it. Most of us just want to live lives of quiet power. The last Council destroyed things, but it's not too late to fix it. Or blow the whole thing up and start over from a better position. I actually believe. And for the other stuff you were worrying about? How this works? Look, it's working. It would be if Judson, Trace, and Kade were running around here now, too."

He was right except in the small details. "Judson has a practice in Massachusetts. Trace has a job in Virginia."

"Neither of them is currently there." Derrick squirmed, rubbing his forehead against my shoulder. Was he planning on just going to sleep? I kind of loved that. Oh boy, I really was still squishy inside. I kind of thought I'd hardened, but it turned out I still had the part of me that wanted to give affection and love easily. Was I going to survive this if I continued to be so soft? Of course, I'd also shoved a knife through someone's eye without giving it much of a second thought. Maybe I was doomed to live in a constant dichotomy of personality issues.

Derrick continued. "Trust them to know what they can do with their jobs and what they can handle. I don't know how much Judson even wants to practice anymore, and for Trace, it was always a cover as much as a calling."

Warden shifted slightly. He closed his eyes. "We're all in love with you. We spent too much time apart. I..."

He never finished what he was saying. Mid-word sentence he simply nodded off in my lap. Derrick was silent, his breathing eventually deepening. I guessed they both needed naps and they wanted them lying on me. I continued to stroke my hands through Warden's hair. It was soothing to me. He'd shown up in my bar, and he'd needed me. It really had been that easy to get me back into this mess.

I picked up my phone, shooting a text to Judson and Kade. Someone had put everyone's numbers back on my phone. I'd purchased it to be a throwaway device, but with all the apps on it now—that had to be because of Kade—it looked like I was keeping it for the foreseeable future. I downloaded a book app and picked up a mystery I'd been wanting to try. The Wi-Fi in here was fast. That had to be from Kade. He really was amazing. I wondered if he even knew how much better he made our lives.

I was going to tell him. While I was in this soft, gooey emotional zone everyone might as well benefit from my feeling this way. It was bound to be shut off any second when either someone pissed me off or the world interfered.

Thank you for this beautiful house and making it so comfortable and easy to be in already. I sent it to him.

A text came immediately back. *I love you, too. You were out last night. I don't think you moved. I checked a couple of times to make sure you were breathing.*

I grinned. Warden made a small sound that was a sigh, and I realized I'd stopped petting him with my other hand. I went back to it, and he settled. I guessed he liked that. Derrick breathed evenly, his hand on my hip. I wasn't sure how he could possibly be comfortable.

Thanks for that. Guess I needed the sleep. Is Trace okay?

He responded fast. *Yes, hold on. I'll have Judson text you. He's staring at a soap opera on a television like he's never seen something so awful before. It's actually kind of funny.*

A few seconds passed and Judson's number popped up. *Hey, Everly. Texting Kade and not me? Should I be insulted?*

I chewed on my lip. *I always think of you as busy.*

Not currently. Just waiting. Trace is going to be fine. They knocked him out to take an exploratory laparoscopic look inside the wound area, but the general consensus from the trauma surgeon is he seems fine. His fever broke this morning, and he is cranky as hell.

Warden shifted again. *When does W get more pain meds?*

Three hours. I should be back, but if I'm not, they're in the room I put him and Trace in. Next to his bed. You sleep okay?

A second text came right in from Kade. *Don't just text with him. Now I'm jealous. Text with both of us.*

I put them into a group text. *How is it where you are? Any place you could go get lunch?*

It was Judson who answered. *That's a good idea. Let's go get lunch, Kade.*

I grinned. They were sitting next to each other and they were texting. *I've got Derrick and Warden both asleep on me. I just ate lunch, and I guess I'm going to read until one of them wakes up. I hate to bother either of them.*

Really? It was Kade who answered. *Lucky assholes.*

Judson's came in fast. *I call the next nap on Everly.*

I'd been really alone for months. That had been my choice and what I'd thought I'd needed. Hell, maybe I actually had. How would I know? I'd told them I needed to be alone and even if they hadn't really given it to me, until Warden walked into my bar I'd felt entirely on my own. Now here I was, with men I should probably have never known, asleep on me, and sending me text messages that made me smile.

Life was really bizarre sometimes.

No time for lunch. They came to get us. Trace is up. Pissed off and up. Grump Trace is no fun. Just in case you wanted to be warned about who we are bringing home. He makes Warden seem easy going when he's injured.

I looked down at Warden. He was completely easy going right now. Adorably, so. I hadn't thought he was handsome when I'd first seen him. His face was too intense, almost too masculine, when I'd first laid eyes on it. But now? He was beautiful. There would never be a time I wasn't attracted to him or think he was among the handsomest people on Earth.

I let go of his hair to run my finger down the slight of his nose.

It was slightly too big to be fashionable. Then again, there was little about me that would land me on a fashion magazine. Even injured, Warden had on perfect clothes that were likely tailored to him. I didn't even know how he'd gotten them, considering he'd had on the pilot's clothes the last time I saw him. Maybe he kept a bag of expensive clothing at Judson's house.

Or maybe he was wearing Judson's, which should have been slightly too tight on him except that Warden had clearly lost weight. I was way overthinking this.

He rubbed against my hand in his sleep. Warden was desperate for touch. I knew that feeling well. I was starved for it, too. Derrick shifted, and I nuzzled against his hair. That's what this was about. The sex with each of them was astronomically good, but it wasn't enough. At the end of the day we were humans and we needed to touch each other in gentle ways that didn't end up with our clothes off.

We were fucked up humans, but it didn't alter our human status.

I went back to my phone. I didn't have any new messages from Judson or Kade. They must have been getting Trace ready to come back. I returned to my book. The plot was interesting. A retired detective dragged back to work to solve the case he never did. It was a trope in mystery, but one I enjoyed nonetheless.

I wasn't sure how much time passed, but soon the door to the house opened. Kade, Judson, and Trace's voices boomed into the room. They were arguing, that much was clear.

"If she's not here and this is just a fucked up way to get me to cooperate with the two of you, I am going to fucking kill you," Trace shouted.

Judson laughed. "Go take a look."

I kissed Derrick's head. "Time to wake up. Think I have to move."

He grunted and opened his eyes. "I'll go see if they need any help."

Derrick stretched his arms over his head, doing that thing that let me see his abs when his shirt rode up. I'd had him half naked in my bed that morning but I'd never get enough of looking at him. I grinned. I hated to disturb Warden so I scooted right, which let me lay his head down on the couch. He sucked in a long breath but didn't wake up. Healing must have been exhausting.

I made my way toward the hall, almost colliding with Trace when I did. He was wrapped up in bandages, his eyes were red and wounded looking, and for just a second as we stared at each other, and then true joy blossomed in his gaze.

If I'd ever wondered if he loved me, and I had, I didn't anymore.

I cupped the side of his face. "If you ever do that to me again, get shot and end up in some weird woman's house held captive for money, I'll fucking kill you myself."

He grinned. "I missed you, too. Congratulations on the college degree. I... I got you something."

"Damn it," Judson shouted from the hallway.

"Thank you, Trace."

Trace swallowed his pills using a bottle of water I'd handed him. Warden was up and we all sat around the kitchen table —the first time the six of us were together since I'd stormed out of the hotel room.

"It was very sudden but death always is, right?" He shook his head. "One second James was chatting about his latest conquest, the next he was dead. I hit the ground just as the bullet struck me right in the side. If I hadn't... I'd be dead on his floor, too."

Derrick nodded. He twisted his mouth up like he was chewing something and then stopped. "And you saw nothing? Not even a red dot or something like that as you were targeted?"

Trace shook his head. "No, it was only seeing James go down that made me hit the floor."

"Okay." Derrick rose. "I'm going to go for a few days."

"What?" I grabbed his arm. "Why? Where are you going?"

He smiled at me in the same way he had after he'd made me come on the bed that morning. My cheeks immediately heated up. Was my grabbing his arm somehow akin to him to his getting me to orgasm with his tongue? I tried to drop my hand, but he grabbed it, linking our fingers together.

"I'll be back in three days tops. I need to know who the shooter is. There are contacts I have that Kade will not be able to find on the dark web. Retired people who still know things. They won't be on any websites. I'll be safe." He looked around the table. "And she better be when I get back. Kade, this is on you. Judson's got his hands full with these two. If she's hurt when I get back, I'm going to be pissed."

Kade nodded. "We're on the same page over this now, Derrick. We all took the oath. Well, Trace hasn't, but presumably he will."

Trace shook his head. "What oath?"

I squeezed his hand. "We can get into that later."

"All right." Trace kissed me before he spoke to Derrick. "See you in three days or less. I'll have information."

"Derrick." I rose and crossed to him to hug him against me. "Trace and Warden have both been shot. You threatened Marcus and they did nothing to you. I got a mediocre warning. Judson hasn't been messed with. We don't know if Trace was the target or if James Robert was. Why? Why Warden and Trace?"

He shook his head. "When we know who, we can find out why. I love you. See you soon, Evs."

I sat again as he left. Everyone was quiet, maybe they were considering what I'd said, but I thought that Warden and Trace were probably pretty preoccupied with how badly they felt.

Trace rubbed his eyes. "Feeling like I missed something. Derrick just came out with that pretty openly. I love you, too, by the way. But are we all just saying it?"

Kade smirked. "We are. I think she loves you, too. She put a knife through the eye of the woman who was holding you hostage."

I waved my hand. I really didn't want to get into that right now. "Judson, I'm guessing you're exhausted. Go take a nap while these guys are fine. I'll sit with them. Kade, can you get a list of everywhere Marcus has ever lived or if he visits some place over and over?"

He nodded. "On it."

Warden winced. "I'm thinking I'm not good for anything right now. My pain pill has worn off."

"It hasn't." Judson got up. "Not for another hour. Don't let him take it early, Everly. You saw yourself he has no restraint when it comes to this stuff. How much did you drink on the pain pills in Everly's bar?"

Warden rolled his eyes. "You deal with that pain over three weeks on the run and see if you make good decisions."

"I really missed a bunch of shit getting shot, didn't I?" Trace smiled.

He was in one of Jud's green shirts. Trace was always the man in black. He was profoundly colorblind and couldn't differentiate most colors from one another. It was easier for him to simply wear black all of the time. He looked funny in color. I didn't like it.

"We need televisions. Is it safe for me to go buy us some stuff? You guys went out today. Presumably I can? I'm not at risk, anyway. They don't seem to give a shit about me."

Kade nodded. "It's fine, but tell me what you want and I'll order it."

"This is going to sound strange but I'd like to get Warden and Trace clothes that are more them."

Trace tugged at his shirt. "What color is it?"

"Green." I stroked my hand down his arm. "I miss you in black."

"Want to see what I got you? Kade can pull up a picture on the Internet. I was thinking if you were about to go off the grid, so to speak, that maybe the thing to do was to put you on a yacht where I'd know you were safe. Presumably, Kade had a similar idea."

Judson's mouth fell open. "I thought of that. Today. A yacht. I was going to buy her a yacht. You bought her one already? Fuck me."

Dr. Smythe stormed off to the kitchen.

"You bought me a boat? I don't know how to captain a boat. I mean, thank you. But other than the little fishing boats we tooled around on lakes and rivers back home, I wouldn't have the slightest idea how to do that. I'd need to take a class."

Kade grinned. "I think the point here was that Trace was going to captain that boat for you."

Trace nodded. "Yep. That's what I was going to do."

I scooted my chair closer to him. "Can you guys give us a minute?"

Kade nodded. "I'm going to order televisions. That was a good call. Anything else you want? Clothes for Trace and Warden. What else?"

Guilt washed through me. "Kade, you just bought me this house. Don't spend any more money. I have an account. Use that money."

He laughed, throwing his head back. "Yeah... that's not going to happen." He stood before he grabbed his computer.

Trace grabbed his arm. "Safe outside? To sit outside facing the beach? Are we visible?"

"Oh." Kade grinned. "Yeah, brother. Sorry. Yes, we can all go outside. We can even walk down to the water, into the water if you want." He pointed out the window. "As long as you can see the house, it's safe. I took care of a two-mile radius. Could extend that but..." Kade rapidly blinked. "I have a great idea. Yes, a good one. Game changer. Fuck. Why didn't I think of this before?"

I got to my feet. "What are you thinking?"

He held up a finger. "Give me a few minutes with this in case it turns out to be nothing. I... I don't want to get everyone's hopes up." He kissed me. "I'm going to the back of the house. The little room no one is using. Okay if I make that my office? I need to put things together. I'll actually need to get my equipment. I'm going to do that."

Kade didn't really need an answer, so I didn't give him one. He was already out the door, his mind not here anymore but on whatever he was going to invent to fix things for us. I grinned. He was really adorable.

Trace pulled himself to his feet as Warden moaned. "Why are you in such better shape than me?"

Judson shook his head. "We all heal differently. It's a different place on the body. They had to undo something that went wrong with you and you had weeks like that. He didn't need much intervention. Or maybe he just handles pain better than you do."

"Not when we were getting beaten at Ben's." Warden rolled his eyes. "Fuck. I'm going to sit on the couch until you deign to give me another pill, Judson."

The doctor laughed. "Oh, you're going to love me next week when I cut them in half and then take them away altogether."

Trace scowled at Warden. "Don't act like you were king of the beatings, Warden. We all went through that hell. I don't remember you doing that with a smile."

"I can't imagine anyone taking Ben's beatings that way." I chewed on my lip.

Warden rose and walked past Trace. "Well done. Now she's thinking about that. Just what she wanted for today. You okay?" He addressed the last part to me.

I touched his arm. "I don't fall apart from the memory of what happened. How could I? I'd be wrecked all day long. I just carry it like a constant companion on my shoulder. Trace bringing it up doesn't make that harder. I always have the load whether I talk about it or not."

Warden nodded. "Did you really stick a knife in that woman's eye?"

"I did." And I still didn't feel badly about it.

"I'm not even sure I could have done that."

Trace pulled himself to his feet, visibly wincing when he did. "Then I guess she's more lethal than you. You wanted to talk, Everly? Outside? I'd love some fresh air and to look at the water even if I'm not up for walking out to it just yet."

"You don't want to get that ocean water anywhere near your open wound." Judson yawned. "I am going to go nap, and when I get up, I will give you more medicine, Warden, and not a minute before. Try to think about something else."

I didn't envy Judson having to dole that out for Warden. Not even a little bit. And I didn't envy any of us next week when he had to cut the meds down. Pain was awful. Warden had held me in the shower when I'd had to endure the water on my back.

I walked over to him. "You'll get through it, and we'll find ways to distract you."

His eyes were wounded, showing the pain he was in better than anything else. "Love you so fucking much."

"Go sit down. I'll be back in a little bit."

He nodded. There were six of us in this relationship. Well, there would be if Trace said yes to the same terms the others did. And they all had needs that I wanted to meet. Certainly, they'd all been there for me when I was lost, and they hadn't really left me alone, continuing to protect me when I'd thought being on my own was what I needed.

I followed Trace outside. He sat down on one of the porch chairs that overlooked the ocean. "You really like the sea don't you? The Caribbean? Here? The yacht? And thank you for that. I really don't know what to say."

He patted the spot next to him on his un-shot side. I scooted in next to him. He didn't speak, so I did again. "Are you as okay as you are pretending?"

"I'm on adrenaline right now. I don't want to be holed up in the bed for weeks. I'd rather do it here. I like the ocean. I can't see the colors, but I feel like I can appreciate the vastness of it, even despite my color blindness the same way the rest of you can. I like sunshine better than cold. Always have. The feel of the sand on my feet... Yes, all of that is a yes. I like the ocean, a lot."

I put my head on his shoulder and breathed him in. He smelled like soap and oranges. "I thought I might never get to smell you again. I thought maybe I'd made a mistake I'd never get to undo."

He brought my hand to his mouth to kiss it. "You came for me. Thank you. I... I'm finding words a little harder than they should be. For all that I'm pretending to be better than Warden, I think he's just more out there with it. But then everyone is being very open in speaking their truths here right now. Confessing their love. Speaking their feelings. I don't mind it, but it's different."

"It's probably what I made them promise me, and I need to ask you to swear to as well."

He shifted. "That sounds ominous."

"Not really; it was sort of spontaneous, but it's turned out to be very important to me. I want you to swear to be as loyal to each other as you are to me. I don't doubt your feelings for me, not even a little bit. I never did. I needed space or maybe I didn't. But that's not the point. I can't do this. I can't be with all of you and think you're plotting against each other. I'm asking you to promise me to be on each other's team, to be for each other what you are for me."

Trace turned his head to look at me. "That's it?"

"That's it. Is that something you can do?" Trace might say

no. There hadn't been a guarantee with any of them that they wanted to invest in each other that way. But it was what I couldn't—wouldn't—compromise on.

"You need this because you can't be working out the world's agenda while you're trying to also figure out all the strings being pulled at home."

Trace caught on fast. He always did. "Yes."

"I'll make that promise. I do. I will be loyal to them. I swear it."

I turned on my side to kiss his cheek. He needed to shave, but I didn't mind the bite of his whiskers. "Thank you. If you'd said no, there would be a big empty hole where you were supposed to be."

"This does work, doesn't it? All of us with you. I'm not sure why, but it does. I'm not jealous of them. Not when it comes to you. I just feel... solid."

I brushed his hair off his face. "You should sleep."

"Think I'm going to whether I want to or not. My eyes are trying to close." He rubbed them. "The sound of the ocean and you. It's very relaxing."

I didn't say anything else, just lay with him until I was sure he rested. He'd been through a ton, and if he didn't think he had to put on a show about how tough he was, maybe he'd get better faster. I needed his brain, his expertise, because we were going after Marcus. I wasn't going to let that man take anything from me. He was the last piece of the Alliance puzzle and it was time to be rid of him.

I left Trace asleep on the lounge outside. The house was quiet. Not that it ever buzzed with noise. This was a weird time. Derrick had just left, and I had to trust he was okay. Kade was preoccupied, and Judson needed a break. Warden and Trace both had to be given the chance to heal. I hated inaction. Well, that wasn't exactly true. I hated it because this time I wasn't in control of it.

I passed the couch where Warden was asleep, sitting upright. He did not look comfortable. My heart clenched. The second he felt like any semblance of himself again he wasn't going to be needy. I'd seen Warden go from warm to aloof in a heartbeat when we first met. It was going to be hard if he did that again, particularly since he was being so open about his feelings right now.

I crept over to him. Not that I needed to be that quiet. It took a lot to wake a wounded Warden, but considering the understandable cranky that was his personality at the moment, I didn't want to poke the bear if I could avoid it. I laid him down flat on his back on the couch, putting a pillow under his head. He adjusted slightly but stayed asleep.

I should ask Kade to order us some blankets. Or maybe I could go buy some. Was that allowed? Kade said yes but then he said he'd order something. It was confusing, and I wasn't clear. I needed some clarification.

Leaving Warden to hopefully sleep through his discomfort, I passed by Judson's room. His door was cracked, and he was face down on the bed. I closed his door quietly. These guys really didn't take care of themselves when things got a little askew.

Finally, making my way to the small room, I found Kade on the floor. He had taken apart one of his computers. I stared for a minute while he didn't see me. Kade's hands moved quickly. He unscrewed something and set it aside. Technology was like a foreign language I didn't speak.

I cleared my throat to get his attention, and he looked up at me. "Did the computer do something bad so you're getting rid of it?"

Kade rolled his eyes. "Funny."

"If only I was kidding." I squatted down. "Can I leave the house? Is it safe? I'm not sure."

He nodded. "You can. What do you need? I ordered the

televisions and Trace some black clothes that I think should fit him. And stuff for Warden, although I'm sure he won't like it since he treats buying clothing like it's a war that only he can win."

I liked that description. It made me smile. "I kind of want to go wandering around one of those big stores that has everything in it and buy things for the house. I don't want to be cooped up here any longer. If it's safe, I'm doing it."

He nodded. "It's safe because according to the satellites sending images to Marcus, you're in New Orleans. I have it on a loop. I'm going to make that safer. That's what I'm working on now. Call if you need anything."

I touched his cheek. "It hasn't escaped my notice Kade that we haven't gotten naked together yet. The plane doesn't count."

He visibly swallowed. "Evy..."

I grinned. "Think about it somewhere in that big brain of yours until I get back. I will."

His smile was huge. "Wherever you live, I'm going to be, okay? Even if it's not permanently here. I don't ever want to be separated for any length of time. Your home is mine."

"Do you think we should be making big promises when none of us are sure there will be a future for us?" I legitimately wanted to know what he thought. There was nothing rhetorical about my question.

He winked at me. "I've got this. Trust me. They won't be able to find us unless we want them to."

"I have some questions about Marcus for later. All of this downtime is giving my mind time to wander."

Kade shook his head. "Everly, we've been here almost no time. It's not a lot of downtime. You should ask Judson for a Xanax."

I supposed I should have been insulted, but he might have had a point. We didn't sugarcoat things from each other.

"Really?" Was I expecting too much? Did I want to rush when caution was the name of the game? "I'll work on calming down. I don't do adrenaline bursts all that well, I guess. Once I'm up I want to stay that way."

"You'll get used to it." He picked up one of the parts that looked like alien tech to me but might have been some kind of microphone. Did they make understanding your computer for dummies classes?

"Need anything while I'm out?"

His eyes lit up. "Yes, actually." He grabbed a key from his pocket. "I was going to go later. Could you go to my storage unit and grab a black briefcase I have in there? It's just spare parts, but I could use it. I opened it when I bought this place. Well, I should say I opened it when I broke into this place to check it out for you."

There was a time I might have thought he was kidding. "Sure. Text me the address."

"Will do. Thanks. Love you." He looked back at his computer. "And fuck, now I'm thinking about getting you naked."

I knew he was. That was exactly why I'd done it. I was selfish. There was part of me that wanted to be on their minds all the time. Back to that narcissist problem I'd told Kade about. When it came down to it, I didn't mind him being slightly uncomfortable as he waited to have sex with me.

Fuck, I could really be such a bitch.

I took Judson's car to the store, which I had to Google to find after I stole the car keys from his room. I assumed it was a rental unless he'd bought it to come down here. Destin had changed a huge amount since I was a kid and the traffic made getting to the store a lot longer than I had expected. It didn't matter.

This was my outing. I really didn't care how long it took to get where I was going. I sent Kade a text, making sure it was safe to use my debit card, and he responded, assuring me it wasn't going to be traced. He'd messed with the chip in the card. I wasn't sure when he could have done that, but this was Kade. He might have figured out how to do that while he was brushing his teeth.

I wandered the store. There were just some things that made a house a home. Or so my grandmother would have said. I liked some throw pillows, and I put them in a basket. I wanted soft blankets if the guys were going to be conking out all over the house napping. Warden could really have used one on the couch, and if it chilled out at all, then Trace probably needed one outside.

I couldn't believe how domestic I was being. I'd never wanted to take care of a house, but these were things we needed to be comfortable. I picked out a few new brands of coffee and food for the fridge. By the time I was done, several hours had passed.

I just had to go to Kade's storage unit—which didn't seem to be very far away when I looked at the map—so I headed that way, thinking I'd buy Chinese food on the way home if I saw a place to do so. I'd just purchased groceries and now I wanted take out. That was so typical me. It was a good thing I was using the money Warden invested for me again because my bar earnings didn't let me be stupid with cash like that.

I sighed. I'd really liked working there. Was it possible to be with these guys and have normalcy too? And did I even want that?

Once upon a time, I would have said I knew myself pretty well. Now I was a mess of contradiction with no idea what tomorrow would bring. We were supposed to live in the present, experts said, to find contentment, and yet this was a whole other issue. I didn't know who wanted to kill me or why.

Oh well. At least there was sex to look forward to, and I really, really did when it came to my Letters. I smiled, pulling into the storage unit. I'd get Kade's briefcase and get back to that.

On the key was scratched the number associated with the locker Kade rented. This place was unmonitored and not like the air-conditioned luxury storage units my father used to store his model car collection in. I'd had to sell all of those after he died. They'd actually gone for a pretty penny.

But now I was traipsing through a place I'd never been before that certainly looked like it had seen better days. That was funny because everything in Destin seemed like it was booming with newness and wealth.

I sighed. I supposed there always had to be a place people went to do nefarious things. Or maybe I was being mean. Maybe this place was perfectly fine and...

I stopped my thoughts abruptly as two men came out of the shadows to stare at me. I turned to regard them. They weren't Alliance. I knew that right away. Even Alliance assassins were dressed in expensive clothes. It was as though everyone in the Alliance had to hide who they were but wouldn't dress anyway other than the most expensive clothing.

The two men in front of me were not that. In fact, I was

pretty sure their clothing, which was ripped and torn, hadn't been washed in a very long time. They stared at me with red, bloodshot eyes and shaking hands.

There had been a time when I'd thought I'd spend my life helping people in need. I didn't know if I still had that in me. "You guys okay?"

The one on the right, the taller of the two, brushed his tremoring hand across his face. "We're better now."

I supposed I could play dumb about what that really meant. "Do you need some kind of help? I'm happy to call someone to come and help you. There must be places close to here that have programs to help you guys get off the drugs. Yes, sorry, I just made that assumption. Your shaking hands give you away. I guess it could be medical. If you're not on drugs, I apologize. In any case, maybe I could get you some help."

I rambled, but I hoped they understood I could help them. If they'd let me. Even as I spoke the words, I knew they were ridiculous and I wasn't fooling anyone. They didn't want me to help them; they wanted to hurt me. My father had called me a bleeding heart when I told him I was going into social work. He'd told me I'd never make any money doing it but then he'd backed off, which I'd thought at the time was because I'd made my case for wanting to work in a field that inspired passion for me so well. By contrast, I now suspected he'd decided I would eventually marry an Alliance man and money wouldn't be an issue.

I didn't know if my heart still bled, but I knew I didn't want this to end the way it was shaping up to. Would every time I left the house end in violence?

Was that just how my life shaped up to go?

"I think we're just fine. The kind of help you could give us would be to spread your thighs and let us have just what we wanted."

Maybe it was the drugs. Maybe they had been decent people before they'd fallen down the rabbit hole and not come back up again. Boys whose mothers loved them. Young men with dreams they hoped to fulfill. A life spread out before them that they'd never get to live because they'd done this instead. There was my bleeding heart.

The one that didn't do that anymore, the one that had dried up, questioned whether they'd just always been assholes. Of course, there were circumstances that made people do what they did. But to corner a woman who was alone for the purpose of raping her? And then probably robbing me and maybe killing me?

"I want to make sure we understand each other. You're going to... hurt me? That's your intention. And I should let you know that isn't going to happen. Not ever. There are two of you, one of me and yet you two are going to fare very badly in this. If you come at me now, I will kill you."

The one on the left laughed. "We might be... as you say... in need of help. But I can say without a doubt, the two of us and you? You don't stand a chance."

I sighed. If only that were still the case.

The knife taped to my back burned. "Please don't do this. Please just go about your way. I'll go mine and we can all pretend this never happened."

They didn't.

I sat on the ground, knife in hand, with two dead bodies on either side of me. I was covered in blood—again—with no idea if the whole exchange had just been caught on video feed or not. I didn't see a camera but that didn't mean there wasn't one. Kade had taught me just how intrusive technology could be. It was a constant battle to keep ahead of it.

Had I done so now?

Well, I didn't hear police sirens or see anyone coming.

I pulled my phone out of my pocket and dialed Kade.

"Hey there," his deep voice boomed through the phone to my ear. "You're still at the storage space? Did the key not work?"

I sighed. "I have two dead bodies. I just killed two men. They threatened me but that's neither here nor there. What do I do with the dead bodies?" He was silent, so I spoke again. "Kade?"

"Sorry, I heard you. What happened? Are you okay? Are you safe now?"

I smiled. "I'm sitting on the ground. My attackers are dead. I think I'm relatively safe. I'm going to go get your stuff out of your locker in a second. But I'm asking about the bodies. What should I do with them?"

The last times I'd been involved in situations like this I'd had others to handle the aftermath.

"Do?" He groaned. "Don't do anything. I'll be right fucking there."

I sighed and hung up. I really was either the person with the worst luck in the world or there was something with my karma that drew this nonsense to me. I must have done something bad in a past life or something. Not that I particularly believed in anything anymore.

I got to my feet. Sitting on the ground feeling sorry for myself wasn't going to get me anywhere. There were things to do and maybe there was the possibility of still getting that Chinese Food. My stomach rumbled. I had two dead drug addicts less than a foot away and I was already hungry. It was as though every time I took a life, some part of me that found horror in this disappeared with it.

I found the bag Kade wanted and locked up behind me just as an SUV skidded to a stop in front of the locker. I had parked a distance away, not knowing exactly where I was supposed to be. Maybe if I'd been right in front, I could have avoided this altogether.

Kade and Judson jumped out on opposite sides, almost simultaneously.

"Are you hurt?" Jud yelled, running over first.

I looked down at myself. "Not my blood."

He spun me around like he looked for holes in my body and not finding them, pulled me against him. There was something wrong about getting blood all over Judson, considering how nice his clothes were. "You're going to get yucky."

"I'll throw the clothes out." I thought about hugging him back, but the truth was that my arms just didn't want to do that right now. He waited a beat before he looked at me. Judson cupped my chin before he narrowed his eyes. "Everly? You okay?"

"I'm fine." I shrugged. "Just hungry."

"You're not." Judson pulled me against him again, this time not seeming to care if I hugged him back or not. He didn't let go. "You can talk to me."

I didn't pull back, which surprised me. I wasn't ready to hug but standing there like that seemed like a perfectly okay idea. "I'm obviously not okay. We have two bodies. What are we going to do with them?"

"That's not what I meant and you know it. Don't run away, Everly."

Where did he think I was going to go? "I'm standing right here."

"You're running away emotionally," he whispered in my ear. "Last time it was physical. This time you're leaving while you stand here."

I sighed. "Judson, when I asked Derrick to teach me how to kill, I thought it would be Ben. There are a lot of people who are dead because I asked that question. And I don't even feel sorry. I think I might be dead inside."

He rubbed my back. "You're not dead inside. They threatened you. It's called self-defense. It's even legal."

I leaned back to look at him. "I have skills the normal person doesn't have. Maybe I could have disarmed them. I didn't even think about it."

"Who would think about that? They might have been out of their minds. What were they on? I see track marks. And..."

I shook my head. "Judson, you don't have to make this okay for me. I did this. I killed two drug addicts. I didn't try to run. They lunged at me, I took out my knife, and that was that. I am a psychotic killer, and I don't feel remorse."

He snorted. "I've known psychotic killers my whole life. You might be living in denial, but you are not that."

"I'm going to get this cleaned up," Kade said, stepping over one of the bodies to walk over to us. "Any evidence you were here is gone."

Judson squeezed me again. "I'm going to take her home. Do you want me to come back and help with the clean up?"

Kade waved his hand. "No, I've easily got this."

He easily had this. Of course he did. I killed two men, and Kade would just erase the whole thing like it never happened. I rubbed the back of my neck. Why did he do this? Because he loved me, and he was Alliance. Oh, it might be in ruins at the moment, and we might be hiding until we could take back control, but there it was.

The Alliance. It was always there. It would never be gone. And if I wanted to kill two men by a storage unit—well, that would be just fine. It would be handled. Why did this still surprise me? I should have been feeling grateful about it, and yet there was something that was still so off about this whole thing, and I wondered if it would ever become my normal.

Would that be okay if it did?

Judson took my arm. "Where are your car keys?"

I pulled them out of my pocket. "Your keys, if you want to be exact. I stole them from you."

He laughed. "While I face planted on my bed, dead to the world, you came in my room and stole my car. I see how it is. Well, we'll just have to get your car from Warden delivered here and then you won't have to steal from me."

"Maybe stealing is one of the things I want to be really good at. Like death. I'm a death giver. I can be a take your stuff person, too."

He kissed my cheek, his mouth lingering there while he spoke in a whisper. "I've killed people. A lot of them. At the behest of the Alliance. I never talk about it but there it is. You are not a death giver. Today, they would have hurt you. Even before Derrick taught you some skills that you mastered, you wouldn't have sat around and taken that. This is going to be okay."

The thing was I was pretty much okay. And that concerned me more than anything else. Who the fuck was I? "I really wanted that Chinese food, and I bought pretty stuff for the house."

"Well, I'll get you some Chinese. You can't go in. You're covered in blood. I'll go in. Just tell me what you want. Keep in mind, I'm not sure Warden has ever eaten take out Chinese. So we may need to get a variety of stuff so he can figure out what he'll eat. He's been to China, but he probably only ate in five star restaurants there."

That didn't surprise me in the least. This was Warden. Of course in this case, Jud was one to talk. "How much Chinese have you eaten?"

He rolled his eyes at me. "I went to medical school. We ate Chinese at midnight while we studied for exams."

"So once or twice?"

He laughed, throwing his head back. "Maybe three times."

We drove in silence except for me directing him to the closest takeout down the street. We were close enough I could have walked. Except, I was covered in blood. Judson had to go buy the food for me while I waited in the car, staring out the window at the cars rushing by on the busy street behind us. Ben would have called them ants. Kade would have called them that, too, when I first met him. I envied them their ignorance and I knew that was a ridiculous thing to think. How nice would it be to be in one of those cars, planning a dinner, a hookup, talking about... nothing.

"I've eaten Chinese food before," Warden rolled his eyes as he spooned some white rice into his mouth. He chewed and swallowed before he winked at me. "Lots of time. More than Jud, I bet."

Trace shook his head. "Judson Smythe and Warden White argue about which one of them is less of a snob, and they're both losing."

Judson grinned. "Because you're such a man of the people? How much did your watch cost that they took in the Caribbean? I bet that's what got her attention, got you held ransom. Where is that watch?"

Trace rubbed the absent place on his wrist. "I miss that thing."

If anyone noticed I was completely disengaged, they didn't say. It might not have been the kind of thing that men like the ones I loved noticed. Or maybe they just didn't have a clue what to say to me since I was so hot and cold on this topic. I didn't even know what to say to me, and I was the one living with my internal monologue.

"Is the food what you expected?" Judson addressed me before he took a bite. Kade was still not back, which didn't seem to concern anyone, and Derrick was off on his mission to contact other assassins.

I swallowed the bite of chicken I'd put in my mouth. Truth was I couldn't taste anything at all. "It's perfect."

His smile was huge. "Great. That makes me incredibly happy. Something should go right today."

I was absolutely not going to spoil this for him. Of course, I need not have worried. Trace was here. He would never let this go.

"She's lying." He swallowed his drink. "She hates it, and she's trying to make us feel better by saying she likes it. It doesn't make any sense that she should think she has to do that since she was threatened, attacked, and had to kill two people today." He raised his eyebrows to me. "You don't have to make this okay for us."

I shook my head. "My god, you can be such an ass sometimes. It's a good thing I love you or I'd take your fucking chopsticks and jam them so far up your nose I could cut out your brain with them."

Warden choked. "She actually could do that."

I wasn't done. "Making it easier on you and not having it pointed out that I was lying would have meant I didn't have to discuss this with any of you, didn't have to rehash again how they said they were going to rape me. How they are now dead because I slit one's throat and stabbed the other one in the jugular. Same knife. I don't have to talk about how the first one never got a second to scream but number two did." I leaned forward. "And how the premiere thought I had afterward was about how hungry I was for Chinese food that I can now not really taste." I shrugged. "Do you think I have a brain tumor, Jud?"

"I think stress does funny things to people." He smoothed my hair off my forehead. "And you're in denial if you think you didn't care. Your first and foremost thought was not about food."

Trace sighed. "Everly, we have watched so many people lose themselves to this. I think I was lost before I found you. Until the day we kidnapped you and you woke up and made that ridiculous run barefoot through the woods, I was lost. I don't want to lose you to it. We're a table full of killers. If you wanted Chinese after you killed them, well, that's not that weird to us."

Was that true? "I killed that woman in the Caribbean who held you captive. I put a knife through her eye. I'd been debating using that move for months. It was almost convenient. Easy. Oh, now I'll shove that knife in her eye. We're super rich. I could have negotiated with her. I didn't even think of it. She threatened, I killed. Same thing today. I get a threat and I react. I'm lethal and not restrained."

Trace threw some rice at me. The act was so bizarre, so shocking and ridiculous, that my mouth fell open in response. "We're throwing food?"

He got up. "I'm on too many drugs right now to fuck you. One benefit of coming off the pills in a few days will be the return of things to where they should be. But I think someone has to fuck you, Everly. In a big way."

Sometimes the things Trace said skirted the edge of me wanting to kill him, sometimes what he said went over that edge. It was amazing I loved him. "Do you think your magic dick is going to fix things, T? Oops, had sex with you now Everly is fixed?"

"Not mine today." He bent over and ate the rice that was semi-attached off my neck. "But I think they're all going to fuck you and that doesn't mean I can't make you feel good."

I trembled with pleasure as he did that. Damn Trace for being right. He was way too cocky as it was. "Trace..."

I didn't get to finish what I would have said because

Warden scooted his chair closer to me so he could nibble on my neck. "Trace is right. Off the painkillers and I'm going to fuck you so hard you won't be able to walk. Can't do that right now I don't think. But Judson can and we can help."

I'd closed my eyes while he said those delicious words, but my lids flew open right then. I almost laughed. Judson's face held an expression of absolute disbelief. The same I imagined was on my own right now. "Have either of you discussed with Judson the idea of group sex and Chinese food?"

Warden smiled, his mouth moving against my neck. "Judson never turns down a challenge even when he's initially a little surprised. Isn't that right, my friend?"

That was true. But there were things about J that the others didn't know or at least I didn't think they did. We'd never talked about whether or not his tie was a secret. Of course, we'd already had sex once since we'd gotten back together without needing it, so maybe I was worrying about nothing.

He rose. Since he'd sat next to me he didn't have far to travel. "I don't turn down a challenge. Making love to Everly with or without you two is not that. But yes, I'm game. The question is are the two of you up for it?"

Warden smiled. "I'm not feeling any pain right now."

"I wouldn't have started what I couldn't do. Besides, the calisthenics will be all on you, brother. I just have to get her going."

I was already going. Judson walked toward his bedroom. "Be right back. Going to grab something."

"More time for us." Warden pushed the food off the table with a bang. I eyed the mess on the floor. "Who's going to clean that?"

Trace grinned. "We'll leave it for Kade."

I doubted that very much. K was just as likely to step over the mess and forget it was there. In any case, I didn't get to think on it very long. Trace pointed to the table, and I got on it, but Warden grabbed my shirt, stopping me from lying all the way down.

"Raise your arms," Warden told me, and I did just as he said. He tugged my shirt over my head with his good arm. "Oh look, you're wearing a black bra. I love that look on you. Dark hair. Dark eyes. Pale skin. Black bra. It's like a painting."

Trace kissed my cheek. "It's the shade I can see. She understands me."

I wished I'd given it that much thought. I'd put it on, end of story. But maybe I subconsciously only had black bras now for that reason. I'd go with that.

Trace dropped some orange sauce on my abs before he pushed me down so that I was flat on my back on the table. In the meantime, Warden unzipped my pants. It was a good thing I'd cleaned up before dinner otherwise this would have been not nearly as sexy.

I cupped Trace's cheek. "Don't hurt yourself doing this."

"I won't. Like I said, I'm going to be frustrated and not able to finish as I'd like. But I'm going to make you feel good. Warden, too. We didn't plan this, but I'm so glad the idea came to me."

I rolled my eyes but winked at him. "You're just getting yourself out of trouble for being such a douche bag."

Warden laughed as he discarded my pants over his shoulder. "Sex and Chinese food. It's a great way to end the night."

"You see through me so well, Everly Marrs. I never thought I'd like that, but I truly do." Trace unhooked my bra. He licked the sauce he dripped on me off my abs. I shuddered. Oh wow. I hadn't thought to like that but damn I really did.

I giggled. "Do that again."

Warden slipped my panties off my legs. "You made her giggle. Seriously, do that again. I loved that sound."

"It was a great noise." Judson joined us, his tie in hand. I blinked at it. He'd bought a black silk one. We'd had this discussion about what color I wanted, and he'd gotten it.

I pointed at it. "My graduation gift?"

"No. This one is a gift to myself used on you. You are getting a gift from me. It's just taking a little time to arrange."

Trace stared at the silk tie. "Really?"

Judson didn't answer but came over to me. "What are you going to say to any of us if this goes too far and you don't like it?"

That was easy. "Stop."

Judson nodded before he started to tie up my wrists. "Proceed, gentlemen, this takes a few minutes."

Warden shook his head. "Just when you think someone can't surprise you."

12

I was naked on a table, my arms stretched over my head and my wrists tied together. If that wasn't strange enough, Trace seemed to be dripping sauce on my stomach and licking it off. Seemed was the key word since Judson had told me to close my eyes and I'd listened to him. I couldn't really see what they were doing to me, but oh fuck could I feel it. In every pore of my body.

He was smart to tell me to do this. Otherwise, I'd have been worrying about each of them. Was Warden misusing his arm? Was Trace doing too much? Was Judson okay with what was happening? But they were adults and capable of making decisions about what they should and shouldn't have been doing. I couldn't look or interfere.

All I could do was enjoy.

A mouth pressed to mine, and I knew it was Trace. His lips were thinner than Warden's or Judson's. He tasted like barbecue spareribs, and it might have been my very favorite taste ever. He fluttered his fingers over my stomach, running them up toward my breasts.

"You are so beautiful." He stopped kissing me just long

enough to whisper in my ear. "I wondered some nights if I'd made you up."

He slid his hand up to cup my breasts. My nipples hardened. I could hardly think.

"I can't see you right now, but I know you're still just as gorgeous as ever, Trace." I smiled, hoping that would push down some of the cheese of what I'd just said. Maybe it would just be better if I didn't talk.

Warden caught my attention, running a finger over the outside of my pussy. "You are, Everly." His voice boomed through the room. "I feel lucky that I even get to look at you."

He kissed one of my inner thighs and then the other. I squirmed, and he laughed, putting his hand on my knee to drag them wider. His mouth returned to the spot he'd kissed last, and he ever so slowly kissed his way toward my core, staying just beyond where I wanted him.

Not being able to see him was sweet torture.

I ached everywhere. My nipples burned, my stomach clenched, every part of my body begged for attention. The stubble on his cheeks cut into my skin—even if I missed the fullness of his beard—and I loved the feeling.

"You guys might be trying to kill me." I squirmed again. It was getting harder and harder to stay still. Judson laughed somewhere nearby on my left. He must have been watching this whole thing. "Jud, how are you going to participate in this? You're not getting any foreplay from me."

His second laugh sounded deeper. "I assure you, watching you squirm and get turned on is an incredible aphrodisiac for me. I'll be good and ready. You're wearing my tie and that is... beautiful."

We were throwing the b word around a lot, and I didn't mind at all. Particularly because they were using it to describe me. I smiled at my own vanity. Sometimes I did need to have my ego stroked just like the rest of me. They should think I was beautiful if they were all going to fuck me.

Warden pressed his tongue inside of me, and I cried out, surprised by the contact. Distracted by all the different sensations, he actually caught me by surprise. My sound was half shock, half pleasure. It was possible to have both, and I'd never known that before.

Continuing as he was, Warden licked the length of my pussy until he stopped just over my clit. He paused there like he wanted to torture me. In fact, I was pretty sure he did want that just knowing Warden the way I did. I could practically picture his self-satisfied smile as he tormented me.

He flicked his tongue over my clit, and I cried out again, this time grabbing onto the table as though it could somehow offer me support. Still, the wood did nothing to help me, and as he massaged my clit again with his tongue, I had no choice but to ride the wave of pleasure threatening to take me under.

I arched on the table, unable to stop the motion, and Trace bit down on my nipple, adding a bite of pain to the whole experience. I was in sensory overload. I couldn't tell one moment from the next. Trace let go of my breast and his mouth was suddenly on mine. He kissed me like he owned me, and I knew with Trace that wasn't an exaggeration. He would if he could.

As he pushed his tongue against my own, we started a battle of mouths. It was funny to think of Trace that way, but even as he loved me, it would always be a war of the wills with each other. He wasn't easy, and he never would be.

"All right, guys. You've got her ready. If you can't do it, and I don't think either one of you should physically try right now since I'm really not in the mood to redo your stitches, then get out of my way and let me."

Warden grumbled something I couldn't make out, and I

heard a chair screech, indicating he'd moved backward. Trace let go of my mouth. "The next time we do this I'm going to be at full stamina and there is no way I'm giving you up."

"The next time you do this you can damned well be alone with her. If you bring me into it, I'm never leaving her alone." Judson's voice was hard, determined. "Keep those eyes closed, Everly. I want you feeling things, not thinking about them."

With my hands tied the way they were, I simply wanted to obey Judson. I knew it was strange that one episode of this, which was all we'd ever had, triggered such a response from me but there it was. Maybe it was just easier to do so, considering he wasn't telling me to do anything that wouldn't give me pleasure in the end.

The wood of the table dug into my back, but it wasn't uncomfortable. I was already sort of floating through a haze of pleasure. Judson moved over me. The heat of his body struck me before I became aware of the slight pressure in the places where he already touched me. He pressed his lips to mine.

Judson's mouth was sweet. He reached down and stroked his finger once over the outside of my pussy. "Look how wet you are, Everly. I love it."

I smiled. "I love it, too."

He laughed, and it was a joyful sound. Judson was so rarely like that I almost wished I could open my eyes to see it on his face. But that would spoil this and I wanted it to last. I had to remember to keep my eyes closed.

He pressed himself inside of me, stretching me as he went. I bit down on my lip, and he rubbed his thumb over it just as he pushed all the way in. "Don't do that. Give us your noises. They're ours. Like you are ours."

Judson pulled out and then drove back inside of me, pressing his cock against my clit as he did. It sent jolts of pleasure through me, and I came off the table, banging my sensitive tits into his chest. Pleasure zapped through me.

He repeated the motion, driving harder into me. It was hard not to touch him, hard to keep my eyes closed. But as he slid in and out of my body, I managed. I was primed and this wasn't going to take long.

"Everly, open your eyes and look at me."

Oh, it was such a relief. The light over his head was almost blinding, but a second later my vision cleared. It was impossible to look away from Judson. He stared at me with a mixture of adoration and what almost looked like anger in his gaze. I held his gaze in my own, refusing to look away, and after a minute it softened. Whatever he'd needed to see from me, he'd gotten.

I came fast and unexpectedly. I had no warning it was about to come. One second I reveled in pleasure and the next I exploded from the onslaught, with no build up to alert me to prepare. I dug my hands against each other, jerking against Judson.

He tensed, every muscle in his body reacting as he came inside of me. My heart beat so loudly in my ears that I couldn't hear past it. I pressed my forehead against him, knowing that it broke the touching rule but not really giving a shit right then. I closed my eyes. The world was going to have to wait until I could hear again.

I sort of drifted after that. Judson undid my wrists, bringing my arms around his neck. I guessed he wanted me to hold onto him, and I did. A minute later he'd scooped me up and brought me over to the couch. My back appreciated the relief from the table. That was fun but now that real life intruded on this moment, I didn't need to have the wood digging into my skin anymore. I curled up on him, my head in his lap as he stroked my hair.

"Long day," Judson said. I wasn't sure to whom, but soon Warden sat down, my legs in his lap. Trace wasn't far. I could hear him picking things up off the floor. That had to hurt, but he was capable of deciding what he wouldn't do.

"You all right, Evy?" Warden squeezed my feet.

I managed to nod. "A little overwhelmed I think but otherwise fine. Are you? I can get up and take care of you and Trace. I can..."

He shook his head. "Stop it. I was glad I got to participate at all. Not sure I could do more right now. Leave it. I'll look forward to a date not too far in the distant future."

All right, that sounded fine. I decided to lie there just like that. There was nowhere to go, nothing to worry about.

"You always tie her hands like that?" Trace set a glass of water in front of me.

Judson shook his head. "Nope."

I guessed that was the end of that conversation. I hadn't dwelled on it, but Judson must have really been embracing the whole trusting each other thing to show them that he did that at all. Now that I was thinking, sort of, it was an interesting thing to consider. Had tying my wrists this time with the other two here asserted his dominance over the whole thing?

Internally, I shrugged. I didn't really care. "You're wrong, you know."

Judson turned his head to stare down at me. "Me?"

"What you said to me. You're wrong." I might not have been making a whole shit ton of sense here, but I understood myself perfectly well.

"Which part?" He smiled down at me. "You're going to have to refresh my memory. The last hour is somewhat of a haze. Either that or I have post-coital haze coming over me."

Warden snorted. "Look at Judson using the fancy words for fucking her."

Judson ignored him, keeping his attention on me. He needed an answer so I gave him one. "You said I belonged to you. To all of you. I don't. I absolutely don't belong to any of you but you all belong to me."

There, I'd said it. Now they could all understand.

He nodded. "I think that's probably true, Everly Marrs. Close your eyes. You're rambling."

I did just that.

I stood on top of a hill overlooking a valley down below. The wind picked up, blowing my white skirts up so that I had to push them down before I gave a show of my panties to anyone watching. I knew that I was asleep, and yet I didn't know it at the same time. Such was the nature of dreams. I smiled at my ridiculous thought.

"Everly." Trace ran to me. He wore his signature black, and he was healed. His color was good. What was he doing on this hill with me? Before I could ask him, he extended his hand and I took it. His hands were smooth, the way that Trace's always were. He didn't do a lot of labor that required his hands to toughen up. Kade's were different, rougher. That was funny. I'd never thought about either of those things before.

He spoke again. "We have to go. You know that right? This was a temporary reprieve, but real life is coming. And we all have our roles to play." He passed me a gun. Where had it come from?

I stared down at the weapon, feeling the weight of it in my hand. I was so comfortable holding it that it practically fused itself to my fingers as though it was part of my body.

"Everly," Derrick called my name. He stood in the center of the other four. Trace stepped away from me, joining the others. They were all lined up.

I tilted my head to the side. It was funny. I should have been feeling something right now. Some emotion should play into this and yet there was... nothing. When it came down to it, I really had become nothing.

I lifted my arm and fired.

I sat up in bed, panting. My ears rang and sweat broke out all over my body. I had... I had fired at the Letters.

"Hey." A cool hand touched my face, and I turned to find Trace next to me in the bed. He blinked awake, and his eyes weren't clear. The room was bathed in sunlight, making it easy to see. "You okay?"

His voice was slightly slurred. He must have pretty recently taken a pain pill. Either that or he was feeling discomfort much more acutely. I wiped at my face. "Yes, sorry. Bad dream."

He snuggled back down. "You were out of it last night, and you didn't budge. I had to practically pay Judson off with promises of future favors to get to stay with you. He thought I might disturb you if I ended up in pain. Well, I didn't. So he can suck it."

I ran my hand over his cheek, feeling the stubble there. "I'm going to get up. You can sleep longer."

"Just a little bit more."

I nodded. "Get some rest."

The house buzzed with noise as I padded my way down the hallway toward the kitchen. Kade was back. He'd made a mess of the table, covering it in equipment and that was fine. After last night's adventure, I wasn't sure we should eat on it anymore. Maybe it would be our useful table instead of our dining table. There were some things that couldn't be disinfected enough.

He looked up as I approached and grinned. "Hey, gorgeous. You were out of it last night, big time. Judson put you to bed and you didn't even budge. You okay?"

"I'm good." I smiled, walking into his embrace for a hug. "Is there coffee?"

"Warden made it when he got up. He's outside starting what Judson called gentle physical therapy. Apparently something last night made him get motivated to push on with the healing process?" He raised a dark eyebrow, and I pinched him, which evoked a laugh.

So far, it had been an easy morning. I didn't trust those. Not after my dream. I'd lifted my arm and fired. Who had I hit?

"Is Derrick back?" I looked around. I hadn't seen him, but Warden and Judson weren't here either. Just Kade and his computer plus the turned on television. He might be back.

Kade kissed my cheek. "Not yet, but he isn't due yet. Want me to get in touch with him about what happened?"

"What happened?" I hadn't followed his train of thought.

He blinked. "The drug addicts you had to get rid of. Don't worry on that. No evidence you were ever there."

"Oh." I winced. "Kade... I'm not normal. Shouldn't I still be thinking about it? The two days you and Warden described. Two days to feel it? I don't. Not a thing."

He pressed his forehead to mine. "I don't feel it anymore. Derrick doesn't. Maybe you just got there faster. The place where the value of human life is so small you don't give a shit whether most people live or die. Let me ask you, would it upset you if I died?"

My mouth fell open. "Are you kidding? It would end me."

"Then you're not incapable of feeling. You just value people differently. Some people count, some people don't. You have a circle, and you decide who's in it."

That rang very true for me, and I wasn't sure I liked it. By the same token, I wasn't sure there was a damned thing I could do about it. "That's not who I was."

"You should kiss that old version of yourself goodbye. She's gone, and she's not coming back. If it means anything, I love this version of you something hard."

I pinched him again. "Yeah, but you're an Alliance psychopath so what does that make me?"

"Takes one to know one, my love."

I supposed he was right. I didn't need to keep banging my head against things, worrying about what I did and didn't feel. This was who I was. And I liked her just fine.

I chewed on my lip. After coffee, I knew I'd forget about that stupid dream. It was time to get the caffeine in me fast.

Derrick came through the door that afternoon as we were all crowded around Kade's electronics, trying to make sense of what he was doing. The idea had been that we'd all wear a small button on our clothes that sent a signal to confuse the satellites. We'd essentially look like someone else. Then we could go wherever we wanted.

I thought it sounded like genius, but Warden thought Kade was biting off more than he could chew even if he did invent the programs for the satellites to begin with.

Kade didn't seem to care one bit what anyone thought. Actually, he was hardly communicating at all. This was Kade totally focused on what he was doing. Completely absorbed in his work...

Who would they have all been if there hadn't been any Alliance?

Derrick's arrival distracted us. I rushed over to him, bringing him into a tight hug. "You're back."

He kissed my hair. "You missed me."

I loved how he didn't ask but informed me. "Maybe I did. Maybe I didn't."

"She killed two people," Trace offered as he passed us walking into the kitchen.

"That so?" Derrick kissed my hair. "They're dead. You're not. Successful time for our side."

He stepped away from me. "I have some news, and, Kade, I'm going to need your help with it if you can pull yourself away from that."

Kade looked up. "I can." He set down whatever piece of machinery he was using. "For now. What's going on?"

Trace came out of the kitchen and Derrick crossed to the couch before he sank down on it. "My contacts helped a tremendous amount. Marcus' people reached out to several assassins." He shook his head. "But no one wants to deal with him. They're all holding out for us to come back, particularly since the word got out that you are back in play, Evs. That said, there are some people who will always take work because they either need the money or they need the kills to just be okay in their head. Certain amount of sanctioned killing so they don't go on a rampage."

That sounded like some ridiculous movie, and yet here we were dealing with it as absolute truth. "Okay. So they found some people."

"They did, and you two," he pointed at Warden and Trace, "can thank your lucky stars they got who they did because otherwise you'd be dead."

Trace touched his side. "Right. A good sniper wouldn't have missed."

"A decent one wouldn't have missed. But Ron Murray is twenty years old, and he missed. Badly. I don't think he was supposed to hit James Robert Michaels. Word on the street is you were the target and he was a whoops. It was an equivalent young guy not trained properly who took on you Warden and ended up dead."

Warden sighed. "I hardly remember the incident. It's sort of becoming a blur."

"The painkillers can play havoc with the brain." Judson rocked back on his feet. "Can we track this Ron Murray back to wherever Marcus is hiding out?"

"That's what I'm hoping." He pointed at Kade. "Can you?"

My K nodded. "Of course. Take a few minutes. Unless they have the kind of device I'm making to disguise us, but since I haven't invented it yet I think that's unlikely."

Derrick smirked before he looked at Trace. "So Kade rambling? How long has he been focused on his project that he's losing communication skills?"

"Not long, actually." Trace grinned. "Fast descent this time."

I pointed at both of them. "You two leave Kade alone. He's fantastic. And adorable when he rambles."

"Thanks." Kade snorted. "You can all kiss my ass. Got him. Not even hard. He really is untrained. How sad for Marcus he couldn't do better than this. Dude was just out wandering yesterday in a totally open-to-surveillance area of Colorado until he disappeared into the zone there that can be hidden." He grinned. "He never seems to have exited the area so we know, pretty much, where he is. I'll need to recalibrate the satellites, and I'll know if I can see in that space. Just a minute."

Judson sat down on the couch, sprawling out. "I'm always grateful he's on our side."

Derrick looked around. "How are things here other than the killing?"

"Trace and Warden are healing. I think otherwise it's been pretty status quo. We had some really good Chinese food."

Warden snorted. "Yeah... it was delicious."

Derrick rubbed his eyes. "I take it there was some kind of sex. Good for all of you."

"Got it." Kade pointed at the computer. "Come take a look. Ron entered this house just a few days ago and hasn't come out."

I looked over Kade's shoulder. It did look like an Alliance lair. Huge and imposing. The first thing they'd told me when they explained the Alliance was that it had to be secret. And yet every time I turned around, it was one exhibit of ridiculous display of wealth after another. I shook my head. Right now I wasn't going to deal with that.

It was another big house and Ron the ridiculously bad sniper was in there with whomever else Marcus had working for him. "Should we watch it on surveillance for a few days?"

"We'll get the satellites to start recording and ding me if anyone comes and goes." He stepped away from the computer. "It'll be good for us to have a sense of who he has working for him as we decide to take him out."

I nodded. "I don't suppose we could just blow up the house."

"We'd have to get in there to do that. If you have an idea how to do that, I'm game." Derrick tilted his head. "I think a sniper rifle would be better with me on the end of it firing. I'm starving. Do we have any meat? I'd love to grill."

13

I stared at the screen. It was the same image I'd been looking at on and off for over a week. The house in Colorado. Few people came and no one left. It seemed Marcus liked living in Colorado. The house where Derrick had visited him to threaten him to leave me alone had been there too. But not this one and not as heavily encased in mystery as this one was.

Warden had been grumpy all day, coming off of his pain meds, but he'd managed to get through his physical therapy with Judson, proclaiming him the worst human being on the planet, which meant he was making incredible improvement from how the day before had gone. I'd take it. The yelling at each other bordered on tantrum-like, and I couldn't help but wonder if everyone was simply getting enough of inaction.

Except for Derrick. He spent an incredible amount of time trying new recipes in the kitchen as though he were on some kind of vacation that included cooking. I chewed on my lip as Kade sank down onto the couch next to me. "Anything new? I didn't get pinged so I just answered my own question. No, there's nothing new."

"How can a house be so full of people and never have them leave? We leave. Judson and Trace went to the dry cleaner today. We had groceries delivered. People do things. Not them." I pointed at the screen. "They're holed up in there like we're in a nuclear winter."

He laughed, throwing back his head. "Thanks for that imagery, Everly."

"You're welcome. I live to please." I rolled my eyes at him. "How are you? Making progress?"

"No." He grinned. "But I will. You can count on it. One day it'll just be…" He snapped his fingers. "Done like that."

Warden crossed into the room and sat down. "The elusive Marcus remains in his house. I never knew he was such an agoraphobic."

"If you had shitty assassins working for you and knew Derrick wanted to kill you, would you go wandering around?" Trace and Judson came in through the front door, T jumping into the conversation right away.

I shook my head. "The question is: when Derrick arrived at his original home and threatened Marcus, why Marcus didn't just kill him right then? Or have him destroyed when he exited the house? Was he so overwhelmingly intimidated by Derrick that he just didn't take an obvious shot?"

Judson shook his head. "Both good questions we don't have answers to."

"I like the 'I'm just so intimidating he couldn't take it' answer." Derrick grinned from the doorway.

"I've had enough of this." I rose. Patience wasn't my strong suit. I'd own it. "I'll tell you what I'm not going to do. I'm not going to sit in this house and wait for them to find us or see if they ever deign to come out. Kade, do we know from the satellites roughly how many people are in the house based on body heat?"

He winced. "It's an estimate. I never thought to improve

that tech. If you want me to break into the CIA or the Delta force databases I can probably..."

I held up my hand. "Guestimate is fine based on what you do have?"

"I think there are twenty-five people in that house."

That was a shit ton of people to be stuck inside and never leaving. We were going stir crazy and we were leaving the house and were only a party of six. Of course, it might have been just enough people to never need to leave. Maybe Marcus was having a constant orgy in there. "Is he big on sex parties?"

Trace blinked rapidly. "Not that I ever heard of, and people do tend to tell me that kind of stuff."

"All right, then we need to get them out of there. Force them to come out."

Derrick nodded. "Easier said than done. How do you propose doing that?"

That was a good question. "What gets people out of the house? Fire. If the house caught on fire we could absolutely get them out."

Trace shook his head. "Too risky. We want them dead, but not until we get to question him. I don't want him to die before he tells me why he targeted me. Judson was running around and he didn't get shot."

"I wasn't exactly running around." He held up his hand. "Point taken. If they'd wanted to take a shot at me they could have."

"Not to mention fire is so... unreliable. Someone could just put it out." Derrick walked over, placing guacamole in front of me on the coffee table. He'd spread tortilla chips out around it. I stared at it for a second. Apparently when Derrick wasn't killing anyone or training me to do so, he made dips. All of the others bent over quickly and started spooning the green dip onto the plates Derrick set down. They started crunching all around me.

I didn't have the heart to tell Derrick I couldn't stand guacamole. It was a mental thing I needed to get over but couldn't. My grandmother had dragged me to her friend Miz Viola's home one afternoon. She was a well-dressed woman who never left the house without a pound of makeup on her face, wearing clothes that needed to be pressed to even be put in her closet. The two old biddies got along like they'd always been best friends, even though I thought they'd met at church only a year before the incident that would forever end my ability to eat guacamole.

Miz Viola had made the dip. In retrospect, even as my mind threw itself back in time, lost in the memory of the sheer grossness of what had happened, it was kind of odd that she'd made it at all. The two ladies were much more likely to drink sweet tea and snack on fried shrimp than the guacamole. But for whatever reason, she'd served it that day.

I'd been eight years old. My stomach turned, and I had to look away from Derrick's creation just to get through thinking about it. I'd put my chip into Miz Vi's dip and looked down to see the largest collection of cockroaches I'd ever seen or would see in my life. They'd been all over the floor, practically swarming all over each other; two of them had climbed up my leg.

I'd dropped the guacamole, and for the rest of my life I carried the association of those roaches with the guacamole, even though they'd technically not been related other than a comment on Miz Viola's cleanliness. My grandmother had been a nightmare about it, blaming me for the bug event. God forbid, the woman ever take my side. I'd never found out where those bugs came from or how they got there. It was always just the guacamole incident in my mind.

"Everly, you want some?" Derrick lifted his eyebrows.

I shot Trace a quick look as I answered D. I didn't need Trace outing me for lying to Derrick right that second, not when I was being polite. Trace could take his observations about human behavior and shove them at the moment.

"I'm still full from lunch. I think if I tried to eat right now, I'd make myself sick."

Derrick nodded, seeming to accept that as true. "Try some later."

"Will do." I smiled even as Trace lifted his eyebrows to let me know he'd not missed any of that and still kept his mouth shut.

The whole memory was... I rubbed my arms, a plan formulating in my head in a sudden rush as though it had always been there. "I know how we get them out of the house."

Judson ate his chip. "How?"

Goosebumps broke out on my arms, bringing with it a surge of pain that I ignored. I could be grossed out later. "Bugs."

Silence met my remark so I kept speaking. "I'm dead serious. Bugs. Fleas. Bed bugs. An infestation of cockroaches. Trust me, it will get people out of the house. If they have to bug bomb the house, they have to leave it."

Kade opened and closed his mouth. "I... Yes, bugs. They would most likely leave the house if bugs came into it, and it's not as obvious as say setting it on fire. They won't necessarily see it coming."

Derrick nodded. "How do we get the bugs in the house? I mean, yes, I agree. I love it actually and, Evs, the fact that you came up with this idea? It's sexy in how gross it is. The way your mind works. Gross."

I wasn't insulted. For Derrick, that was a compliment. He was more impressed with me the darker I got. For both of us, that could be deadly, but I wasn't afraid of the hard stuff.

Kade drummed his fingers on the table, and I caught another look at the guacamole. I was really going to need to get away from it or get them to put it away.

Judson narrowed his eyes at me but didn't say anything else. It was Warden who finally spoke. "How do we get the bugs in there? That's not any easier than setting things on fire. That's not like Kade crashing their computers."

"They clearly have a tech guy. That much I know. I made a gentle tug at their firewalls and found them very strong. I didn't push harder to not give us away, but I can work on it. If you want me to."

I shook my head. "No, don't. I know this was my idea and maybe that's why I'm focused on it. But there has to be a way to get the bugs inside."

"I know a guy who has bugs. I mean who could get fleas. A lot of them." Trace's announcement had us all turning around to face him.

Derrick's mouth fell open. "You have a guy who has bugs?"

I laughed. I couldn't help myself. That was hysterical. Trace had officially shocked Derrick. Pretty soon everyone was laughing. It was the most ridiculous, wonderful moment. Here we were, sitting in the living room staring at a screen at a house, waiting for people to come out, and talking about Trace and his bug guy. How had this gotten so normal?

How had it gotten so fantastic?

I leaned on my elbow. They were mine. There were lots of things in the universe I was unsure of, but how they felt about me wasn't one of them. I blinked. When had that happened? How was it so easy? Not very long ago I'd left them and now here we were. I chewed on my lip, which hurt because I'd been doing it a lot lately. I needed to stop, find some gross lip-gloss I didn't like the flavor of, and put it on so I'd be less inclined to taste my own lip.

Truth was I knew the answer to my internal query. I'd

been one hundred percent certain of their feelings for me the day I'd left them. I'd known it. I just hadn't been sure of my own. These days, I knew how I felt for them. I loved them. I just didn't know how I felt about it.

"Everly?" Warden touched my cheek. "What are you thinking?"

"I'm mulling over life." I smiled at each of them. I could think about the nature of our relationship and how I found myself in this odd situation another time when I was alone. For now, I needed to focus. They needed to get rid of Marcus so we'd all be safe and they could go ahead and take over the Alliance. And I could... well, I didn't know what the fuck I was going to do, but I'd figure it out later.

Trace winked at me. "I think for a second there you were really happy."

"I was. I'll be happy all the time when this is done."

He laughed, throwing his head back. "No one is happy all the time. Ever. The best we can all hopeful is contentment and no one in the Alliance is ever that. Sorry, Everly, your life is bound to be torn up in angst and disgruntled moments."

"Well, just so long as you all keep fucking me then I guess I'll be fine."

Trace jerked. He hadn't expected me to say that. I slowly smiled at him. Trace wasn't the only one who could say mouth dropping things. I shook my head. "Surely there must be a way to get bugs in the house. Enough that they don't see them come in and then they have no choice but to get out of there so we can get a good look at all of them."

"Well, I'd probably be the perfect person to do that, actually, had they not already tried to kill me. I could go pretend I wanted to change sides and drop the bugs. But since they've already scarred me up with one bullet, I'd really rather not risk another one." He shook his head. "Guess I'm not helpful right now."

He was right. He couldn't go walking in there with the bugs and somehow get them into the house. The absurd nature of this entire endeavor hit me at once and yet I couldn't dismiss it. This would work. I knew it in my gut. No one was going to stay in a house during a bug infestation. I shuddered even thinking about it.

"Warden and Trace, you both got shot at. My question is would they shoot at all of you or was it specifically just them? And is there a way to test it? Like for example, Judson could go in if we knew he'd be safe."

He stopped chewing mid-way through a bite, and I watched him visibly swallow the chip in his mouth. "Me? I'm not really the subterfuge guy."

"That's why you're perfect for it." I actually had no doubt about Judson's ability to lie. All of these guys could summon up fabrication when they needed to. They lied about their entire existence to most people every day. The problem wasn't that he couldn't pull off a trip to see Marcus, the problem was that there was no way I was sending Judson out alone where he might very well get shot and die.

Judson lifted his eyebrows. "Do you want me to go to Marcus'?"

"If we can guarantee your safety, yes. Only so far as you can do some snooping and drop off the bugs."

He winced. "So we're really going with this bug thing? And I'm not certain how we're going to guarantee my safety."

"Me." Derrick sat forward. "I've already been in and out of one of his houses and not gotten killed. You weren't targeted. I think you'd be fine, but just in case, we go in together. Me to argue for them to leave her alone and you to act like you're going to betray her."

Judson jumped to his feet. "Me to betray her? What the fuck? You think I would? That anyone would believe that?"

"Yes." Derrick didn't even flinch at Judson's temper. "You

want a return to the old ways of the Alliance. That is the last thing anyone heard you say before you disappeared mostly from sight. In the hotel while we fought for our lives and you had no idea. While you made that speech they applauded you for."

Judson put his hand over his heart. "If I had the slightest idea what was happening upstairs I would have been up there with you. I never would have stayed in the banquet hall and made a speech."

"Everyone knows that." I rose. "And as to that, Jud, you can let that go. You couldn't have gotten into the elevator. They were blocked off from everyone except apparently my father, who may have been coming to kill me. He was at the very least working with Ben. And none of that matters because I killed him." I'd finally gotten to the point where I could say that and feel nothing at all about it. Or at least it didn't feel like it was going to pull me under into a pit of self-pity. "So please don't worry on that account."

Judson crossed his arms across his chest. "I'll do it. Work on the details. You can count on me. I'll get the bugs in the house."

I glared at Derrick. "Do it because you believe it can work. Do it because you want to. Not because Derrick just emotionally manipulated you to do it by bringing that up."

Derrick shrugged. "I'll go with him and keep us both alive. Sorry, Judson. I don't do that on purpose. It's just how I'm made."

"You didn't used to be this way, actually." Warden sighed. "Not when you were younger. There was no one more open than you. You losing the ability to do anything but win came after Alyssa."

I didn't want to open the door to analysis this way. I was pretty sure we'd all fair badly in the "who was mentally the least unhealthy" discussion. It wasn't the time to open these doors, and maybe I was lost in a good case of denial, but I didn't know if we ever needed to do this. Why strip bare to our soft underbellies when we had to stay strong?

My psych professors would have been horrified, but I was all for bottling up my shit and dealing with the explosions or meltdowns when they happened with some booze and pills. Yes, I had officially become that woman. I was perfectly comfortable in my box and fuck anyone who tried to take me out of this.

"Okay. Not now." I held up my hand. "We've already done the pretending thing. Trace did it really well at the bar the last night we were together in Boston during the aforementioned killing-of-my-father vacation."

Trace snorted. "Is that what you're calling it?"

"Don't encourage her." Jud shook his head. "And for the record he didn't manipulate me. I saw what he was doing straight off."

I ignored the exchange. What was the answer? "They won't see us coming if we just arrive. The six of us together. They won't take any shots if we have Derrick with us. And me. They don't know it yet, but I'm deadly. We ring the doorbell and go inside."

I walked to the screen doors and looked outside at the beach. I'd gotten used to the sound of the ocean so much I didn't notice it that often. But it was a soothing sound and it somehow led some credence to the idea that what we did here was important.

Background noise mattered in life.

"We tell the truth. We're done with hiding. Done with bullshit. We don't want a war. We want nothing." I looked over my shoulder at Trace. "We don't say a thing that isn't true. We tell them they can take the world and fuck it for all we care, we want to be left alone, the six of us to get on with getting on. We tell them all they have to do to never have a problem from us again is leave us alone." I turned to look at them. "That's what we want, right? If that isn't what you want we should get that out there now. Who here still has dreams of world domination?"

Trace shook his head. "Don't look at me. I'm done with it. I want you, Everly. I want to be where you are. Tell me where that is and I'll fit my life around it."

Oh how times had changed. Not so long ago—and yet sometimes it felt like two lifetimes had passed—Trace had been suggesting I fly around the country following them. "You're sure?"

"Positive." He nodded. "Kade? Do you want out? Can you stay away from interfering with things?"

My K blinked rapidly. "I'll never stop doing whatever I have to do to keep us safe. But can I leave the rest of it alone? Easily. I told Everly, my home is with her. Judson?"

Judson nodded. "My practice is over. I've been away from it too long. You can't vanish like I do and have any hopes of it continuing. But I'd like to try to reestablish elsewhere. I don't need the Alliance to be happy." His gaze met mine. "I need you."

Goosebumps broke out on my skin. These men were laying their souls out in front of me. They were braver than I was. I didn't even belong in the same emotional category.

Judson turned to Derrick. "Mr. Attempted Manipulation? How about you? Ready to stop?"

He shook his head. "There will never be a time that I won't be prepared to kill for this family. Other than that, yes. I want quiet. And don't worry, Evs, I'll never make guacamole again. If you had told me you had such an aversion, I'd not have done it in the first place."

My cheeks heated up. "I thought I covered."

"Took me too long. Did you not think to say something when I bought the avocados?"

I held out my hand. "You could have done anything with them. Hold this thought. Warden?"

He nodded. "I'm done with it all. I can make money without needing to be in everyone's business. I had years of this. I'll gladly put it aside if that is possible, but do you really think it's going to be that easy?"

"Maybe. Maybe all it will take is to say Marcus we're done. Leave us alone."

Warden rose and crossed to me. "And when he says no, no one leaves the Alliance and demands the five of us take an oath to him and locks you in his fucking basement?"

I waited for the cold terror his words should have evoked. Instead, I simply remained calm. "No one is locking me in another basement. I'll slaughter the whole house first."

Warden searched my face. I didn't know what he looked for, but whatever he saw had him nodding. "I'll destroy the world before I take an oath to him. We get what we want or we leave bodies in our wake. Screw the Alliance. Let the world burn."

I loved his pronouncement so much that I kissed him—hard. He smiled against my mouth before he returned the embrace. Kade walked over, taking his place and kissing me the same way. I felt Trace before I opened my eyes to see him. He slipped his arm around me, taking me from Kade. His lips were soft, but his embrace spoke of ownership. Derrick was next. He made no preamble of gentleness. His mouth felt almost punishing. And finally, it was Judson who kissed me like he needed me to live.

We were all in this together and one way or another we'd know soon what was going to happen.

———

Warden slipped into my bed that night. I opened my eyes. If

they'd worked out a schedule of who was with me when, I didn't know it. I loved them all. It didn't matter who it was. I just loved that one of them came every night.

I cupped my W's cheek. "You're up for this?"

"I'd better be because I can't go another night without putting my cock inside of you, Evy."

His words made me wet almost instantly. I squirmed my way over to him, pressing on his good shoulder until I pushed him flat on his back. "I'd promise to be gentle with you but I'd be lying."

Warden's lips were cool against my own, and for the longest time, we didn't do anything but kiss. I smiled against his mouth. This was a little bit like being back in high school. Even knowing the excitement that was coming, there was something so incredibly wonderful about just making out like a teenager again.

I didn't know if he understood why I grinned or if he was just happy, but he smiled against me too. With his good arm, although he was getting strength back in the other, he rolled me over so that I was under him.

I ran my hand over his face. "We're all here because you showed up at my bar. Thank you for that."

He stared at me, his expression turning serious. "I love you. I tried to stay away, to give you what you wanted, but I couldn't. It was selfish, but I needed you. I almost didn't come because I didn't want you to see me weak. But I couldn't deal with the idea of dying and not looking at your beautiful face one more time."

I kissed him, leaning up to reach my lips to his. "I love you, too. I'm dark inside. Don't tell me I'm not. I really am.

But my love for you is real. If there's anything left inside of me that was me before, I had to kiss that part of me goodbye. I have it to give to you."

He ran his thumb over my lip. "Sweetheart, whoever you are, that's who I love. You don't need to be sunshine and light for that, if anything, I like your rougher parts. They match my own. And I don't think you were ever as... innocent... as you're remembering yourself being. You weren't afraid to run off barefoot from the house in Vermont. That took internal steel and a sophistication a lot of people don't have. Trust me on this, most people crumble when faced with that stress. You didn't."

I ran my hands over his chest, holding onto his shirt like it was a lifeline. This shouldn't have been sexy, and yet speaking my truth in the darkness pressed to Warden was maybe one of the most vulnerable things I'd ever done. And with that came intimacy. I wanted him more than ever.

"I did in the basement."

He pressed his forehead to mine. His breath was warm. "Anyone would. You survived, and you are so strong now it's almost frightening to me. Part of me wants to protect you. Wrap you up in a bubble somewhere and just love on you from now until I die."

I wrinkled my nose. "I might die first. Death is unpredictable that way."

"I'm older than you and more nefarious. Let's assume I'm exiting this life first. It's a pretty good chance. But you'd never let me do that anyway. You're too strong. You always were. I won't stifle you, Everly. So if I seem like I'm battling sometimes, that's what it is. I'm not... giving by nature. I don't think of other's needs. But I'm trying."

I shook my head. "Maybe you don't know yourself as well as you think you do."

He pressed his weight down on me slightly as he kissed

me. Again and again. This time it wasn't easy going, this time it was heated. I loved feeling surrounded by him. We undressed each other, and despite my proclamation that I wasn't going to go easy on him, I made sure to be gentle, particularly when taking off his shirt.

I ran my fingers through the dusting of hair on his chest. We were both brown haired, but Warden's was significantly darker than my own. He shuddered as I ran my fingers through it, stopping to touch the slight beard on his face. His hair was soft. He'd hate that description so I didn't say it to him but that didn't make it any less true.

I slipped my hand around his hard cock, and he flared his nostrils. "It's been a long time for me. This might be over very fast if you're not careful there."

I smiled at him. "I'll be careful, sort of."

"You like tormenting me."

"Only in the bedroom." I kissed his chin. "Lie back."

He nodded. "Makes more sense for you to be on top right now."

That was just what I'd been thinking. I climbed on top of him, running my thighs against his cock just to feel it jump against me. He widened his eyes and then grinned at me. "You are so beautiful. You know that right?"

I lifted my eyebrows. He believed that. I could see it in his eyes. Even with all my scars and everything he'd seen me go through, he really did think I was beautiful. "When you look at me like that, I feel that way."

"Good."

I rubbed against him one more time before I slipped him inside of me. My muscles stretched to accommodate him, and he closed his eyes as I pressed down on him. A second later, he lifted his lids, his gaze heated.

I moved over him, rubbing him over my clit until we both panted for it. He wasn't wrong. It had been a long time since he'd done this and it was going fast. That was okay. The harder and faster we moved the closer I got myself.

My body tingled, my breasts tightened, and all over I was close. But I wasn't quite there yet. Warden jerked inside of me, coming fast. He groaned, and I imagined he knew that I hadn't come. I smiled. It was okay. I wasn't the one who had been injured and just getting back to myself. That had been fun even if it was over and...

He pulled out of me fast. I moaned. I might have liked a minute or two to feel close to him even without the orgasm. This kept happening to me. It might just have been where I was in my own head. I didn't mind in the least. I still got to feel close to him and there was something seriously nice about how it felt to lie there connected afterward. Although, this seemed really fast for Warden and...

I'd no sooner thought that than his mouth came down on my pussy. He pushed my legs apart to get closer to me. I cried out. My clit was swollen, I could feel it, and his tongue on me was almost too much after the friction of what we'd just done.

"Just breathe," he spoke in a low tone. "You taste like heaven. I'd never leave you unsatisfied. You're my woman. You coming is the most important thing to me right now."

I listened to him. I closed my eyes and did just as he said. I breathed. His tongue massaged my clit in a circular motion and soon I was panting. Goosebumps broke out on my arms. I was close... so close... and yet I couldn't get there.

He pulled back but only to replace his tongue with his finger. The change in sensation was jarring, but as he spoke to me, his words were just what I needed to hear. "I love you."

I came hard. I wasn't going to question how much I'd needed him to say that.

Warden outright snored, his head pressed against my chest as his good arm was slung over my body, essentially pinning me to the bed. Usually, he was more of a deep breather but not tonight. He was out of it and he was sawing wood. I stared at his handsome face, touching the scruff that would soon be a full-on beard. If anyone outside of here knew how sweet he was, they'd never believe me. He crumbled people's entire existences financially without giving it another thought.

He scared the people who worked for him.

I pressed on him just slightly, kissing his neck while I did, until he rolled over. He muttered something but didn't wake up. Most of the time I'd love to be held like that. When it came down to it, I had a soft center that loved romance. But tonight I'd needed to move.

I grabbed Warden's shirt, which was huge on me, and put it on. The air conditioning was on high, and I rubbed my arms, wishing I could calm down enough to enjoy lying in the bed with Warden, snoring and all.

But I was too wound up.

I walked slowly toward the living room. The television was on low and Kade lay, silently, eyes closed. The door to the outside was cracked open, and I walked toward it. Kade laughed in his sleep, and I grinned. He must have been having great dreams.

The light on the porch was on, illuminating the house and part of the beach. Trace wandered toward the water. If he'd gotten any farther, I wouldn't have been able to see him because he would have lost the light.

I opened the door quietly and then slid it closed behind me. I looked over my shoulder back into the house. Kade slept on, unaware that I'd ever come and gone. I walked toward Trace, finally catching up to him when he reached the water's edge.

"Hey." He turned at the sound at my voice.

Trace extended his hand. "Hey."

I linked our fingers together. "No sleep for you either?"

"No. Trying to avoid taking a pill. I like how my head feels alert, but I'm hurting a little bit."

I winced. "Take the pill. It's nighttime."

He shook his head. "Not if I can avoid it."

We stepped closer to the water, letting it rush over our toes. In the darkness, it felt like it was just Trace and the moon out here looking at the ocean together. The sea rushed up, covering our ankles.

"You're beautiful in the moonlight."

I lifted my gaze to meet his. "Thanks. You're not really the compliment type, Trace. You're more likely to tell me everything I'm doing is wrong and order me around. Don't go sappy on me now, love."

He didn't laugh, which was disappointing since I'd tried to be funny.

Instead, he pushed my hair off my face. "I do think you're beautiful."

"Thank you." I kissed him in the moonlight with the ocean rushing away from our feet, leaving us covered in sand up to our ankles.

He was quiet again for a long moment. "You're welcome."

"Did I hurt your feelings?" I squeezed his fingers in mine.

"No." He shook his head. "I was just wondering when it changed. You're right. I'm not really a compliment guy. But I do want to do that for you."

I stepped closer to him until he drew me right up against him. There was no space between us. "Am I making a huge mistake suggesting we go to Colorado and just walk in? Pretend it's the time of your grandfathers when there could be civility in the Alliance?"

He stared down at me. "I don't know. But don't make the error of saying that was your suggestion. We are going to do what you tell us to do. That is how this has worked since the moment we got you back from Ben. The months away... it devoted us to you. We love you."

I'd never get used to hearing them say that, and I did seem to be ridiculously needy for the words. I wasn't going to overthink it. Maybe that was just what people in love did, they talked about it. I didn't know. I'd never gotten to see it as a child.

Maybe I'd been needing it my whole life.

"That doesn't mean you should let me lead you into a ridiculous idea."

He placed his nose on my hair as the ocean rushed up against us again. The tide was officially coming in.

"I don't think it's a ridiculous idea. I think it might be a little naïve to think that the same people who took a shot at Warden and me would be willing to talk. But it's worth a try. I don't want you going without me. That might be... wrong. I might make things worse. I can't see it anymore, Everly. The plan. The layout of anything. It's like... a blank slate for me out there. I'm not helpful."

I squeezed him tighter. "You were able to read me so well that you could tell what I was thinking when I wished you couldn't. You've still got it. You're just healing."

"Why don't you like guacamole?" He kissed my temple. "Or hate it would be more accurate. Do you not like avocado?"

"I like avocado but I hate guacamole. It's a whole story about cockroaches."

His eyes widened. "That's where you thought of the bugs. I see the correlation now. Ugh. Yes, cockroaches. Don't tell me. I don't want that imagery. I like guacamole and Derrick made it really well. Of course, if he keeps this up with the cooking we're all going to be too fat to keep doing anything at all."

I ran my hands over his chest. "There isn't a pound on you."

Something crashed in the house, and we both jumped, turning to stare at it. One of the windows in the living room shattered. Trace took my hand and we ran together toward the house. He should probably not have been running, but I wasn't going to worry about that right now.

Or maybe it was fine.

We ran into the house the same time Warden, Judson, and Derrick arrived there, too. Everyone had been sleeping.

Kade was on his feet. "Sorry. I didn't mean to break the window. I just threw my shoe. I wasn't aiming for the window."

I rushed over to him. There was glass but most of it seemed to have been outside and not in. Still, I had to ask. "Are you hurt? Did the glass get you?"

"No." He was staring at the screen. "I woke up, and I checked the systems like I do whenever I get up, and we were breached. I don't even know how. There's one man who could do it in the whole universe, and if they managed to convince Mercer who never wanted anything to do with helping the Alliance other than the bare minimum, we are truly fucked. He's better than me."

I didn't believe that for a second. "Kade, you are the best. Everyone says so."

"Only because they don't know that son-of-a-bitch Mercer. He was better than me. I'm not looking for compliments. I'm just telling you the truth. Mercer is in that house with Marcus. They're like the most obnoxious people with the letter M in their first names ever."

I blinked. "Mercer is his first name? Never mind. That doesn't matter right now. Okay, we were breached. What does that mean?" We'd left the door open when we came back inside and a sound caught my attention. I whirled around. "Is that...?"

"Helicopters." Derrick ran to the door to look out. "Black ones landing on the beach. It's bad if they're negating all sense of being seen to land here. Fuck." He ran into the kitchen and pulled a bag out of one of the cabinets. "Guns."

No wonder he spent so much time in the kitchen. "There are three helicopters landing. Six of us. And we're not in Vermont where Judson has the whole place set up like it's high ground. If they start shooting, we're all dead."

Derrick spun around. "What do you suggest?"

"I don't know what I suggest."

Kade pounded on his keyboard. "Mercer, that asshat, is sending us a message. If we stay calm they won't hurt us."

Warden stalked over to Derrick. "Give me a gun."

I couldn't blame him. He'd already been shot. "Do we believe them, Kade?"

"No, fuck. I only believe the people in this room."

Derrick and Warden raised their guns as a woman walked into the room. "That's too bad, Kade. That might make the next bit of time very uncomfortable."

Derrick's hand shook. That was the first thing that caught my attention. The next was that Judson choked on his breath from where he stood on the other side of the room. It was like my brain didn't want to work. I stared at this woman. I'd seen her before, but I'd never met her. Sometimes it felt like I'd gotten to know her quite well and other times she was an abyss of misinformation, presented by the men I loved from whatever perspective they saw her.

To Judson she was his beloved twin sister. To Derrick she was the love he'd not been able to satisfy. To Trace she was the reason we were all in this mess. To Kade she was something he'd rather not deal with even in memory. To Warden she was a whispered confession that he'd never liked her.

Alyssa Smythe Norris. Who was apparently not dead after all.

"Sorry to just burst in like this. I was actually hoping you'd all be asleep but Mercer told me that you guys were aware that we're here. It's a pity. This could have been a lot more pleasant. Go to sleep in one bed, wake up with another. Oh, Derrick darling, do put down that gun. You're not going to shoot me. Warden, you might, but please keep in mind the people I have with me now are much better shots than the others that went after you. One word from me or any move from you they don't like and you're dead. Painfully. Lower your weapon."

I could hardly think from one breath to the next. I turned to look over my shoulder. Judson was pale; he held onto the wall. None of my guys had known this was possible and they all looked the most out of it I'd ever seen them.

They were the secret keepers and this was a truth they hadn't foreseen.

I stepped forward. "Alyssa, right?"

I wanted to make sure. This was all so bizarre it was possible I was about to be in one of those situations where suddenly there would be a triplet I never knew about. An identical sister we never knew about.

She smiled at me. Her grin was cruel. It was a funny description, and one I'd attributed to the Letters when I first met them but wouldn't anymore. She had no mirth in that beam she gave me. "Everly, right?"

Her response snapped me out of my stupor. Oh, okay, I could do this. She was a bitch and we were doing that thing women did when they greeted others they didn't like. It wasn't nice and maybe there would come a time when that wouldn't be the case. But tonight was not that night.

"Not dead, I see."

She shrugged. "Sleeping with my husband and my brother together, I see."

"Everly." Trace shook his head at me. I wasn't sure what he did or didn't want me to do right then. I'd love to take his advice since my trip to Ben's basement had prepared me to handle all the worst things in the world but not what to do when a woman who was supposed to be dead came back.

She walked past me over to Judson, touching his chin. "Take this as a good thing, Judy. I've been wanting to get you back for years. I just had to have things set up."

"What in the ever-loving fuck?" He batted her hand away.

A muscle ticked in her jaw. "Spending time with trash doesn't mean you have to sound like them. We're done with this. We're all going home. No not to Colorado, once you found that place we moved. Kade, darling, you are making Mercer nuts. It really would be so much better if you'd work together." She stepped away. "You will forgive me Judson. You always do."

I couldn't stand it anymore. I ran over to him and wrapped my arms around him, bumping her out of the way when I did. His arms came around me, and she groaned.

"This is just so bourgeois. Okay, I'm done. Knock them out."

I didn't know what happened next because there was sudden movement. The men she'd brought with her—I hadn't even focused on them, maybe there were ten—yanked masks over their faces as they pulled out spray bottles. The room suddenly stunk, and as Alyssa sauntered outside, I found the room spinning.

Judson grabbed onto me, but he was falling to the floor, too.

I hated fainting.

I woke up with the worst hangover I'd ever had. My mouth was dry and sticky. I coughed, hard, and it only made the sensation worse. What in the ever-loving fuck did I drink last night? I looked around and the reality of what happened rushed back to me.

I rubbed at my eyes. I was in a bedroom. Light streamed in, and I wondered, briefly, exactly how many times this had happened to me. I was knocked out, and I woke up elsewhere. A moment like that started this whole fucking mess.

The bedroom was decorated in greens and browns. Unlike the first time I woke alone in a strange place, I no longer cared to know what it looked like other than the fact that I wasn't where I wanted to be.

I struggled out of the bed. It was lucky I wasn't tied up in a basement. I'd count my lucky stars if I thought I had any left. The guys weren't with me and that was problem number one. A black dress was hung over the door to the room, clearly indicating I was supposed to wear it. I sighed. When was I supposed to put that on? Now, while I felt like I'd drunk a bottle of tequila? No, I wasn't going to do that.

There was a bathroom connected to the room, and I went into it. The place was fully stocked like it would be in a hotel and a shower sounded heavenly. There were things to be learned in constantly going through this kind of bullshit. There really was no need to rush, at least not yet. I could run downstairs. I could scream. I could make a scene. It was just as likely that I was on another island somewhere and not knowing everything I should would mean I got nowhere fast and just ended up hurt again.

If any of this had taught me anything, it was that I needed to be the smartest person in the room even when I was surrounded by geniuses.

The truth was that Alyssa might be the smartest person I'd ever met. She'd clearly faked her death, leaving both her husband and brother devastated by her loss. I needed some details I hadn't pushed for from Derrick and Judson on how she'd died. Or didn't die.

I put on the shower and waited for the water to turn hot. Hopefully wherever this luxurious hellhole turned out to be had hot water. I wandered over to the window and looked out. There were palm trees and oceans in the not too far distance. Okay, I was somewhere tropical. I'd bet this was an island. The Smythes did like their islands.

Did Alyssa want me to put on the black cocktail dress in the middle of the day? Were we going to wear formal wear all the time while we did whatever this was?

Maybe I'd wander downstairs in my bathrobe just to see what happened. I smiled. I loved that idea. That was just what I was going to do.

I walked away from the window, dropping my clothes on the floor like a petulant teenager as I approached the shower. There was hot water, so already this kidnapping was looking up. I closed my eyes and let the heat move through me. One way or another I'd get through this. I was a survivor, and Alyssa might have fooled the world but now that I knew she lived, she was going to wish she'd never shown her face to me.

One way or another.

15

I brushed out my wet hair and pulled it back. The bathroom was well stocked. Unlike her brother, when Alyssa kidnapped me, she didn't fill the place with my own stuff, but I could make do with the products she had in here. I smiled. I wondered if there was a place to leave reviews online about how your kidnappers treated you.

Service was great but I've had better food... four stars.

All right, I'd really lost it now. After putting on the pair of pajamas I found in a drawer, I wrapped myself up in the white cotton bathrobe and left the room. I was not putting on that dress. It was my passive aggressive fuck you to Alyssa. They could force me to do it, of that I had no doubt, but I wouldn't make it easy. If Ben had taught me anything, it was that being nice to the person who wanted to hurt me did nothing to improve my situation.

I hadn't seen a clock, but I guessed it to be mid-morning, which proved to be wrong. The first clock I passed in the hall showed it to be quite earlier than I thought, just seven. Maybe I didn't know how the light filtered inside here. Maybe it was just brighter.

Men with guns walked through the hall. One of them nodded to me, and I did the same back to him. Yes, I'd seen him, and I acknowledged he had the gun. That was the subtext I got anyway. One gun wasn't going to take out ten, and so whatever inclination I had to grab it out of his arms and shoot him passed fast. I was going to be smart about this. Quiet and deadly. In the meantime, I'd smile at anyone who smiled at me. I believed the word my grandmother would have used was disarming. Hopefully they'd just think I was a non-threat.

Warden sat at the kitchen table when I entered, a cup of coffee in front of him. He was fully dressed in khaki shorts and a blue collared shirt. He blinked at me before he grinned. "You look comfy."

"I'm not in the mood for dress up right now." I leaned over to kiss his cheek. "You're okay? Where are we?"

He nodded. "For now, I'm okay. But make no mistake. While we are in Hawaii—I saw a letter on the counter with the address— and, as you said, being dressed up like this is a vacation, we are in Alyssa's version of Ben's basement. I did a quick look before the guards stopped me. I've seen Trace. He's still out cold, in the room next to mine. Other than that, I don't know where anyone else is or if they're here at all. Enormously glad to see you."

I nodded. "The dress up basement. Got it." I had suspected as much myself. I poured some of the coffee. She could make this all look as pretty as she wanted it to be but we were in hell, and hell dressed up was still just hell in disguise. There was no way to make it heaven even if you put it in a pretty black dress and made the residents sit in designer furniture.

I took my coffee and sat down on Warden's lap. I wouldn't overthink the need to do so. I wanted to feel him next to me.

I was strong; I could handle this. But it was nice to know I wasn't doing it alone.

He leaned his head against my back and kissed me through my bathrobe. "You okay?"

"Yes. We should assume we're on camera, right?" I leaned back against him. "That we're being watched."

"Considering Mercer is here somewhere, I'd say yes. Kade was always better than him but now maybe they've switched roles."

As though we'd summoned him, K arrived in the kitchen. He was still in his clothes from the last time we'd all been together. He rubbed his eyes and stared at us. "Why do you two look so much better than me?"

"We showered." I patted the chair next to me, and Kade threw himself down in it before he pressed his forehead straight down on the table. Yeah, he was pretty hard off still.

Warden and I shared a look before I placed my hand on the back of Kade's hair, running my fingers through it. "You should go back to bed. You're not missing anything. We're all on camera. We can't plan an escape, and if you tell us which room is yours, we'll be sure to get you if something exciting happens."

He lifted his head to meet my gaze. My poor love, his eyes were red-rimmed. He looked like he had the worst hangover in the universe. "How are you so good at this?"

"Experience." I shrugged. "I get kidnapped a lot."

He put his head back down and groaned. "Don't stop petting my hair."

I pretended he'd put a please on that order and went back to doing so. Kade was grumpy. His head hurt. I'd already seen Warden and Trace when they weren't at their best. So far only Derrick seemed to manage himself nicely when he was in pain and maybe that was because it had happened to him so much.

"Have you two talked about how this is going to play out?" Kade spoke without picking up his head. "Mercer's watching, for sure. But I don't give a shit. I'm not saying anything he can't hear."

I looked at Warden, and he shook his head. He hadn't followed Kade's thinking either. "No. I'm not sure I know how it's going to play out."

I rose from Warden's lap and went and poured Kade some coffee. If he really wanted to talk instead of sleep, he was going to need to be caffeinated. I placed it down in front of him, and he managed to sit up to drink it. Instead of climbing back on Warden's lap, I sat down across the table from them. I needed to feel the weight of what was happening, and it was best to do that on my own.

He sipped it and then spoke again. "Makes sense why she shot Trace and Warden. You two were always mistrustful of her. Warden you turned her away when she propositioned you at her engagement party." I gaped at him but didn't interrupt. The layers of intrigue these guys kept to themselves was ridiculous. Alyssa asked Warden for sex at her engagement party for Derrick? There wasn't enough coffee in the universe for this shit.

Kade kept speaking. "She'd never hurt Judson. If she's to be believed, she was eventually coming back for him, and she always wanted Derrick, whatever she did to him."

I pointed at my K. "And you? She didn't shoot at you."

"Mercer is here. He wouldn't like me dead unless he did it." He sipped the coffee again. His color was getting better. "I'm sorry about this guys. I missed it. He must have been in and out of our system."

I shook my head. "Stop it. You don't control the world. I've told you that before. You kept us pretty safe and got me out of trouble. We should be apologizing to you. That wasn't a one-man job. You needed a team. You and Mercer together."

A wave of emotion swept over his gaze as he regarded me. "Why are you so good to me, Everly?"

"I'm in love with you, Kade." It was important to say it, a lot, right now. "And you, too, Warden."

He squeezed my hand across the table. "I love you, too."

Kade nodded. "Me, too."

"You're not dead, Kade. Go on. What else?" I needed to hear what he thought I didn't know, what he was avoiding saying.

He took a moment, and then he did again. "Trace will be with us. We know that. But Derrick and Judson? This is Alyssa."

I got up to pour more coffee but mostly so I could step away from what he said, putting distance between myself and the words he'd uttered. "You think Derrick could go back to Alyssa and Judson side with her over us."

I took a long sip of my drink even as it burned the inside of my mouth before I turned back around. Warden lifted his eyebrows slightly. "What Kade said is hard, but I'll admit to thinking it myself."

"I'm one hundred percent sure of Derrick's love for me." As I spoke the words I realized I meant them. He was as loyal as one person could be to another, and she had betrayed him on what must have felt like a cellular level. "And Judson's too."

Trace entered the room. He'd dressed in a pair of jeans with a black t-shirt. I really needed to see if she'd given me anything less fancy than the dress to wear. The guys were neat but casual looking. He stared at me for a second before he shook his head with a grin on his face. "Talk about passive aggressive. What have I missed?"

"We're discussing whether Judson and Derrick will betray

us. Everly is sure of them." Kade filled Trace in. "I'm less sure."

Trace winced. "Derrick is secured. It's going to make Alyssa nuts, but he is one hundred percent devoted to our Everly. I wouldn't have believed it possible, but Everly makes Derrick solid. He's back to how he used to be before the Alliance made him a killer. Slightly off kilter, but brilliant and trustworthy. He'd do anything for her. I get that because so would I." He walked over and kissed my cheek. "But Judson might be a problem."

He was wrong. "No, he's not."

"Everly, you don't understand the connection they have. Judson broke rules for her and he never does that. That is his twin sister. He always thought despite all her flaws that she walked on water."

Religious analogies aside, they hadn't seen what I had right before we were all knocked out by whatever gas they'd used on us. She'd touched him, and he'd knocked her hand away. He didn't like to be touched indiscriminately, and he hadn't wanted his twin to even touch him. At the same time, he'd held onto me as we were going under. Judson loved me. I didn't have to compete with his sister even if these were normal circumstances.

I shook my head. "You guys are wrong. You'll see. Judson won't betray us."

"I hope you're right." Warden sighed. "If you can still see anything other than betrayal everywhere you look, then you're not as dark as you think you are, Evy."

"Or maybe I just see the world accurately this time. I promise you, I'm not beyond seeing the dark edges. Before we get out of here, things will get deadly."

Judson strode in. She'd given her brother exactly the right clothes. He was in dark pants and a light blue button up shirt he'd rolled up to the elbows. All three of the men in the room stared at him for a long second.

I sighed. "We were just discussing whether or not you're going to turn on us for your sister."

I wasn't lying to any of them anymore unless it was to save their lives. Or if I ever got to do something like throwing a surprise party. Did people even get to do normal things like that?

Judson sighed and strode to the coffee. "I can't blame you all for your worry. I'd do the same thing but I can assure you that..."

Trace elbowed him. "I'm sure we're on camera. And Everly took your side one hundred percent. Your sister has gotten to see enough of that, I imagine. Let's not antagonize her anymore."

"Good call." Judson took my hand and tugged me to him. "This is a fucking nightmare."

The cursing told me all I needed to know. Jud was on edge. "I'm going to save us all. Somehow."

"Everly, she was always..."

She strode in the room like she walked on air. If I'd wondered about the dress I needn't have bothered. She was in her own version of what she wanted me in, only her too-fancy-for-breakfast attire was pure white, like she could get married in it. I tried and failed to not roll my eyes.

"Oh good you're all here."

As if she hadn't known that. I hated the sound of her voice. "Derrick isn't here."

"Derrick is occupied." She smiled at me with nothing but pure malice coming from her. "We had quite the reunion last night."

I swallowed. She wanted me to think they'd had sex. I didn't believe that for a second. If she'd actually been in Derrick's bed she wouldn't have to brag about it this morning. Being well loved gave off an aura that was impossible to miss. Good sex with him would have made her glow. I knew from personal experience.

I didn't doubt they'd had a reunion. Now, I needed to worry about his health. "Is he in the hospital?"

Trace choked on the intake of a sip of coffee.

She ignored me. "I'm sure he'll be out soon. There is food you know. Not just coffee. If you are all going to think to plot escape or my death, you should do it on a full stomach. The sooner you're all fed we can start the real work of making this work between us."

I stared at her. If she wasn't careful, I was going to put a knife through her eye. I knew how to do that now. I could even try for more accuracy this time. Judson's movement caught my attention. His hands weren't steady as he poured his coffee.

This was going to be hell on him. Derrick, too, wherever he was.

She wasn't just another enemy. This opponent came with enough emotional baggage that it could have filled this entire house.

"We're in Hawaii?" I changed the subject. "You kept us knocked out a long time."

"We are." She smiled. "But don't think to get away. One word from you out there or any attempt to escape and one of the guys will shoot you in the head. They're getting to be much better shots. You took out most of my most experienced men. That was really something in the hotel. I mean, to even shoot your father, Everly."

I shrugged. "You might be surprised how easy it is to kill your father. Yours is dead, right? Otherwise we could try it. Too bad. It's an experience I think perhaps everyone should try. Really, with a gun it's just point and click."

She opened and closed her mouth. If she was going to do

crazy—and it seemed Alyssa wanted to somehow combine utter lunacy with who could be bitchier—then I was going to do it bigger than she would.

Alyssa slammed her hand down on the counter, all the façade of calm suddenly gone. "Listen, we are going to get something straight here."

Derrick took that moment to come in the room. He had a black eye, and for a second I could only see red. She'd either hurt him or had him injured. No one hurt the men I loved. He must have seen death in my eyes because he quickly came over and wrapped me in a hug from behind. It looked affectionate, and it was, but I understood his second purpose was to restrain me from launching myself at her.

"You're still my husband, Derrick. Kindly get your hands off of her while you're with me."

He shook his head and didn't let go. "I only promised until death did us part. You died. Just because you faked it doesn't mean the death certificate doesn't count. You're not my wife. You're just some crazy lady who I have to deal with now and probably have to put a bullet in your head. Sorry, Judson."

Judson didn't answer. He watched the whole scene with his eyes wide. So far, and I only had two instances to go by, it was like every time Alyssa showed up part of Judson seemed to check out. I wondered if that was a new thing from the trauma of this whole insanity or if that had always been the way between them. Even he had said Alyssa was impossible to resist, difficult to say no to. I could now see why. She simply plowed forward and demanded she have what she wanted.

I could admire that if she wasn't the worst person on the planet. That was saying a lot, considering I was really pretty awful myself.

"We are going to sit down and talk now." She looked me

up and down like she was really seeing me for the first time. "Are you in your bathrobe?"

I nodded. "Yes."

"I left you a dress. Are you blind? Do we need to get a doctor to see you?"

I shook my head. "No. I just didn't like the dress."

"I am not dealing with you like this. No one told me you were so obtuse."

Who would she have talked to about me? Pretty much the only people who truly knew me in the last eighteen months or so were in the room here, and she hadn't been conversing with any of them. I almost asked her but thought better of it. There were men with guns, and I didn't have one. I had to keep that in mind even though I was seriously pissed off. Only children couldn't get control of their tempers.

I'd have a temper tantrum later when I was armed.

"Go put on some clothes," she ordered me. "And everyone meet me in the conference room. Whether you live or die is up to you. Well, not Derrick and Judson. You two I would never hurt." She actually batted her eyelids.

I turned in Derrick's arms. "You liked that? That was the woman you pledged to love forever?"

"I was young. I thought she was elegant." He kissed my temple. "Second time around I decided I preferred a woman who pulled a gun out of my hands and threatened to shoot me."

I touched his eye, and he winced. "You need some ice. What happened?"

"She thought we might get friendly. I stopped it. She decked me. I'll be fine. It's nothing."

I sighed. "I have to go get dressed. I may push issues before this whole thing is over but not on this. I'll put on the dress she picked out since I'm to be her living doll at the moment."

"Kade." A man I'd never seen before entered the room. He wore a black silk shirt that was too big on him and a pair of jeans. His blond hair was shaggy, puffy, like it was too long but didn't want to grow down, just out.

Kade jumped to his feet. "Mercer, you piece of shit. What the fuck?"

The other man had the good taste to look down at his feet for a second. "Kade, I'm in love with her." He took a step back. "Sorry, Derrick."

D laughed. "Take her."

"Fuck me." Judson turned around, gripping the counter.

I tugged out of Derrick's arms and walked to Judson. "Come with me. I've got to go look pretty. I could use help with the zipper."

He nodded but didn't look at me. "Okay."

"Thanks." I took his hand in mine. "We'll be right back. Oh, Mercer is it?" The man turned to face me so I spoke again. "I'm Everly Marrs. Is everyone here in love with her?"

He blinked. "Not everyone. The guards are getting paid but some of us are. Like you guys."

I didn't know who or how this worked for Alyssa, but I could promise him—although I would say nothing for the sake of not giving anything away—that they were nothing like us. I loved these men, heart and soul.

I wasn't sure Alyssa had either of those things.

———

The dress fit like a glove, and Judson noticed. That much he responded to. He had otherwise not said a word since we'd gotten in the bedroom. When I tried to speak, he put his finger to his mouth. We were being watched, and so far what we'd all said had been pretty innocuous, things she would expect us to say. He didn't want me continuing. We weren't safe just because we were in our bedroom.

But this was a huge problem, because if we couldn't communicate, how would we ever work together on any attempt to get out of here?

He walked up behind me, zipping it up. I felt the slight tug of the material as the dress tightened on me.

Judson bent over and kissed my neck. "You make that dress. It's stunning on you."

"Are you okay, J?" I used the letter on purpose. I knew we were in that kind of tension. The Letters kind of stress.

He breathed against me, and when he spoke, it was in a whisper. "E, I feel like I might explode, like every bit of me is destroyed. When this is over, whatever is left, I don't know. If we live through this, feel free to lock me up because I will be crazed."

I turned and hugged him to me. I answered him the same way he had, a whisper in his ear. "Hold on to yourself, Judson. When this is over, we'll put you back together the same way you put me back together."

He stared at me for a moment. "She's my sister. How could she have done this? How could she have let me think she was dead? Fake her death? I mean... fuck. Fine. Fake her death. Tell me. That's my twin sister. We shared life before we had... consciousness."

"I don't have an answer for you. But we'll figure it out. I promise we will."

He nodded. "Turn around. Let me look at you?"

I stepped back and spun so he could look. I should have hated the dress. It was open straps in the back so some of my skin showed through. The evidence of the beatings I took in Ben's basement was evident, viewable by anyone who saw me. Yet, right then I didn't care. They were my battle wounds, and I was going to war.

It also wasn't lost on me that Judson had called me E. It was a result of me calling him J. I understood why it happened. And yet, he'd sort of just made me a Letter.

I could do this. I could be E.

I kissed him on the lips. "You can stay in here. Take a nap. Don't go to this meeting. Why bother? You know she's just going to poke at all of us."

"I need to be there. This is my torture, and it's being plunged on all of you like some kind of virus, like a plague. I won't leave any of you to do this alone. You're my woman. And they have really become my brothers, even if that is really fucked up."

I didn't let go of him. "If you're coming, then you can't fall apart. Not now. Not until later. That sounds cold, but we have to be. Right now, we're not allowed to feel anything about this. If you can't do that, then stay here."

I wouldn't baby him. Judson wouldn't do that to me in the same situation. Sometimes you needed the person who loved you to tell you to suck it up and deal. He could stay here and have a breakdown, but if he came with me, we were J and E.

That was how this worked.

He nodded at me. "Got it."

I really believed he did.

16

There were similar decorating styles between Judson and his sister. They both liked clean lines and big open spaces. It was ridiculous to notice things like that given the circumstances, but life was made in the small details. Maybe it would matter.

We sat around the table, the six of us and Alyssa with her four men. She used to have eight. That was bizarre to think about. How on Earth had she managed that? I couldn't fathom it. I was barely treading water loving these five men. How did she make sure they all got what they needed from the relationship? I wasn't at all sure I was doing that.

She and I could be besties, comparing notes. How did a woman love multiple Alliance men at the same time in this modern world where they had to pretend to be people they weren't? But she was a psycho bitch—and I *hated* that word but it applied—and I wouldn't ask her for advice on what kind of gum to buy, let alone how to love anyone.

I stared at them all. It wasn't clear to me that she loved anyone at all. Or maybe she did. I didn't know her, and I hoped I didn't have to.

For a bad person with a plan, she didn't say much.

I looked around. Next to her was Marcus. Bland Marcus who no one could understand how he did things or why he did. Well, it all made sense now. He wasn't. He was the face in front of Alyssa. Alyssa who couldn't be out front both because she was a woman and because she was technically dead. Next to her on the other side: Mercer. Alyssa and her M men. I could do a whole word play with that if I had the time to contemplate such things.

Mercer had probably been the one to take over the elevators in the hotel, to lock Kade out. He was the reason the Letters couldn't get to Derrick and me that day. But my father could. He'd be the person to get a definitive answer from on that subject. I chewed on my lip. Not now but maybe someday.

I didn't know the other two or who the four she had lost were, only that she'd had them and that I garnered quickly from Kade before we sat down. Mercer had let that much slip.

Alyssa placed her hands in front of her, and she linked them together. I stared at her nails. She had a French manicure. How had she had that done? She'd been stuck inside a house and hadn't come out. Oh, wait. That was probably bullshit. Mercer could outplay Kade. At least for now. Kade would figure this out, of that I had no doubt.

"You have been nothing but problems for me." She sighed, her shoulders going up and down. I knew she was considered beautiful, that Derrick had wanted her, that she was glamorous, but right now she just looked brittle to me, like she hadn't had enough time in the sun or never smiled. Her dark hair was long and silky, her cheekbones high. I would have killed for her perfect-for-clothes figure. And yet... the look altogether wasn't working for her. Alyssa looked like a woman about to break.

I just had to push her over her edge.

One way or another.

"How so?" Trace asked her. "Because the last time I checked, I was minding my own fucking business and you had someone shoot me. You killed the mark I'd been working on for years. Warden, too. I'd say you've bothered us a lot more than we bothered you. We didn't even know you were alive."

She waved her hand in the air. "You killed four of my loves. You two are still here. In the end, you've hardly even been inconvenienced. The whole thing brought lovely Everly right back to you. How... charming."

Trace opened and closed his mouth. I took that chance to jump in. "We killed four of your loves? How did we do that? Last I checked, we hadn't killed anyone except..." The truth dawned on me. "The hotel. Ben and the other Alliance council. Were you with the entire Alliance council? Were you with *Ben*?"

Her facial expressions remained solemn. "I loved Ben very deeply. I am who I am because of him."

"He is who you used to fake your death." Derrick sat back in his chair. "They kept me tied up, while they hurt you. And then they dumped your body in front of me."

"Well..." She scrunched up her nose. "They dumped *a* body in front of you. It wasn't me, and you didn't look that closely. I don't blame you. It was horrific looking. Ben gave me a look-see before he brought that poor girl in."

A muscle ticked in Derrick's jaw. "You planned it with Ben from moment one?"

"Oh no, my darling. Of course not. I screwed up. I went to him, trying to work with him to improve your situation, gave away my knowledge of the Alliance, and he tortured me. Just as you thought. Just as he did to sweet Everly over there."

This woman made me want to choke on her bullshit endearments. Sweet? I'd show her sweet when I choked the life out of her body. I shot Judson a quick look. He stared at his sister, and I couldn't get a clear reading from him how he was doing. I'd told him to hold it together, which I knew was asking a lot. Was he doing it? Maybe I couldn't just kill her. This was his twin sister. He might want her alive and somehow rehabbed.

Fuck this entire situation. If someone was dead, they should stay dead.

"So he tortured you and then you ended up having sex with him?" This was the first time Judson had spoken since we sat down. He narrowed his gaze as he asked his sister the question. There was no emotion to it otherwise. He might have been asking her what car she decided to buy.

She smiled. "I turned his desire to hurt me into his desire to fuck me. It wasn't that hard. Well, I shouldn't say that. Ben didn't have sexual desires at first, not that I could tell. I managed to bring him around. I'm that good. In the end, we loved each other. For a while, I worried you were about to do the same thing, Everly, considering how you seem to be collecting men."

I threw up a little bit in my mouth. I couldn't answer her because I was too busy trying not to full on vomit on the table. Sex with Ben? She had sex with Ben consensually? And thought I might have been trying to do the same?

Warden put his hand on the back of my neck and rubbed, slowly. The action caught my attention enough that I managed to shove down the vomit before it came up.

The gist of this, and she was still talking, was that after she'd seduced Ben. They'd concocted the whole idea of the fake death and a taking over the Alliance. It was convenient because she just so happened to keep falling in love with men who could help her do this.

If either Mercer or Marcus—the ridiculous M men—saw

that they were being used in this contorted plan, they didn't indicate it. Neither did the two nameless jackasses who completed this ridiculous farce. Four men, all being used, being dragged around by their dicks in the name of love. It was pathetic, but it was also dangerous. These people were dangerous and they helped rule the world.

"To what end?" Trace looked bored, as though he'd already gotten over the novelty of faking one's death and wanted to get the fuck on with this. It was amazing I could read him so well when it used to be so much harder. "You shot at me, shot at Warden. Why? Killed a man who you could have used for your own agenda somehow. What was the purpose? Or are you just floundering in the wind, hoping to feel important because you have somehow managed to pull the wool over the eyes of people who really didn't care if you lived or died?" He held up his hand. "Sorry, Derrick and Judson cared, and I gave a shit that they were upset because even when I didn't like them that much I kind of still did."

Judson laughed. I was so surprised by the sound that I jumped in my seat. He shook his head. "Thanks, Trace. I sometimes didn't hate you, too."

Kade put his head in his hands. Somehow he was making this all his own fault. If I could have reached him under the table, I'd have kicked him in the shin. Kade had to quit blaming himself every time something went wrong. He didn't control the world.

Alyssa pointed at me. "You are making them soft."

"What do you want? We're not here just so you could have a coming out of the coffin party. You're not dead. Woo-frickin-hoo. What do you want?"

She sighed. "I need your father."

"Do you have a Ouija board?" I wished I had bit my tongue the second I said it, but once I'd gone there I just had to keep going? "A medium? How about that woman on TV from Long Island? She might be available. Or that dude who talks to the dead in front of the whole room of people. What was his name?"

She slammed her hand down on the table. Okay, I'd pissed her off, but Derrick was grinning, so I'd call it a win. "I am trying to be nice to you."

"You had two of my loves shot. I get pissed when people do that." Kidnapping I could apparently forgive pretty easily. "My father is dead. I killed him the same time I took out Ben."

I was pretty sure that Derrick had killed Ben. My memory of everything leading up to shooting my father was fuzzy. It was like a violent blur and then bang... Dad was dead... and I left the Letters. I'd needed space. They'd only pretended to give me some. It was our version of a love story, as fucked up as that was proving to be.

"I am well aware. Everly, I think we should get some things straight between us. I am trying to be nice to you. I didn't have you killed when I could have that whole time you were wandering around Baton Rouge, a lost little girl pretending you could do it on your own. I respected the effort even if you would have fallen on your face without Derrick watching every step you took."

He cleared his throat. "Not true."

She shook her head. "No point in patronizing her, Derrick. She would have fallen apart in a heartbeat."

We'd gotten off track, and I didn't give a shit what this woman thought. "You were being nice to me," I reminded her to get her back on the subject.

"Yes. Judson loves you, and I do love my brother, whatever he thinks right now. So I left you alone, and then I had you warned to just go about your business. You could have stayed alive and left alone if only you had stayed in your cheap apartment and worked at your nothing bar."

Things were starting to add up for me, the small details that hadn't always made sense. Alyssa interfered with things to a large degree, using her own twisted look at the world as some kind of roadmap. "You tried to have Warden and Trace killed. Why? I get why you left your brother and former husband alone." And I noticed she left the fact that Derrick loved me out of her explanation. She clearly didn't like that at all. Was Derrick supposed to pine for her forever? I bet in her mind he was. "And Kade? Was he because of your deep-seated love for Mercer over there?"

"Mercer asked me to not kill Kade. He did hope the two of them could someday team up to do brilliant things together." She ran her long fingernails up Mercer's arm, and he smiled at her like a dog might do with an owner who scratched him behind the ears. Any second now, he might actually start panting.

She continued. "And I did try to have Trace and Warden killed. They had no place in my new world order. Warden interferes too much in what I'm trying to do economically and Trace has always just pissed me off."

That was pretty much what we'd figured. Warden ran his finger over the back of my neck. He was okay and didn't want me to freak out over that statement. So much could be conveyed with just the smallest touch.

"And you want what now?"

She sighed, throwing her brown hair over her shoulder. What was it that the entire world had found so tantalizing about this woman that they were obsessed with her? Even her brother had thought she all but walked on water and was willing to forgive her all her faults. I didn't have siblings, but I figured it was more common than not to actually dislike the person. Sibling rivalry and all that. Had it been a twin thing? And why was Derrick, who saw through people so effortlessly, taken with her? She must be really, really good in bed.

Like the best blow job giver in the world...

"I want to get into your father's inner vault in the Alliance headquarters."

What the fuck was that? My confusion must have shown on my face because Kade answered my unasked question. "In New York City, it's where the records are kept. The ones that your father forged so that we all got kicked out."

I sat up straight. "Were you sleeping with my father?"

"Well, you're sleeping with my brother so I don't see what the difference was."

In all of the years that I'd known my dad, he had never brought a woman home. Ever. He had seemed like he was too consumed with his work to be dating. And he'd never been powerful enough to be one of her top men. But that hadn't meant she wasn't sleeping with him.

It was hard for me to digest this. Alyssa had a lot of men in her life, and more power to her for liking a good fuck, but she wasn't in a closed unit like I was. I would never... stray from the five guys I had. It was us and only us. That was how this worked for me.

Alyssa wielded sex for power as many people had done before her throughout history. And that seemed to include my father.

"Did you sleep with him to get him to mess up the background of these guys so they'd be thrown out of the Alliance and then let him spin in the wind when it fell in on his face?"

She rose and walked over to me. Warden tensed while the others all got to their feet. I put my hand out in the sign of stop. I wasn't afraid of her. She needed something from me. I wasn't going to die right now, and I knew how to survive hurt.

I didn't want to have to do that again, but if the scars on my back indicated anything, it was that I might have once been a girl made of sand but I was a woman with steel in my spine now.

I wasn't the one feeling so bothered by this moment I'd had to get up and move. I wasn't the one with the nervous energy.

Her own men hadn't budged.

I was a woman who'd jammed a knife in the eye of a woman who held Trace prisoner. They should be quaking in their boots to let her near me, armed guards or not.

Still, I kept still, and I smiled. Two could play the charming woman game.

"You were a surprise, Everly. I didn't see you coming. I didn't expect you to be kidnapped and brought into this. Ben and I had to figure out what to do about you. Your father was frantic as he should have been. Not for your safety, of course. Other than me, all women are expendable in the Alliance. You should know that by now. When the five of them no longer find your pussy exciting, they'll dump you because you'll have nothing to offer them."

I blinked. If she had a point, she should make it. Emotional wounds could still be inflicted on me it would seem. Not because she'd stated that my loves would be done with me when they got tired of me—that could happen to anyone in any relationship, and I felt as solid in mine as was possible to be—but because she'd told me that my father was more concerned with her not being found out than with what happened to me.

There were more important things to be said than how I felt. I'd told Jud to hold it together. I had to do the same. So I forced myself to swallow. When I spoke, I actually sounded calm. "Why throw them out to begin with?"

"I wanted my brother back. I wanted Derrick back. The

others I didn't care what happened to them, but I wanted them powerless so they couldn't investigate what happened to Derrick and Judson. The fact that they had pseudo-friends was an inconvenience for me. But then you came around."

She acted like I'd done that. They'd fucking taken me from my apartment. Derrick had drugged and kidnapped me. I was the poster child for Stockholm syndrome, which was neither here nor there at the moment.

"Then you were such a problem. We were chasing you all throughout the country. You kept moving. You didn't die when..."

The door opened, and a woman I expected never to see again entered. Was this just the week for people who should be gone to reappear? Constance, Judson's housekeeper who had given me to Ben, came in carrying coffee.

My mouth fell open. Damn it, I should have known she was with Alyssa. She'd all but told me that. She was loyal to the Smythes. She always would be.

Judson pounded on the table in a movement similar to his sister and stormed away to stare out of the window. He was breathing deeply, evidenced by the up and down movement of his shoulders. He hadn't known she was here either.

Constance put the coffee down on the table and embraced Alyssa like she was family. Alyssa held the older woman close before she let her go. "Come on, Judy, come say hello to Constance. She practically raised us. Surely you can forgive her for what role she played. She tells me she gave your little girl a warning and sweet Everly didn't take it."

Alyssa walked over to her brother and placed her hand on his shoulder. He jerked, and I rushed forward. She wanted to mess with me, fine. She wasn't going to hurt Judson or any of them while there was breath in my body.

"Oh, brother. Still got that problem being touched?"

He turned around slowly, pushing her hand aside. "E, it's fine. Seriously."

"What a cute nickname. You call her E?"

She didn't know they were the Letters, hadn't known they would take me, and what plans they'd made since then.

But Constance did. She smiled. "They all made her call them by their first initial. Seems he's adopted that for her. You will forgive me, Judson. You and your sister belong together. The two most beautiful babies I'd ever seen. You were both towheaded as children. Bright. Funny. You did whatever she said. And I swore to your mother I would always protect the family. I've done that."

Judson kept his thoughts to himself. He put his hand out, and I took it. He linked us together, silently indicating to his sister he had no issue being touched. By me.

"Get to your point, Alyssa." He spoke to her. "You want into the vault. Go ahead and do it."

"I can't." She put her hands on her hips. "If I could have, I would have. Although Jeb was more than happy to end Everly's life—I think he thought he was sparing you another round with Ben—he left his entrance coded for your finger-prints. I think at the end of the day he didn't trust me that much. He wanted me to have to... persuade you to open that vault for him."

I swallowed. My father had wanted to kill me. I'd suspected it but now to hear it from someone who knew...

Trace was up against me, taking my other hand. He brought my fingers to his mouth. "Fuck her. She doesn't know why your father did anything. Even if she was sleeping with him. Only he knew what was in his heart. We can suspect his motives, we can believe he was going to do the wrong thing, the awful thing, but none of us know. He might have been coming to kill Ben."

I appreciated what he tried to do. I really did. And I

wanted to be cold inside, to be dead to pain, to be strong. The one tear that fled my left eye that I quickly batted away was all the pain she was getting from me today.

"You want to negotiate for the use of my fingertips?" I held up my hand. "To open my father's vault because somewhere in there he has something you need. What is it? Proof that a woman can be in the Alliance? Proof that your family should have leadership of it? Something you need is worth negotiating with me."

Mercer finally spoke as the totally bland Marcus sipped his coffee. "I designed the lock for him before I fell in love with Alyssa. It requires you to also speak into the door and show your eye."

"How did you get all that information to code it? Never mind. Of course, you're Alliance. You got it through satellites or something else that is going to make me never want to get naked and get in the shower again because someone is always watching. Don't tell me."

Kade shook his head. "Probably simpler than that. He recorded you."

That was only slightly better. "The bottom line is that you could get that open by cutting off my finger and using recordings of me to open it and a visual representation of my eye, but you are afraid something will go terribly wrong and you'll never get it. Mercer made it Mercer-proof and you don't think you can get Kade to cooperate since he is probably the only one who could undo what he did if you kill me." I took a long breath. "Better to negotiate with me to get me to cooperate. That's it right?"

"Why, Derrick." Alyssa clapped her hands together. "Your little whore is also smart."

I rolled my eyes. "I won't even consider doing it until you promise me certain things, and I'm going to be honest with you, I'm not sure I can trust your word. So I'm going to need some assurances. Some lethal assurances. Are you ready to deal with me like that, Alyssa? Because I'm not playing around. You want that lock open? I'll give it to you. I don't give two shits what's in there. But we're not leaving here until I have what I want."

We stared at each other, and for the first time, I was one hundred percent certain we understood each other.

17

There was silence in the room. Alyssa finally spoke again. "We have guns to your head. Why would I negotiate with you?"

She knew the answer to that, she just wanted to hear me say it. "Because if you kill me or if I decide to end my own life to stop you from doing what you want, you may never get in that vault. And, yes, I could be pushed to such a place that I could decide to go that far. I'm not suicidal but don't assume that doesn't mean I won't take any means necessary to screw with you the way you have with me."

Alyssa crossed her arms over her chest. "What do you want, Everly?"

"I'll go with you to New York, and I'll get that vault open for you. When I'm done you're going to let us all go and be done with us. I don't want the Alliance. I don't want anything to do with it. I want to go off with the five of them and live some kind of life that you stay entirely out of. We won't mess with you, we won't tell anyone what you did or how you did this. You can have whatever life you want—as long as you stay away from us."

She smiled but showed no teeth. "That's not fine. You have my brother. You have my husband. I've never let them go, not really. It's fine if you want to sleep with Derrick, but he remains my husband. Mercer wants Kade. We can't just separate."

We'd stalled at the first point, and I hadn't even gotten to the hard stuff yet. "Then this is over. That's non-negotiable."

She grabbed onto her brother's arm, and this time he didn't wince. Maybe it was because he still held my hand or maybe he had just been ready for it. "Do you want to be out of my life, Jud? Do you want me to be dead to you again? I know you're mad but this is you and me. You know you're going to forgive me. Do you want this... this no one... making deals that involve you never seeing me again?"

"Alyssa..." Judson sounded exhausted. "I'd be thrilled if I never had to see you again. Give Everly what she wants so she can give you what you want. Then we can all be done with this charade."

Derrick spoke from across the room. "We're not married. If you want me to actually kill you to put a period on that sentence, we can go ahead and get there right now."

Her two men jumped to their feet. The two whose names I didn't know stayed seated. They sure didn't seem loyal to her. I filed that away in the back of my head as something that might or might not be useful later.

I met Derrick's gaze. He was serious, but he had to know as well as I did that if gunfire started right now, he'd be dead, along with Warden and Trace, and not the fake kind. They'd keep me alive until I wasn't useful. Judson would remain with Alyssa so she could prove some kind of point, and I didn't know how it would eventually end for Kade. All of that was unacceptable to the nth degree.

"This part is easy, Alyssa. Don't play all your cards now." I dropped my hands from Judson and Trace, to touch her arm.

She stared at it like it was a foreign body she'd never seen before. "We should stop arguing like we can't be civilized. This part is easy. At the end of the day, you want me to open that lock, and I'm telling you that I will. I absolutely am going to do that. I'm not even going to put up a fight. You have to give in on some easy things. You have to leave us alone. No more shooting at Trace and Warden. No more threatening us in any way. We stay away from the Alliance. Don't lose the ballgame now that you've just gotten to the ninth inning."

While I was speaking to her and wanted her to understand what I said, I used my baseball analogy on purpose. That was for Derrick. He couldn't blow this now. I wouldn't lose him to temper. I wouldn't bury him because he was pissed off.

"Okay. I'll leave you all alone."

And she would. I'd see to it, because if she didn't, I'd tell the whole Alliance what she had done. And if there was anything I knew about the short tempered misogynists running the Alliance, it was that they were going to be really pissed that a woman had gotten the upper hand on them.

But before that I had to keep us all alive. "That is so great. I knew you could be reasonable, and so can I. There's just one more thing before then that we'll have to agree on before I'll go with you to New York and get that locker open."

My body buzzed. I had no experience with any of this, and it really was just me making this up as I went along. I could be doing everything wrong. I knew from firsthand experience that sometimes people just had the upper hand on things. Alyssa wasn't stupid. She'd managed to survive this long.

"What's that, Everly?"

I walked over and took one of the coffees Constance had brought in earlier. I took my time drinking it. I couldn't look at anyone. She was going to refuse what I first offered. Of course, if she surprised me and said yes, I'd have been thrilled, but that would be stupid on her part. No, I needed her to walk into my second offer.

I needed her to think I didn't know what I was doing. And maybe I didn't.

"I want you to give each of my guys a gun. They'll still be outmatched while we go to New York. But that's the only way I can be sure they can defend themselves and you'll keep your word."

Marcus spoke for the first time. "That's insanity. We're not giving them guns."

No, of course they weren't. "They have to be allowed to defend themselves or the second I get finished here they're going to be in danger. I won't have that."

Warden lifted both his eyebrows slowly. If he saw what I was doing, he at least had the good sense to not really indicate it, and Trace was keeping quiet from his usual disclosure of whatever I hoped to keep hidden.

"Derrick is a trained assassin. He doesn't get to have a weapon in this house. Not until I'm sure he's on my side."

I ignored the last dig. She was always going to say things that might hurt me just to get that rise. Mean girls were always mean girls even when they were psychopathic power wielding lunatics and not just sixteen-year-old social climbers. Although, at sixteen I might have found it to be the same kind of problem.

I walked over to Derrick. "He's the problem? You don't want to arm Derrick? You have a house filled with trained assassins."

Their peers hadn't been able to kill Trace or Warden but this was different. Anyone with minor training could point and click at close distance or when someone was sleeping. They couldn't stay awake for the next however many days this took, watching their backs. Not alone, anyway, and I wasn't going to leave them here either.

We stayed together. That was how this worked.

"Fine. Then they come with me. We all do this together."

She lifted one eyebrow, one perfectly sculpted eyebrow. She was clearly a person who had time for that kind of thing. I hadn't had any time to even consider my own. When this was over, I wanted to be the kind of person who could go get her brows done.

Alyssa was trying to figure out what I was thinking. I could see it in the tilt of her head. If only she understood how readily my mind wandered in periods of stress to the ridiculous and mundane. Eyebrow shaping. Fingernails. How much I really wanted to eat pizza right then. With mushrooms.

"I didn't plan for it to be anyone except Mercer who came with the two of us. It would practically be a girls' trip."

Visions of getting massages with Alyssa hit me hard. I did *not* want that. "Maybe we can make it more like a double date."

The more we moved the more chances we had to get away from this woman. I'd open the lock if we had to, but I wasn't above running away from her either and regrouping now that we had all the information we needed. We'd always been playing this game with one hand behind our backs. We couldn't know how to win if we didn't know against whom we were matched.

"I like that." She waved her hand in the air. "It's been too long since we went to New York City. One thing about having to pretend to be dead is that you don't get out as much as you'd like. Mansion to mansion, it got terribly boring. In the meantime, today let's go to the beach."

I wasn't going to the beach. There was already a shark circling me on dry land. I wasn't going to risk my luck with the Pacific Ocean.

Mercer indicated his head, and Kade rose. Right now, it looked like he was tied to the other tech guy. I met his gaze, and he nodded at me. We'd gotten what I wanted, and he was acknowledging it. I walked forward fast and kissed him square on the lips. He wrapped his arm around my back, drawing me close.

I pressed our foreheads together. "You'll get us out of this."

"I just keep fucking up." He kissed my cheek. "Don't count on me to come up with anything. I'm why we're in this mess."

I shook my head. "I'm always counting on you, Kade. Don't give up."

I stepped back. It wasn't going to be Derrick who made this all go away. There were too many guns, and despite his tough guy attitude, a bullet just as easily killed him as it would me. Warden and Trace had survived being shot. I wasn't going to take a third risk.

"I'm going to be in my room," I announced to the general population. If the cameras Mercer had on us were trailing me, maybe they'd miss something on the guys. That was a small chance, but one I took anyway.

"But the beach." Alyssa laughed. "I'm still convinced we can all be friends. You can keep sleeping with my brother, Everly. And Trace, Warden, and Kade, too. We'll share Derrick. I mean, he's my husband, so that'll be on my terms, but that'll be fine because you're sleeping with my brother."

I rolled my eyes. Some statements weren't worth dignifying with an answer.

DERRICK

I didn't remember Alyssa being this ridiculous, but then again I'd seen her through the eyes of my hard dick most of the time when we'd been together. It wasn't that I found her to be that physically attractive, actually. She was pretty, but I'd been a professional baseball player and a rich kid before that. I'd had plenty of women in my life and most of them had been more than pretty. On the physical side of things, I couldn't really complain about how the women I fucked looked.

Of course, none of them held a candle to Everly, and I didn't think she knew how physically attractive she was. Or if she cared.

Alyssa blathered on. I used to love the sound of her voice. It was so sophisticated. She'd been exactly the kind of girl who had never been interested in me before her. Well-educated, wealthy enough to match my own, and from the right Alliance family. My father had always told me I'd never be able to get anyone like her. But then she'd been interested.

And I had fallen for it hook, line, and sinker. Damn if I hadn't loved her. I truly had. I'd mourned her, sworn revenge, and this whole time she had been alive? There was something sick and ridiculous about that. Worst thing was that she'd never loved me, and I'd known it.

Of course, now she seemed obsessed but that had nothing to do with loving me. That was pure old-fashioned jealousy. I'd moved on. I half expected she showed herself for that reason.

I stared at Evs as she left the room. My gorgeous girl. Nothing about how I felt about her was based in rhyme or reason. The funny thing was... on paper she was exactly like Alyssa. Well-educated, Alliance family, beautiful. She would have checked off the entire boxes, the same ones that Alyssa had. The difference being that she wasn't without compassion, without a soul.

So we had fifteen guards wandering around with guns, and I had to do something about that so that Everly could be safe. If I polled the other four guys she was in love with, I'd almost guarantee they were on the same page. Except maybe for Judson. Poor guy was shell-shocked, but at least he hadn't lost his mind and turned back to his sister.

Not that I thought that he would. Judson loved Everly. We all did, and fuck us all because not one of us knew what the hell to do with that except to practically smother her and promise her whatever she wanted whenever she asked for it.

Instead, we were all in this house in Hawaii together with fifteen armed guards. Fifteen I'd seen. There could have been more. But I'd start with fifteen. I'd kill Mercer and Marcus. They might even thank me. There was something wrong in their devotion to her. Elijah and Jedidiah, too. They were minor Alliance members that I hardly knew.

The four of them. What were they getting from Alyssa? Anyone could get their dick sucked for twenty dollars if they wanted to. And Alyssa wasn't really that good at that. I smiled.

My *wife* shot me a look. "What are you grinning at?"

"Nothing at all, actually. Come in my room again and I'll forcibly remove you. I don't hit women, but if you put your fucking hands on me again, I will kill you. I will do that."

Everly had left. I had no reason to be standing here at all. Wherever she was, I'd never be far. So long as I drew breath from my body. Fifteen guys. I could take them all. But Everly hadn't wanted me to. I'd picked up on her signals. She had some notion I shouldn't die. The big heart on that woman. Somehow Everly could be both brutal and kind. I hadn't known both could exist in the same space.

EVERLY

I stared out the window. The beach really did look inviting and Constance dropped off a bathing suit. Well, a two piece skimpier than any I had ever worn before. It would show every mark on my body and I was sure that she meant it to. I stared at the pink strings that were supposed to be my bathing suit and threw it at the door as Constance left.

I wasn't going to act like I was on vacation when I was absolutely not.

The door opened and closed, Trace coming in. I leaned against the window as he walked toward me. I shook my head. We couldn't talk about things. It might have been better if we just all stayed away from one another until we were in New York. Even then, maybe not. Technology was going to make this miserable.

He wrapped me up against him, neither of us speaking. Finally, he said something. "Did I ever tell you about the day I decided I was going to figure out how human beings got to Mars?"

Well, that couldn't have been more surprising if he'd said he wanted to wear a bunny costume and hop around. That was a huge shift in conversation, but I supposed it was a safe topic. What did Alyssa care why Trace wanted to get humanity to Mars? "No. I mean, I know it's your objective. That's why you were after James Robert but no... the details... I don't think so. We might have discussed it a little but that was back when I was still trying to escape you rather than, you know, get you in my bed and love you forever."

He rubbed his nose against my hair. "Say things like that to me forever. I was nine years old and everyone was looking at Mars through a telescope in my very expensive private school. The teacher looked like the actor Bill Hader. I didn't know Bill Hader back then but when I look back at it now he looked like Bill Hader."

"Funny how memory does that." I let him pick me up and walk me over to the bed. We lay down together, facing each other. It was strange to do this knowing both of us would stay totally dressed.

He leaned on his elbow. "He used to wear a bow tie. With everything."

"Well, you remember it so it worked. He was memorable." I touched the whiskers on his cheeks, loving the rough feel of it.

"Right." He nodded. "The thing was he kept talking about the Red Planet. The Red Planet this, the Red Planet, that. And then the asshole stops the whole class and he says oh, Trace Hill, you can't see it because you're colorblind. Class, Trace has a disability. And he just starts screaming about it. Or at least it felt like he did. On and on. Or at least it felt that way. All the eyes were on me, their perfect working eyes that could see the red of the planet Mars."

I winced. "That must have felt really awful. I'm pissed on your behalf. It was not his business to expose you like that."

"A different time. I'm just enough older than you that things like privacy laws weren't exactly followed. I stormed away from the telescope and stared at my desk like I could drill a hole in it with my gaze. But rather than cry, which is what I'd have done if I wasn't afraid someone would report to my father that I was a pussy—his word—I got focused. I didn't know about the Alliance yet, but I knew that I could somehow grow up to do something, and I swore it would be Mars. One way or the other, even doing what the Alliance wanted from me in terms of careers, I've worked toward it ever since."

Just from this one story alone I felt like I knew him even

better than I ever had. "If we leave the Alliance, you never get us to Mars. Why not go yourself?"

He pointed to his eyes. "I'm broken."

"Trace…"

He kissed my lips. "I don't mind anymore. I like my eyes. They're what I see you with, and I wouldn't change a thing about them. I wouldn't alter a cell in them, a connection in my brain. You are the most beautiful woman I've ever had the privilege to gaze on. And I don't care about Mars. Oh wait, I just heard that. Your last name Everly Marrs. I am getting Mars. The better version."

My mouth fell open. "Did you plan that? How long have you been planning the Marrs, Mars connection?"

"Literally just now. I'm not that creative."

I laughed. It was the best feeling in the whole damned world until it wasn't. My laughter rapidly changed to tears until I was weeping against his shoulder. I didn't know even what for. Maybe it was simply that once again everything was fucked up.

Trace didn't say anything. He held me, a strong wall against whatever might come through that door next to screw with my equilibrium.

When I was wrung out from crying, so much so that I should have fallen asleep, a strange peace came over me instead. Trace had told me that whole story about Mars and it was beautiful in how exposed he'd made himself doing so. He wasn't a man who showed vulnerability easily and yet he'd spoken to me, knowing we'd be heard.

I lifted my head to stare at him. Hell in a handbasket, he'd made that all up. There might be reasons he wanted to go to Mars but none of it was because of his broken eyes. He lied. I couldn't indicate I knew. Why had he done that? What did he want me to know in that story he'd needed to convey like that for me to hear? The Mars comment. Not being that creative.

Yes, he was. He was the most creative, conniving person I knew. So good, I'd fallen for it.

He'd given me a backstory. A reason for him doing what he did. A fake one, but nonetheless a motivation I could carry forward if I wanted to, as an explanation for how Trace became Trace. We were in Alyssa's house, taken prisoner. It had to be about her. Alyssa's backstory. How did Alyssa become this way?

What was her vulnerability?

She was a woman, born with Judson into an Alliance household where she shouldn't even have known the Alliance existed. Judson had once said Alyssa was extremely charismatic, better than him, smarter. He'd been unable to keep secrets from her. She'd learned of the Alliance.

A smart, dynamic personality told of a secret organization she'd never have a hope of joining except to marry a member, who could only tolerate that she knew, and deliver more Alliance babies into.

She did just that. Then Derrick floundered, not advancing. How was she supposed to be satisfied with her peripheral role if the starring player with her couldn't be counted on to handle advancement? She broke all the rules. Exposed her knowledge to try to push Derrick forward and she was punished for it. The men who would later be her lovers, who she would use sex to control, sent her to Ben's basement.

I knew that place all too well. I'd been beaten in it. So had she. Alyssa might have had at one-point scars on her back that matched my own. I didn't see them today in her white cocktail dress that exposed her back. Judson offered to fix mine, and I'd declined. They were battle wounds, but she might have felt differently. Someone fixed her back for her.

She was never rescued. She never had anyone who turned around and betrayed Ben for her, no one offered money. Jud hadn't known she'd been taken and Derrick was tied up, restrained from helping her. There would never be the chance of rescue. She spread her legs for a sadist, when she wasn't a masochist and likely would not have consented to it, and so it began.

Everyone who ever hurt her became her captive... sexually... until she controlled them all. Then she moved on. Forget those who hurt her, she'd taken those she needed. All of it until she could control the Alliance.

And the only thing in her way was me, and a lock she couldn't open.

Was it possible, given the same set of circumstances, I could have been Alyssa?

When I spoke, my voice was hoarse. "Funny how you can really get to know someone when you study their circumstances."

She'd been surrounded by Alliance men her whole life. As was evident to me all the time, they didn't know how to love, and they had almost no one to show them how. My five had me, and I was arguably as fucked in the head as they were.

"I know, E. It really is screwed up, isn't it?" He kissed my lips. "I really do love *you*. My smart, beautiful, woman."

Judson had dubbed me E and Trace confirmed it. I was a Letter, and I had all the information I was going to need to strike. My way.

I used to hate being on airplanes. I still didn't love it, but since I'd spent the whole night waiting for someone to burst through the door and drag me off to who knew where, I was tired enough to not really care where I spent the day. I'd kept the guys away from me. If Alyssa wanted to send a goon in or fuck with me herself they weren't standing in the way. Plus, I really felt like we were all better off watching our own backs for one night. We looked like less of a threat individually than we did as a group. Better she thought we weren't united.

For me, I knew I was less likely to screw up saying something that they'd hear, something I would wish I hadn't said. Of course, the tradeoff for that was that I didn't sleep.

The plane buzzed, and I didn't feel like sleeping now either.

Derrick didn't have that issue. With his legs stretched out before him, he dozed in his chair like people who would kill him in a heartbeat didn't surround him. The dark circles under Kade's eyes told me he had also not gotten any sleep. He looked out the window, ignoring any attempt Mercer made to speak to him. It was interesting watching their interactions from a distance. Mercer had beaten Kade twice now, but it was like he wanted Kade's attention. I chewed on my lip and watched.

They were roughly the same age, but it was like hero worship. Mercer wanted Kade to be proud of him, to work with him on something. That was good information to have. I wondered if Kade knew, and I couldn't ask him.

If it was possible, Judson was paler than even the day before. He was starting to look like a ghost, as though seeing his sister alive was sucking the life right out of him. He sat next to me, staring at the floor. On my other side, Warden read a book he'd found on the plane. It looked like some kind of thriller.

Trace winked at me from across the plane. "How you doing, E?"

"I'm just fine, T." I winked back at him.

This seemed to set Alyssa off. She'd been quiet since we'd boarded but now she started chatting again. I didn't really listen to what she said. It was something about the life she was going to have when she came out to the Alliance. Marcus was going to bring her onto the Council. I tilted my head, less interested in what she was saying than what she wasn't.

How were she and I alike and how were we different? Well, I could start cataloging the differences now and write a book about it. But fundamentally, she and I had both endured Ben's basement. When it came down to it, I was pretty sure that she was still there.

I changed from chewing on my lip to biting on my fingernail. Now wasn't the time for me to use that insight, just to hold onto it. We had a long flight ahead of us, and I wasn't knocked out on medicine that would make me not know the hours ahead. I needed to rest. Exhaustion wasn't going to help me, and it wasn't going to make this easier on Kade either. Or Judson.

Reaching out, I stroked the side of J's face. "Take a nap."

"I don't think I can sleep." He linked my finger in his. "Don't worry about me."

"Our mother used to sing him to sleep. Isn't that sweet? That was the only way Judson could get a good night's sleep."

I put my head on his shoulder. "Okay if I put my head here or too much pressure?"

He leaned his head on top of mine. "It's fine."

Something about what I'd done stopped her from talking. I didn't care to analyze it too much. I stayed like that on his shoulder, not moving. Warden reached out without lifting his gaze from his book to place his hand on my knee. He squeezed. That movement might have meant anything. It could have been an indication he liked that I was trying to take care of Judson or a signal to stop. I was too tired to try to figure out all of this non-verbal communication. I was going to take it as Warden just wanting to touch me and leave it at that.

I didn't want a gunfight on this plane. I wanted to open the lock and have Alyssa go away. If that couldn't happen exactly that way, then so be it. I'd deal with it then. I was starting to understand her better. Judson jerked slightly in his chair then settled down, shifting his head until I could feel his breath on my forehead. If he'd fallen asleep, I didn't dare wake him by moving. I had no choice. I just had to go to sleep, even with Alyssa on the plane and fifteen armed guards ready to kill us all.

———————

"Everly." Warden's voice in my ear woke me. There was movement. Everyone was rising, and I realized I didn't feel the plane moving. We'd landed, and it hadn't even roused me. That was really saying something.

My waking up must have jarred Judson because he lifted his head. He yawned and leaned back in his seat. "Sorry. I didn't mean to do that."

"I fell asleep, too."

Alyssa looked like she hadn't wrinkled at all. "So this is going to be how this works. Mercer owns an apartment in Manhattan. We're going there. Well, the guys are going with my guards. I don't feel like delaying this inevitable again. Let's go get this done then we can all go back to the apartment and celebrate."

She seemed to have completely forgot the whole we were never going to see her again bit of this arrangement. Alyssa was lonely. She wanted us to big one happy family while she took over the Alliance like she'd completely forgotten she tried to kill two of my guys.

I rubbed my eyes as Derrick spoke. "I'm not leaving her. I'm not going to some apartment while you go off with Everly."

"Consider that spoken from all of us." Warden rose. He looked strong, healthy. If his arm hurt him, he gave no indication. "She isn't going off with any of you alone."

That was when the men with guns all rose as one. It was an impressive show and one I wondered if they'd practiced.

I held up my hand. "Alyssa, we made some agreements. Everyone heard you make them. You claim to have loved Ben, to have made him yours, and I believe you on that. If Ben was anything, he was honest. What he said he was going to do he did, right?" I stepped toward her. "He said he'd burn me with a cigarette, he did that. He said he was going to slice up my back, that happened. He said he was going to tie me up and leave me on the porch all night to almost freeze to death, that happened." I hoped some of this triggered a reminder in her. It was sick that I was doing this, but I'd do whatever I had to right now.

"He helped make you," I continued. "So you should be living up to your word, too. We agreed that you would leave us alone. I expect you to live up to that."

She didn't smile when she spoke to me. "I don't break my word. If you want to be left alone that is what you will be. But you will live to regret it."

I gifted her with a fake smile. "Great. Let's get this done. If they can't come then you don't get anyone else either. Just you and me."

Alyssa nodded. "That's fair."

It really wasn't, but I'd emotionally manipulated her into not knowing what she was doing. That was a dirty trick, but I was willing to play that way if needed. It seemed her guys either didn't notice or they didn't correct her. Whatever was going on with Alyssa's men it wasn't love, at least not in the way I understood love to be.

Were they so dependent on her that they just did whatever she said even if she was wrong? Someone should have been telling her that I had no right to order her around in a kidnapping situation. But her loss was my gain.

The Alliance was powerful, but it seemed to be by emotionally stunting themselves, by sidelining the women in their lives until they could never really know them, never really love them, never share their lives fully; they had left themselves vulnerable to emotional manipulation disguised as love and presented in the form of sex.

I didn't think I'd done that to my guys.

They seemed perfectly fine informing me I had to do things differently or getting in my face about things. They were also free to leave anytime, as I had been when I'd taken off. I wished Alyssa could have done that. The day I'd stepped away from those I'd loved to give myself space to rediscover who it was that I wanted to be was the day I'd finally gotten out of Ben's basement.

Of course I did have a tendency to find sympathy for my kidnappers, so maybe it could have been that.

But I liked my explanation better.

I followed Alyssa out of the plane, pausing to stare at each of my guys as I did. "Ready to be done with all of this? Because if you want something different now is the time to let me know."

"Just be safe, Everly." It was Kade who spoke for them. "I don't like you going alone but at least it's just the two of you. Be... extra cautious."

I nodded at him. "You guys, too. I love you."

"Isn't that sweet?" Alyssa twirled her hand in the air. "You guys are so ridiculously verbal. Judson wasn't raised like this. It's just not done."

He leaned against the side of the plane. "Love you, Everly."

I covered my mouth to stop from laughing. Derrick did one better, he pulled me to him and kissed me straight on the lips. "Listen to me carefully. In all ways that matter in the universe, I love you. I didn't know I could love like this. Be careful."

Warden grinned as he pulled me from Derrick. "You're going to hear about this later from me. I don't like that you're doing this alone, because I love you."

"Okay guys." I shook my head. "Point made."

"Not quite yet." Trace hugged me tight to him. "You got this. I saw what you did and well done." He paused. "My love."

Alyssa yanked my arm, and I almost punched her in the face. "Oh and obviously if I don't report back to my loves," she said the word like it tasted badly in her mouth, "your guys die."

I rolled my eyes. "Obviously. Let's just get this over with."

WARDEN

This was going to go very badly. Everly didn't even realize how badly, but I had enough experience with catastrophes to recognize when I was stepping into one. Oh, sure, we were in a car headed to Manhattan. From the outside, I'm sure it looked like any other SUV filled with people on their way somewhere.

No one would know that inside the car was a driver who worked for Alyssa, Judson, her brother who looked like he was about to have an aneurism, two men hiding guns between their legs, and myself.

I might have preferred to be in the other car with Derrick. At least in that one I could have been certain that if bullets started flying we were the ones firing them.

The third car would have been equally as problematic. Kade hadn't said anything in days. For all that Alyssa had been Derrick's fucked up wife, he and Trace were managing this the best of anyone. I ran a hand through my hair. Yes, I would have liked that car better except that someone had to look out for Judson until he pulled himself out of this funk, and that someone was going to be me.

"So how about the state of the markets? Anyone lost any money lately? That's not my fault. This is just me keeping my hands out of it. What is the world coming to if Alliance men can't count on at least being secretly wealthy?"

Judson rolled his eyes at me. That was good. That was at least a response. I kept speaking. "So how did you meet Alyssa? Are there dating sites for finding women who have gone off the grid like this? Fake your death dot com?"

The guy next to me shifted in his seat and looked at the floor. Now, that was interesting. He was uncomfortable.

Maybe things weren't as perfect in Alyssa la-la land as she'd have liked everyone to believe. I wondered... People always wanted what they saw others have. I'd made a lot of money in my life knowing this.

You could be worth a billion dollars and you might lose it all because you were so desperate to make two billion since someone else had it. These guys had just met Everly. She wasn't just sleeping with us; she legitimately loved us. I wasn't sure how the fuck we'd pulled that off since all five of us were completely unworthy people. But since I loved her more than breathing, I wasn't going to complain.

I was even going to figure out how we could all be happy forever if only we could get out of this mess.

Judson was going to get an earful about his family when this was all over and I was sure he wasn't ten seconds away from having a nervous breakdown.

"Hey, Jud, did you see how beautiful Evy was when she left? I mean... don't you just feel lucky you get to look at her every day?"

He side-eyed me.

Come on, man, catch up to what I'm doing here.

Judson was arguably the smartest out of all of us. Surely, he could...

"When I really feel lucky is first thing in the morning. I never thought I'd like it... sharing a bed with someone. I mean, it used to be that sex was sex. I wanted it and then I wanted them to go home. I even envisioned someday having a life where I could have my wife sleep in another bedroom. But the way she looks when she's first rising? When she's not quite awake? The way she clings to me? I'd never trade a second of that. There's nothing more beautiful than having the woman you love next to you first thing in the morning."

I swallowed through the lump in my throat. I'd wanted to play this game to manipulate the guards but yeah, he'd nailed

that. For that reason alone, I'd be happy to share her with
these guys forever. How could I not when they loved her just
as hard as I did?

We were all getting out of here alive. So help me. No
matter who I had to kill.

Being alone in a town car driven by someone I didn't know—
and wasn't at all sure if he was Alliance—with Alyssa was hell.
Fortunately, without the audience of her brother and Derrick,
she didn't talk.

Instead, she looked out the window. About twenty
minutes into the drive, she finally said something. "I've always
loved Manhattan."

"Have you gotten here much in the last years?"

She sighed. "Ben brought me once. We've had to be somewhat remote. But no matter. I've clearly been able to run
things from afar. Soon, I can come out of the shadows."

"How did that work exactly? Ben would just bring men
home and you'd what... seduce them?"

Alyssa tugged on the edge of her hair. "Did you know that
I went to the best schools in the world? The very best
boarding schools to start. I'd see Judson on holidays since
they were, of course, not co-educational. Just the women.
From there, Harvard. I started graduate school there, too."
She looked out the window. "Did you go to college? I suppose
I should know that... oh, yes, you just graduated."

Where was she going with this? "Yes, I did."

"I tell you this because I want you to understand that I'm
smart. Ridiculously so."

Of that, I'd had no doubt. But it wasn't because of her
resume. The circumstances upon which she'd been born, the
money she had, that had gone a long way to open doors that

allowed her to use that intellect. That only made the decisions that she made that much more difficult.

She tugged once again on her hair. "In the end, seducing a man is easy. I wanted to be Alliance. I wished it more than anything in the world but do you know what I've found? They're all lost little boys. Every one of them, even Ben who had more spirit than most."

Every time she spoke of Ben, I wanted to choke her. My hands actually itched to do so. But I had to get through this so strangling would have to wait until later. I wasn't going to be dealing with Alliance after this, but so help me, I might just kill her in ten years when I showed up on her doorstep and stabbed her in the eye.

It was ridiculous that I felt so much better having those thoughts than the ones I'd been having. I actually preferred feeling deadly. It was healthier. Despondent and slightly panicked really didn't work for me.

"Is that so?" I wanted to keep her talking. This was information collection. If life was kind to me, and it rarely was lately, I wouldn't need to know any of this stuff. But if I had to continue to manipulate her emotionally without her knowing it and turn this into a long con that even Trace could be proud of, then I had to keep this going.

"Haven't you found that?" She turned to look at me. "Even my brother, right? They're so needy in a way I have to believe can't be true of all men everywhere. The ants are luckier than the Alliance men. They don't have any idea that they don't have at least a semblance of control over their lives and they get to make connections with their loved ones. The Alliance takes all of that." She shrugged. "Surely you must see that Everly. You control them by leading them around by their dicks. I get it. And it's not even *hard* to do." She laughed. "Sorry, bad pun."

That wasn't even a really good pun. That was the equivalent of a fart joke. Not that I didn't sometimes love a good fart joke. Maybe I just wasn't in the mood.

"I don't control them." I had nothing to lose in this conversation. "I never did, never could. We're a team. That's how this works for us. I'm not any more important than the rest of them. Whatever I'm doing I'm not getting it done by sex. They're hugely more experienced in that regard than me."

She rolled her eyes. "Oh, never underestimate the power of the virginal girl."

Now it was my turn to laugh maniacally. "I wasn't a virgin. I can promise you that. Not a virgin. Not even close to one."

"I wasn't talking about your hymen and whether or not you broke it or how many times you had your clit rubbed." She scooted closer to me, running her hand through my hair. "I'm talking about your soul. When they met you, your soul was a virgin. And boy, is that the most addictive thing in the world. You caught them in your net, and you didn't even mean to."

Whoa, okay. What was happening here? She was touching me and not in a way I wanted her to. Yes, Alyssa was hitting on me. Her hand was in my hair, and she was trying to give me a come-hither-I-want-to-fuck-you look. The problem? I wasn't even a little bit interested. I was a love is love is love girl and I had no problem with whoever anyone chose to love. I was all for it. If I didn't have five guys taking up all the space in my heart, I could have imagined loving a woman. But not psycho Alyssa. No thank you. *No*.

I had the only Smythe I wanted. His sister could drop dead.

I pushed her hand away. "Not interested. That clear?"

She pouted and then shrugged. "I was momentarily interested in seeing what the hell my brother sees in you. I can't fathom it. He was raised to love someone better than you."

"You just said they couldn't love. That the Alliance screws all of that up. He wasn't raised to love anyone. He was raised not to, right? "

She pointed at the window. "We're here."

That was convenient. She wasn't going to have to answer my statement. I actually didn't disagree with her. Judson was too good for me. All five of them were, but I wasn't giving them up so that was all there was to it.

Our driver pulled over, and we got out of the car. If she didn't have guns pointed at my loves' heads, I'd have run for my life. I was a smart woman. I would never end up in a horror movie where I didn't go out the front door when the killer was in the house. Taking off down the street wouldn't solve this problem. I had to face it head on.

The building itself looked like any other office building in Manhattan. I'd have loved to have spent some real time gaping at the size of the buildings in New York City and feeling great about being there. The truth was, like Hawaii, which had been on my bucket list, everywhere was just a place right now. I didn't give a shit where we were, not while Alyssa was in my face.

We walked in together and the inside of the office building didn't look any different than a million nondescript offices I'd visited before in my life. I hadn't considered the problem of getting to the locked area itself.

I turned to Alyssa, but she didn't stop to speak to me. Instead, she strode toward the guard in front of her. Was he one of her men? She pulled a gun out of her pocket and while I watched, shot him in the head.

I gasped as the man who hadn't even had time to be stunned hit the ground.

I guessed that was a no. He hadn't been hers, and he was no more. I stared at his dead body on the floor.

"Come on, Everly, sweetheart. We have things to do."

19

I stared at the dead body on the ground. I didn't know who this person was, and I was getting a little tired of the body count in my wake. I could almost guarantee he was an Alliance member. No way would an ant—to steal from Kade who learned it from Ben and now Alyssa—guard this place where they stored their prized possessions.

"Everly." Alyssa snapped her fingers and kept walking.

I pictured punching her in the face. Whack. I'd break her fucking nose. "How many people are going to have to die to get to my father's vault?"

"It's not a vault. Just a big locker. I don't know how many people have to die. As many as have to."

I hurried to catch up to her. I felt like I might as well have carried a death scythe around with me. Hey, watch out world, Everly Marrs, was coming and when you see me, you will die. I rolled my eyes at my own thought. I hadn't killed that man. I hadn't even known he was about to die, but now the person who got off the elevator when we did stared at us with wide eyes.

I didn't know if he recognized me or if he knew Alyssa or

if it was just strange for him to see two women in this building. I'd imagine it had never had one visit in all the years it had been in existence. I grabbed him, pulling him all the way out of the elevator.

"Run, and if you value your life, then don't look back or tell anyone you saw us here. We're both incredibly evil people. Go."

He looked like my father, in the sense that he wore similar, conservative clothing and a bow tie. My father had sometimes sported one. Was this one of the places where all the accountants working for the Alliance hung out? Had he known my father?

These were all questions I wasn't going to get answers to because instead of asking them, I shoved him hard, hoping it would make him move faster. The elevator doors closed behind us.

Alyssa glared at me. "If I didn't need your voice to get that lock open, you'd be dead right now."

I had to get that gun from her. Or find my own. The second I opened the door for her she might very well shoot me. I'd ripped a gun out of Derrick's hands once just because I'd shocked him by trying to do so. I might be able to pull that off twice.

The little I knew about any of this was that I had to be ready to take any and every opportunity when it presented itself to me.

"We didn't need to kill him. He gets to go home to his family."

She lifted her eyebrows slowly, in an annoying way that told me she was doing it for show. Had she looked in the mirror and practiced that move? Read it in a book? How can I look like I'm about to say something of significance 101?

"Did you know that man?" She hit the button to take us down to the basement.

"No, I don't have to know him. People don't have to be personally acquainted with me to not be killed."

She shook her head. "You're going to regret that when he calls the Alliance authorities and we get killed."

"There is no Alliance right now except you. Who are they going to call?"

Alyssa blinked. "I... I suppose that is true."

"It is, and if you're about to come out of the closet, so to speak, about running things, who cares if he saw you? I mean... enough. Seriously. No one else has to die."

She didn't comment which made me more concerned than anything else.

The elevator door opened, and I followed her into the basement. It was well lit and looked more like a storage area, like the one where I'd killed the drug addicts, than any basement I'd ever been in. Her heels clicked on the floor. I hadn't noticed the sound earlier, but now it was nails on a chalkboard.

I stared down at my sneakers. I was lucky to have them. She could have insisted I dress like her again. In fact, she'd all but suggested that before we left Hawaii. It was like she wanted to play twinsies with me. I didn't understand her.

I stared at the numbers moving by me as I hurried to keep up with Alyssa. What were in all of these lockers?

"I liked your father. He was a little bit blathering, but I did. I have to admit it was pretty hard-core how he had your mother killed. No sex really to speak of after that until me."

Oh, no. This was not happening. "I don't want to discuss my father with you. However you knew him, whatever you did. Keep that to yourself."

"It's just sex. God knows you've had enough of it. How is my brother?"

Nope. Wasn't going there either. We must have reached where we needed to be. My father's locker. This was where he presumably kept all the books he'd used to discredit the guys under the direction of Alyssa. She pointed toward it. "Open it up."

I stood in front of it, staring at it for a moment. Number 333. I reached up to touch the numbers. I'd been through so much of his stuff when I'd sold the house, when I'd taken down his life, which was really what disposing of things for the dead entailed. The removal of an active life to one that would fade away.

I'd hardly let myself feel anything about it at the time. I'd had to survive the experience, regain some sense of normal, find myself again. I couldn't deal with the fact that I'd killed him. But now, standing in front of number 333, I felt a sob rise in my throat. Alyssa was not the person for me to have a breakdown with, and if I'd learned anything at all in that time where I'd wrenched myself back from the pit of despair, it was that I could survive things.

Opening this door wouldn't bring my father back to life, it wouldn't rewind time so I shot him again or didn't, it was nothing. It was just a door. Still, I reached up to touch the number. Did it mean anything? Had he selected it or was it randomly assigned? Who did the assigning?

"Everly, sweetheart."

Fuck, I really hated how she called me that. "Why the sweetheart?"

"Because that is what Judson says about you. When he talked about you the day you killed my Ben and shot your father. He was on a stadium calling you kind, calling you nice. If Judson thinks you're a sweetheart, that's what I will think, too."

So in other words, she was fucking with me. Fine, so be it. I stepped forward. The lock looked pretty easy to operate. Mercer had made it for my father, which meant all of the locks in this place had their own ways of entering. The secrets behind these doors... I didn't even think I wanted to know them.

"If you could go back and never know about the Alliance?" I regarded Alyssa from where she stood, almost too close to me. "Would you? Would you make it so you were kept in the dark? Lived your life. Went to Harvard. Fell in love with Derrick but never knew about any of this, would you do it?"

I hated to even ask her that question because that meant that I'd never have been with Derrick. She'd have been his life, not me.

"I can't imagine like that. My brain stays in the here and now. What do I have to do to survive? Who do I have to do to survive? What can I do to never be out of control again? How do I make myself more powerful? Those are the questions I ask myself. Not... speculation or bullshit." She put her hands on her hips. "Do you? Do you think you'd rather not know?"

When faced with my own question, I knew the answer immediately. "No, I'd want to know. I... I might have denied or felt differently before but not now. I've changed. And the people I have in my heart now are worth it. The pain."

I touched the lock. It made a clicking noise. Okay, then it would be my voice and my eye print. Why had he done this? Why had he thought I'd ever get here? I knew the answer. He hadn't. My father never intended for me to know the Alliance, which meant at the end of the day, he'd considered my being able to do this an impossibility. He didn't want this lock opened, ever. And yet here I was, doing it.

Sorry, Dad, even after your death I'm always fucking up your plans.

KADE

Something was wrong. I couldn't really put my finger on what but this whole place screamed "get out" to me. I'd grown up on comic books and science fiction. I knew when to listen to that little voice inside of me that screamed run. I'd spent my life paying attention to it and I was still here.

I stared at Mercer. He didn't seem concerned. This was his expensive apartment. I followed real estate. Having never officially bought an actual above ground house until I bought Evy hers, I was still sort of obsessed with it. This was a five million dollar apartment at least, and it overlooked Central Park from the West Side of New York City. Old building but refurbished. Prime real estate. He was proud of it, and he wanted me to be impressed.

That much I'd cued into. It was bizarre... I'd hardly thought of this man, and he'd been outthinking and outgunning me for years basically to get my attention. What was the thing people said? Even negative attention was better than no attention at all.

I really wasn't cut out for this. Right now I should have been designing a button Everly could wear so she could never be spotted by satellites. I was good at that. I was bad at people.

Except with her. I was good with Everly. Or... for some reason she didn't mind the ways I did things the wrong way. I'd never loved a woman before and somehow it wasn't a problem that she also loved the four other guys I could tolerate in the world. Oh, who was I kidding? At this point I cared about them.

"Derrick." I got up from where I sat on the couch, catching D's attention. Sometimes I preferred to think of them as Letters. It was easier for us to do hard things together that way. "We need to get out of here."

I had the attention of everyone in the room right then, even the guards who were going to try to stop us. Derrick lifted his head and met my gaze. Unless you knew him, you'd never know he was tense. I'd watched him play enough baseball to know he had the slightest tell when it came to stress. It was in the way he held his shoulders. I could see it now.

Mercer walked over to me, putting his hand on my arm. "Everything is fine. I know this is shit right now, but Everly is going to be fine. Alyssa will get her back."

I believed he thought that. Whatever was about to explode, he hadn't had a hand in. That was interesting. Still, there was something just on the peripheral of my consciousness, and so help me, I wasn't going to ignore it.

Maybe it was a beep. Was I hearing a beep? Fuck it. I grabbed the gun out of the holster of the guard closest to me and before I'd even lifted it all the way up I fired.

We were getting out of there.

EVERLY

The door swung open, and I stepped inside the locker. Inside it was huge but organized. Everything was pressed against the wall with a white sticker label on the outside. I was in a dire situation, but I had to smile. This was what our whole house had been like when I put it on the market. My dad had labeled everything, even the spices. On the outside it would say pepper and he'd have stuck another label on that said pepper-spice.

Everything was cataloged.

He was a murderer who was probably going to kill me. I was all but sure of it. That shouldn't have surprised me. He'd had his wife, my mother, executed. My feelings for him were so complicated. I wasn't sure I'd ever get an emotional consensus inside myself with how I felt about him. He'd been my only parent, the one who'd taken care of me when I'd skinned my knees or had my feelings hurt.

"Perfect. I can't understand why he didn't just give me what I wanted." Alyssa scooted by me, walking over to look at several binders to my left. "I need to prove my family's long term Alliance membership. The men are going to object to me. They can't have any leg to stand on when it comes to my genetic superiority."

My father slept with this woman, had screwed up my Letters lives for her, and he wouldn't give her a genealogy report? Why not?

The dead couldn't give me answers, so I had to be smart about this. Maybe he thought she wouldn't like what she found. Judson's family had been high up in the Alliance a long time. They were important, but she'd needed to marry Derrick because his family had been more connected somehow. That was strange. I walked over to the books and followed the names until I got to the letter N. I pulled out the book.

Alyssa muttered to herself on the other side of the room. She was looking through files. "Your father is a pain in my ass. Why does he have so much stuff?"

I ignored her. This had clearly been his role in the Alliance, to hold onto the genealogies. I flipped through Derrick's binder, finding his last name, Norris, and looked through it. His family had been in the Alliance a long time, so long there wasn't record of the first person admitted into that. Was that true for all of them? I grabbed folders. W for Warden White. D for Kade Doyle. H for Trace Hill. S for Judson Smythe. I needed to look through his fast. Alyssa might want to see her family's folder any second. She might even be looking for it now.

She just didn't know my father as well as I did. He was psychotic, but he was organized, and I'd lived with his methods my whole life.

I flipped through Warden's book. Same thing. Long term Alliance membership. If anyone ever got ahold of these books, the people in them were seriously screwed. I quickly set W aside. H... I at least knew where to flip to quickly. Nothing different. D... Same deal. I grabbed S. Funny, how I was back to letters. Every part of my life being dictated by an initial, this time the last name.

Or maybe not, maybe I was on the wrong track and finding nothing of importance. I stared at the S. Immediately, I knew why she'd married Derrick and what she wanted today. The S was traceable. The Smythes weren't in the Alliance as long as the others. Oh, they'd been in a long time. If this was accurate, my father tracked the first Smythe to come over just after the founding of Jamestown. But not before that.

Ustis Smythe had been granted entry because of a favor done for another Alliance member. What kind of favor had earned entrance? It had probably been deadly or he'd saved a life. Something of significance. But they weren't anciently connected. The Smythes hadn't been leading the Alliance since before the birth of Christ. They could be challenged for their ruling.

This was why Alyssa wanted the books. She wanted to hide this. If she was going to convince the Alliance to listen to her as a woman, she couldn't have them finding cause to say no. I wondered if Jud knew this, and then I dismissed it. He didn't. As far as my J was concerned he was Alliance royalty. I had to do something about this.

Alyssa started dropping folders onto the ground. It was a perfect opportunity. As quietly as I could, I dropped the S folder into the discard pile and rounded on Alyssa before she could notice what I'd done.

I pushed her, and she fell. I'd never had a playground fight, but this felt similar except that I needed her gun. I hadn't wanted anyone to get hurt and that included myself. I didn't want to kill Judson's sister. What would that do to him?

I ripped the gun out of her waist where she'd shoved the gun into the decorative belt she wrapped around her dress. She gasped and jumped for me, but I took two steps backward, the gun pointed at her by the time I'd found my footing. It was ridiculous how much more settled I felt holding a gun. Weaponry was like my love in this moment, my death wielding security blanket.

"We're done here. Nothing is going to happen to you if you behave. Come on. We're going to get my guys. You have access to this place now. We won't lock it."

Besides, if she did, I could get in again the same way I had before. You and I are done here. Move."

She shook her head. "What were you doing over there?"

"Remembering my father. Move it. I'm not kidding. I regularly kill people. So unless you want to be the latest name on my murder list, you're going to move your ass, now."

I didn't know what made her move. I expected more argument from Alyssa. She'd never complied, not once, without having some lengthy discussion about it. Even after she made agreements, she seemed to forget what she said or compromised on. I really didn't care. To have her just comply? It stank of manipulation.

Still, I was getting what I wanted and that was what mattered. If I had to figure out how to out play whatever move this was later, then I'd do so.

I'd get my guys, get back here and grab the things she shouldn't see. Then we could go disappear somewhere. Somewhere Kade would hide us in the world. He was good at not being found. Alerted to Mercer, he wouldn't be so easily found this time.

Or maybe we could kill Mercer. I was holding a gun. Maybe it made me more bloodthirsty or maybe it came down to the fact that Mercer was an enemy. He wasn't collateral damage.

"You can't pull that gun out on the street." We'd stepped into the elevator and were heading back to street level. "I'm not going to fight you. We do need to go back to the apartment so I can show you something and tell you what happens next."

I hadn't been wrong. She did think she was in charge even though I was armed and she wasn't. Still, she was right. I put the gun under my shirt in my waist. It would be harder for her to grab it than it had been for me.

She stared straight ahead. "Everly, I think you will find that you and I have more in common than we don't. You can forgive me. You're pragmatic enough to do so. When you see what is happening next, you'll get on board. Just like your father did." She turned to wink at me. "The Marrs family is smart and creative. You'll get through this."

I hated her with a fury I'd have thought I saved solely for Ben. But then again, she was Ben's creation and the mold he'd had to shape her with hadn't been wonderful before that.

She was a nightmare who'd been given shape to become a monster.

I wouldn't be here. I wouldn't let my guys turn into the shells that were her men.

The car we'd come in pulled up as we stepped outside like a scene from a movie while the sounds of Manhattan struck my ears. Taxis beeped their horns and somewhere in the distance sirens blared loudly. People walked and ran everywhere. A dog barked. Lights flashed to add to the extreme nature of the place. There was just enough sensory information in Manhattan to dull all my senses entirely. I couldn't pick out all the details so my brain decided to focus on just one: Alyssa.

She got in the car, and I was fast on her heels. I waited for her to give an address to the driver, but she didn't. He must have known where we were going.

"Try anything and I won't kill you, I'll injure you in a way you won't recover from. Do you think you can lead the Alliance if you can't walk? Or with one ear? They're not real kind to people needing assistance, are they?"

She looked out the window. "There's no need to be dramatic, sweetheart. I'm giving you just what you wanted."

That was what was making me so nervous. Still, I kept my facial features neutral and said nothing. In silence, she might spill what was going on in her head.

The sounds of sirens seemed to be getting louder and ahead I saw flashing lights. Where were we? I really didn't know New York, and I looked for a street sign. I couldn't see one because the street was blocked ahead by fire trucks with flashing lights.

"I'm sorry, ma'am. I can't get through." The man driving the car finally spoke. He had a British accent, which I might have found interesting if I didn't want to know so desperately what was happening ahead.

She nodded. "I know. Come along Everly. You're going to want to see this."

"You know what this is?"

Alyssa nodded. "That building that's burning up ahead? That was Mercer's home. I set it ablaze. Well, Bryce, the man driving the car, he did that for me. I'm afraid sometimes you have to cut your losses and move on."

I ran after her. "What?"

"You're in shock, understandable." The car we'd just gotten out of blew up. The sound hit me as hard as the heat, which knocked me into Alyssa. She held me close like we were friends and she had every right to do so.

My mouth fell open as my ears rang. People rushed onto the street. This had to look like terrorism and it was... in its own, different way. "I don't understand," I hollered at her.

"We don't need them at all, Everly. The Alliance doesn't need another man or one female behind the scenes. It needs me. It needs you. I killed them. My brother. My husband. My lovers. Your lovers. They're all gone. Set to blow up and then I killed the man who made that happen. There is no one now but you and me. It can be just me, but I don't want that. Be my sister, Everly. We can rule. It's a dawn in the Alliance. Or I can kill you and you can join those five pathetic souls you opted to waste so much time with."

I couldn't believe what I was hearing, and I stared at the blaze in the building ahead. I didn't have to listen. She was a huge liar. And yet I did... she'd blown this up. I'd let her into my father's locker, and she'd killed all of them.

I cried out, a sob wracking my body.

This woman who had killed my loves had hurt them so many ways. It wasn't enough that I hit her in the eye, but I did it, consciously and with thought. She'd given Derrick a black eye. It mattered that she get one, too. Alyssa stepped back, taking two steps like she was stunned I'd just decked her. My hand ached. I'd never really learned how to properly throw a punch.

They were dead.

Red descended over my vision.

I didn't remember firing the gun right into her head. But that was what I did. Time seemed to still and then catch up to me.

The truth was... you couldn't fire a gun on the Upper East Side into a woman's head with a million cameras watching. Not without someone seeing.

Not without Kade alive to fix it.

I didn't even care. Tears streamed down my face, and I stood there waiting for someone to come do something about the woman dead on the street. The woman I hadn't even considered not killing.

She'd taken what was mine.

I dropped the gun on the ground, and I waited. For whatever was coming next. There was no life left for me. They'd all burned to death while I'd foolishly thought I could get us out of this mess.

I'd never been equipped. I was just a foolish girl who'd led five men to their deaths. When the rain pelted down on my head it felt appropriate, but that was all I could feel.

20

I went through the steps of being arrested fairly silently. Having dropped the gun to my side, I wasn't a threat to anyone, and I'd let them put the handcuffs on me without giving anyone a hard time. The question was what I was going to do now, and in the end, what I decided to do hadn't even really been a choice.

Everyone I loved was dead. Alyssa could have been lying. I wasn't stupid. I'd not seen bodies. Warden hadn't been hauled out, his body black and charred on a stretcher. I hadn't watched them trying to revive Trace from smoke inhalation. She might have been lying. But she wasn't. She'd killed all of them. Her brother. Her husband. All of the men she'd been sleeping with. All of my loves. They were all dead.

Well... almost all of them. I stared at the face of the detective speaking to me, fairly certain he was Alliance, and what was more, he was one of Alyssa's men. The worst kept secret in the world must have been that Judson's sister was alive. Or maybe not. Alliance men were great at secrets.

I waited for others to come in, to join the interrogation. As far as I could tell there weren't any cameras on me or a two-way mirror, although I couldn't be sure since those things were meant to be hidden by design.

This man who gave me no name glared at me across the table. His hand tapped on it hard. "I didn't blow up the car or burn down that building."

"I know you didn't. He shook his head. "But you did... you are a killer."

"I am." And just like that I was sure my hunch had been right. He was Alliance, and he was Alyssa's. If I lived another day, I might see Alyssa everywhere I looked, but I strongly suspected this was my last day on the planet.

Feeling that way, it was freeing in a disastrous, monstrous, miserable way that left me to feel like I would never not know the pit of despair that meant the Letters had left this world. "I've killed a lot of people actually." I tapped the table. "Write this down. I'm confessing. That's something that will be helpful to you, right? A confession."

I wasn't thinking clearly and yet this felt like absolutely the right track. They were dead. There had to be accounting for what happened—for *all* the things that happened—and I had to be punished for them. The Letters were dead because I hadn't been able to outthink Alyssa, because I'd left them alone, and thought I could manage a psycho woman who had been out for death. They'd tried to warn me, and I'd discounted them.

At what point had I decided that I knew better than everyone else?

At what point had my decision making become so poor?

I wiped the lone tear rolling down my cheek, and after a second, I tapped the table again. "Get a recording device or write this down. I'm making this easy on you."

He tilted his head to the side. "What was it that they even liked about you?"

I leaned forward. "I give a fantastic blow job. That's what

Alyssa did right?" I held up my hand. "Never mind. Just write this down. You need this to go away, and you want to get rid of me. So listen up or write it down."

He set his phone down in front of me. I highly doubted this was protocol but then nothing about this would be. When this was over, it wouldn't be the police or the FBI or anyone in law enforcement who took me down. It would be the Alliance, and before that happened I had to confess. I had to say aloud my truths so the universe could hear them... and if that didn't make a hill of a difference, then so be it I would still hear the words with my own voice. I would acknowledge *my* truth.

"I've killed a lot of people." Alliance man wasn't stopping me so no one else could be listening. "My first time was in a surgery center in San Diego. I took out two of your Alliance assassins." My throat threatened to close up, and my eyes burned. These were hard words to say. "They came when Derrick Norris was waking up from surgery. That was just the first time."

I'd confessed all my truths to a man who should have turned around and used them against me. Instead, I sat alone in a cell with someone bringing me three meals a day and otherwise leaving me alone. This was strange, disconcerting, and didn't make any sense to me. I rubbed my eyes. Maybe he was setting me up to be killed in a terrible way.

I pulled my knees to my chest and held back the tears that threatened. Ever since I'd said the words, told him and the universe what I'd done, I'd been on the verge of hysteria. One sharp remark, one badly spoken word, and I was going to lose my shit.

I missed the Letters so acutely I could hardly breathe

through it. The other times we'd been apart from each other had been different. The obvious change being they'd not been dead. I rubbed my eyes, a headache forming. But even beyond that huge fact, the first time I'd doubted them and thought they harmed me. The second was that it had been my choice to leave.

Now, I was responsible for them being completely gone from the universe. There would never be a chance to hear them breathe at night. I hadn't realized how much I loved that, how differently they all slept, how it felt to be alone with one or in a bed with two or more of them.

I'd been privileged to have so much love and was shattered that it was done.

I really wished the Alliance would be done with me. Get it over with. Maybe if there was an afterlife, good or bad, I could join them there. And if there wasn't, that was fine too. I'd prefer nothing to...

The door opened to this small room where I'd spent the last two days, and I got off the cot. It wasn't the man I'd been speaking to. I didn't even know his name although he'd told it to me. To me, he was Mister Alliance. This new person was... wearing a cheap brown suit and a tie that was halfway down his chest.

I swallowed. He looked different from any other Alliance man I'd seen. They were always flawlessly put together in expensive clothing. Even my father lived that way.

"Ms. Marrs, come with me."

I took a deep breath. So here it was. The next step of whatever would be. My hands shook, and I put them in the pockets of my jeans. I didn't know how many days I'd been in these clothes with all of the air travel. Four days? Five? I had to stink to high hell, but it didn't matter.

I followed the man from the room. My limbs didn't want to work. Every step I took seemed harder than the one before it. This wasn't terror, this was grief. The knowledge struck me hard. I'd mourned my father but my feelings had been mixed up in a bowl filled with anger and betrayal. This was different. I'd stepped out of the room into a world where five people I loved more than I did anything else were no longer breathing.

He motioned toward the front of the building, and I stopped walking. The man in the brown suit pointed at the door. Crowds of people wandered around us, living their lives, doing whatever they did at this jail. I didn't even know where I was.

They couldn't possibly be letting me go. I'd confessed to murder. A lot. I'd told them all the things I did. Mr. Alliance had loved Alyssa and...

I stared at Brown Suit. "What's going to happen to me when I go out there? Couldn't you just... put something in my coffee? Will it hurt?"

He lifted his eyebrows slowly. "I don't know what you're talking about. You're being released. You're free to go."

Brown Suit wasn't Alliance. He really didn't know. I rubbed my arms. "Okay. Thanks. Have a... nice day."

That was a ridiculous thing to say but I did tend to fall back onto manners when I didn't know what else to do. The sun shone in the clouds, a stark contrast to my mood as I stepped out onto the Manhattan street. I had no phone—they'd not given it back to me—or money. All of that seemed out of the ordinary. I should have gotten all of that back, but it was more like they were acting like I'd never been in there at all.

I looked around. I could go back to Destin if I could figure out how to get there. That was my home. Kade had bought it for me. And...

I saw Mister Alliance striding down the street toward me. It shouldn't be possible to be shot outside a jail in the middle of the day in Manhattan, but I knew even before he lifted his arm that was about to happen. I had no way to defend myself, no weapon, and nowhere to go.

I just had to hope that no one else got hurt.

It was the explosion of red on the man's head as he fell backward into the street that alerted me he'd been shot and not me. I whirled around. A car screeched to a stop next to me, and the door flung open on the side of the backseat, facing me.

"Evy, get in."

TRACE

FORTY-EIGHT HOURS EARLIER

"We are seriously fucked." I looked at the five guys I'd somehow agreed to share Everly with. We all loved her, and I'd never ask her to choose. Why would I do that when it was taking all five of us to keep this woman we adored alive and well? Fuck. Fuck. Fuck.

Judson held out his hand. "Let's not get crazy. She's in the police station. They caught her... shooting my sister." He shook his head. "That's not important right now. We need to focus. She's with the cops. We have easily gotten people out of the hands of the police before. Kade changed the video. Our people do what they do. She's home to us in twelve hours. We'll feed her, and Warden will get some great wine and the whole thing can feel like it never happened."

He wasn't wrong. That's how we could have done this five years ago—hell, five months ago. Five weeks ago, maybe. But now? "We don't have any power. We don't have people, and we can't get her out without either of those things. Besides, I could be wrong, but the police here have always been filled with Alliance. Maybe some of them are your sister's goons. I don't accept that they all just blew up in that apartment."

By the end of my little speech, I shouted. I wasn't particularly angry with Judson, although I'd have loved it if he could suddenly get back into his sharp, lethal, leadership mindset and out of the holy-shit-my-life-has-been-a-lie version of him that had been present the last days. Not that I could blame him. If my dead father appeared here right now, it would throw me for a loop. He had never turned from Everly, and for that, I was grateful.

We'd gotten out after killing everyone in that apartment. I had to give Derrick credit, he really did know how to disarm people, and I'd taken out three of them myself just using the chair I'd been sitting in. Almost as soon as we were out, the whole building had gone up in flames. I'd never doubt Kade's intuition again.

He was quiet. Our resident tech expert had ended up hand to hand in a death struggle with Mercer. I was glad for him that was over. Warden wasn't saying much either. In fact, they'd all gone silent.

This was such a screwed up situation. We'd run to the vault to grab Everly, only to find she wasn't there. Coming back in time to see her loaded into a police car put a period on this day.

"There's a solution." If the others couldn't see it, then I would.

Derrick ran a hand through his hair. "Does it include me having to go into that police station and kill all the Alliance members? I ask because I am recognizable, and I imagine there is even a limit to what Kade can cover. I'm not saying I won't do it. I will."

That was so true. For all of us. There was nothing we wouldn't do for this woman. Even the impossible.

"We take back the Alliance. We announce it right now. Go back to the vault. Make the announcement. And gather whoever comes to us. Get our girl out."

Warden ran a hand through his hair as the rain pelted down. It kept starting and stopping. "Trace, that seems like it's going to take some time. That is going to take... days at least. That's too much time."

"We don't have a choice. Unless someone else has a better idea."

Judson stepped forward. "We can halt them from doing anything to her, taking her anywhere. That much we can do today. Come on. We need to go to the vault. Trace is right. But before we take control of the Alliance, we'll make Everly safe. That we can do."

This was the Judson I'd been waiting for. He was going to call a cessation to any and all Alliance activity in preparation for new leadership. Whoever had her now wouldn't so much as be able to move her from one room to another without breaking Alliance law, which would result in their immediate execution.

I picked up my phone. We needed a car, and we needed it yesterday.

EVERLY

NOW

I knew that voice. It couldn't be. I stepped toward the sound. Maybe I was dead. Maybe I had been struck and that sound,

Warden's low voice, called to me to come with him. I paused by the car. I wasn't in my right mind. Maybe I was losing it altogether. Maybe...

A strong hand yanked me forward, pulling me into the car as he shut the door behind us. I was face to face with Warden. I touched his face, not even thinking not to, running my fingers over the long slope of his nose, feeling the whiskers that were long enough to almost be a beard. He smelled right and...

"Everly." The car jerked forward, and he drew me against him. Who was driving? I couldn't see them. "You okay? We knew there was a possibility they'd go for you because they know they can't now and..."

I shook my head wildly, my hair going everywhere, falling in my eyes. I could hardly see him. That was fine. I couldn't breathe either. I didn't need any of that. "How?" I somehow managed to get that word out.

He drew me to him, bringing my head to his forehead. "Did you think we weren't okay?"

"She killed you. Burned you to death." I choked on every word until I sobbed against him.

"Well, that at least explains why you went around confessing to things, even things you didn't do. You didn't kill both those people in the Caribbean. According to Derrick, you only took out one."

I didn't even remember what I'd told the now dead Mister Alliance. There was only Warden and the words he was saying... we. That meant they were all okay? "She didn't kill you?"

Reality rushed back into my brain, but it felt more like fantasy. How could this be happening?

"No, she didn't kill us, and we didn't know you thought that. I'm sorry, love." He kissed both my eyes. "Have you eaten or slept?"

They'd brought me food, but I hadn't touched it. "No."

"Okay. We're heading home now. All will be well."

With the knowledge they lived came other problems. "We have to run, and I killed Alyssa. I have to somehow make that okay for Judson and there is no making that okay. I…"

"Judson is not upset with you. Hold on." He grabbed his phone. "We don't need to run. I'll explain it all but first…"

He clicked a button on his phone, and Judson's voice came over the speaker.

"Are you okay? You got her? I know Derrick took him out. That much I've heard. Report. Is she hurt? I'm ready on the plane…

"Jud," Warden interrupted him. "She's okay physically. Maybe a little dehydrated. She hasn't eaten. But she needs to hear from you specifically. She's…"

"Darling," his voice was low over the phone. "I know you were in an impossible situation. We can speak more about it later. But all is well. I promise. I love you."

The tears flowed freely down my cheeks. "Okay, Jud. I… I am sorry. I would never cause you pain and I…"

"Yes. I know. See you in just a few minutes."

Warden disconnected the call. "See? It's okay. And Derrick is too if for some crazy reason you worried about that. He's the one who took out the guy on the street, obviously. There won't be more than that. Things are going to get under control."

There were so many questions in my mind that I couldn't vocalize them all. Instead, I pressed my head down on his shoulder. He was here, and he was okay. His heart was beating.

Warden had always been wonderful about knowing exactly when to be quiet. Right then, he just held me and that was what I needed. I lifted my head. "Who is driving this car?"

He cupped my cheek. "Man's name is Edward Stewart. He works for us now. Well, he sided with us. We've taken back over the Alliance, almost. We've started the process. No war. No schism. The old fashioned way. We're going to make a return to the days of my grandfather. Things will be... civilized and I know it's hypocritical, but I don't mind destroying things to rebuild them right now."

We had people again. And Alyssa was dead. Was any of this possible?

"Come here." He tapped his lap, and I lay down in it, placing my head where his hand had been. He ran his hands through my hair. It was so soothing, so bizarre to feel him alive when he should have been dead. "You're safe, and for the first time, we'll be able to assure that."

"Are we going back to Destin?"

He shook his head. "We're keeping that house. It's yours. We don't really get a say in it. We thought you'd keep it. I couldn't imagine you getting rid of it since Kade gave it to you. But we're all in agreement. We need a headquarters as much as a home. We never thought about it before because he's so private but then..."

I interrupted him. "Are we talking about Vermont? Please don't get me wrong, I love it there. It's stunningly beautiful. But I don't want to hide on an island and never see anyone again. I need a town. Oh, forget it. I'm not getting a say in this. I'm..."

"It's not Vermont," he interrupted me right back. "Montana. We can easily convert Derrick's home into what we need. It's big enough, remote enough. There's a town. And we can have Alliance meetings as needed there."

I loved that house in Montana. "Derrick is okay with that?"

"Haven't you realized that we are always okay with whatever you want? You aren't just... our woman. It's more than that. Something we've all realized. Don't worry about it now. Just rest. We'll all be on the plane together. And things will move from there."

I believed him. Whatever was left to figure out, we would... together.

By the time I got to the plane I'd pulled myself together. I was tired to the point of delirious. If someone had told me that aliens landed and they wanted to give us a one-way ticket to Trace's Mars I would have believed we were on our way there.

Everyone turned when I boarded the plane. Out of the corner of my eye, I saw the pilot I'd met when we'd first returned to Boston. Derrick's pilot. He was here. We had people.

I needed to say something to these five men who had come to mean more to me than anything else. When Warden stepped around me to enter the plane, I finally found my voice. "I'm so glad you're all not dead. So glad."

"The confessing makes sense. She really did believe we were dead." Warden rubbed my back. "But we're all fine. Thanks to Kade. Thanks to Judson. Thanks to finally figuring out what track we're supposed to be on."

Trace was closest and gave me a tight hug. He smelled so good. I pressed my nose closer to him. "Love you."

"Me, too."

I hugged each of them, feeling their strong arms, their presence on the plane with me, their individual natures, the way they filled me up inside. I didn't really care what we did next. I was just so glad we were going to get to do it.

Derrick's home—now all our home—showed in the distance. I leaned forward in the car to get a better look. Next to me, my D smiled. "I think she's glad to be home."

"I am." I still hadn't slept. I'd tried several times on the plane but hadn't gotten there. I wondered if it was possible to get to a place where I wasn't going to have to sleep at all.

The house was as we'd left it the day we'd left to go get Derrick's surgery. Had it been that long? Someone had cleaned it, but he had a company that came and did that. Maybe he'd been home while we'd been separated. But I was struck just the same how nothing had changed within the walls when everything altered elsewhere.

They'd been right. This was where we needed to go.

The rooms were divided up. Derrick had plenty of them, and in the meantime, when he did talk, it was about renovation. He was going to make this place even bigger.

Trace walked over to me, taking my hand. "Come on, beautiful. Let's go take a shower."

That sounded like a wonderful idea. Although, I wasn't sure I could rinse everything that happened off of me, ever.

21

WARDEN

I watched her go upstairs with Trace. Everly was exhausted. I could see it in every move she made and every word she didn't say. This had hit her as hard as anything I'd seen. She thought we were dead, and it had... wounded her to her very soul. I understood. Thinking she was dead would end me. I loved this woman, every ounce of her soul, every thought in her head, every cell on her skin. I loved her until I couldn't think for loving her.

"We're set up." Warden pushed back from his computer. "Firewall is steady, and I don't think we have any direct challenge right now. You should be able to work."

I was going to get us going. The first thing I had to do was stabilize the economy. Everly would like that. She could see that there was good to be done on our end. I'd never been focused on that before but now, if we moved forward the way we wanted to, it had to be with some altruistic ends or we'd never get our girl on board.

And we needed her to buy into this or it wasn't going to work.

We didn't agree on very much except for things that came to Everly. All five of us couldn't have picked a restaurant to eat dinner if we'd had to in order to save the world. But we could make decisions when it came to putting her first, and we could easily do what she told us as if we were born to do so.

I would follow her to the pits of hell and then carry her out when she needed to leave. I'd do anything for her, forever.

There was no question. If we were going to do this, if we were going to be the Alliance so that we could keep the world around us consistent, then she had to lead it. Everly was going to have to lead the Alliance.

I ran a hand through my hair. I really didn't know what she was going to say when we told her. If she said no... this would all fall apart.

EVERLY

The hot water pounded down on me, and I closed my eyes. Trace stepped into the water with me. I hadn't invited him in, but the invitation had been implied given that I hadn't thrown him out of the bathroom when I'd dropped my clothes and gotten under the spray. He pulled me up against his chest and started rubbing shampoo into my hair.

I sighed. There was something so nice about having my hair washed by someone other than me. I'd never get enough of it.

"Tilt your head forward. Keep your eyes closed." I did as he instructed, happy to take direction right now. The shampoo rinsed out of my hair, helped by Trace's gentle hands. When my hair was clean, he washed me with soap. "I like taking care of you. I never get to do this. I'm the one who plots and pushes. But I want to be gentle with you, Everly. I want to love you."

I leaned back, arching my neck until he could kiss my lips. He joined our mouths, and I drowned in the moment as the warm water surrounded us in its embrace. This was our cocoon.

Finally, I pulled back just enough to be able to say the words I needed to say. "I love you, and I know you love me."

Trace scooted around until he sat down on the built-in shower seat on the other end of the shower. He extended his hand, and I took it, walking toward him. His smile was fast. "Do you think Derrick was thinking shower sex when he had this installed in here?"

I shook my head. "He had almost nothing to do with the design of this house. But I certainly love that this is so convenient."

He nodded. "Me, too."

Trace drew me closer to him until I straddled his lap. His hard cock pressed up against the entrance to my pussy, but as we kissed, he made no indication that he wanted to hurry this along. Instead, I stayed right there, straddling his lap while I made love to his mouth.

"I thought you were dead twice now, Trace." I ran my fingers down the side of his face. "So help me, if you do that to me a third time I am going to expire from the worry of it."

He shook his head. "I don't plan to spend a day being away from you, so you won't need to worry about that."

I loved that idea. It was crazy and probably not at all doable. People had to spend days apart, and yet right then it was just what I needed to hear and what I wanted more than anything. I didn't want to be without him or any of the others ever again. It that made me needy, then so be it. I was needy, and I didn't give two fucks.

I reached between us, feeling his cock, running my hand over the top of it. He moaned against my mouth and let go of my back to pinch both my nipples. A jolt of electricity traveled up my spine. "Yes." I didn't say as much as groaned that word. He took that to mean just what he should have and did it again.

I shuddered. I loved the nip of pain right now. It was cleansing like the shower itself, it was bringing me back from that jail cell, from those hours of being in that dark place where they didn't exist anymore.

He replaced his hands with his mouth and sucked. I ground against him. Pain and pleasure mixed together, and he wasn't even inside of me yet. He lifted his hips, pressing harder against me. I panted. I wanted more.

I lifted myself up to grasp his cock hard in my hand. He pulled back to look at me, raising his eyebrows. "Want it?"

"So much." I pressed myself down on him, letting him stretch me, letting him fill me up. I moved quickly. I no sooner had him inside of me before I moved again, pulling out and doing it once more. He moaned. Yes, he liked that and that was just what I wanted. I leaned forward to rub against my clit on one of the passes. I shuddered. This was heaven.

He tugged my head forward until he could reach my lips. I understood what he wasn't saying. I could have it my way... to a point. This was Trace. He wasn't gentle, not even when he was caretaking, and he wanted to kiss, so damn it, I'd better comply.

I was happy to obey because we were going to get off, and it was going to be the sweetest thing ever. We drove into each other, it was like both of us needed to get to a finish line but neither one of us could cross it without the other. I dug my nails into the back of his neck so hard I was sure I would leave a mark. He growled, jerking his hips up one more time. My body burned for release, it practically demanded it.

My breath caught in my throat, and I knew it was happening. I held on for dear life as pleasure seemed to storm through my body, leaving me trembling in its wake. I gasped, biting down on my lips. Inside me, Trace grew impossibly hard a second before he finished.

I collapsed on top of him but he held me to him. Both of us were nothing but limbs and laughter. I loved how it felt to have so much joy post sex that I could do nothing but giggle. Trace bit down on my shoulder, his own laugh a low one.

"You might be trying to send me to an early grave, Everly."

I looked up at him and smiled. "I told you. No more dying."

He nodded. "That's right. Come on. You need to go to bed."

My stomach grumbled. "I need to eat something."

"That, too."

———

By the time I'd choked down a granola bar someone had left by the side of my bed, I was practically asleep sitting up. I turned off the light and drifted. Two people joined me in the bed, and I rolled to the center to accommodate them, hardly waking. I was pretty sure it was Kade and Derrick. Arms tightened around me while someone else pressed my head against his chest. Kade. I recognized the slight cinnamon to his scent.

I tried to open my eyes, to tell them how much I loved them being there, when I heard a door open and close. One of the others was coming. I really wanted to...

Derrick put a hand on my head. "Sleep, Evs. Nothing to do until tomorrow when there will be lots to do."

"Need anything? I just came to check." It was Warden's low voice.

I didn't need a thing. Just more of this, so much more.

With wakefulness came clarity. I'd no sooner opened my eyes than the reality of something hit me hard. Next to me, Derrick breathed deeply. Kade was also out cold and my head was still against his chest. He snored lightly. I hated to move either of them, but given that I'd just realized it had been days and days since I'd taken the pill and Trace and I had just... yep. No condom.

Kade lifted his head, staring down at me. "Something wrong?"

I kissed him. "Might have gotten myself pregnant last night."

He blinked. "Really?"

Derrick tightened his arms around me. "That would be okay, Everly. Things are going to be different now. You're going to be safe. Baby would be safe, too."

Neither of them was freaking out or even bothered about this. "Guys, I was shot at yesterday."

"Yes, but now things have changed." Kade got out of bed. "You have to have this explained, and I guess talk to Trace? There are things to do about this if you don't want the baby. We'd need a... what is it called?"

"Morning after pill," Derrick got out of bed. "Do you want that, Evs? Up to you?"

This was a lot. "I want coffee."

And, no, I didn't actually want a morning after pill. But I did want to... discuss this. And probably with Trace, since this wasn't actually Derrick's or Kade's responsibility. Except that we were all doing this together in this still-undefined-in-how-the-fuck-was-it-going-to-work relationship we were in. I might not even be pregnant. This was way ahead of itself.

I got out of bed and managed to pee and brush my teeth before Trace knocked on the door of the bathroom. When I opened the door, he leaned against it. "We forgot."

"Which one of them ran out to tell you?"

He shrugged. "Derrick. How are you about this?"

"Well, first off, I've already dismissed the morning after pill idea. I don't know why. I just don't want to."

Trace nodded. "That's entirely your choice."

"Right. And... I might not be pregnant so this is neither here nor there. Truly. But everyone keeps saying we could keep the baby safe. They didn't even seem disturbed by the idea?"

Trace put out his hand. "Come out and we'll explain. Have some breakfast. It's too early to worry, but the thing is, gorgeous, if this happened, if you got pregnant, it will be more than okay. I never thought about kids other than I should have one to continue on my Alliance reign. But other than that? I didn't care. I would... love this. So if it happens? We call it a surprise not an accident."

I liked that a lot. I wasn't a woman who had accidents... but life sure did like to take me by surprise.

I pulled my knees to my chest and watched the guys doing their best to stay busy while they waited for me to ingest coffee. If I could, I'd have put it in an IV and injected it straight into my veins. I took another long sip of the life affirming liquid and set it down on the coffee table in front of me. I did love the view of the mountains and the lake through the window. It was peaceful here.

Judson strode toward me then settled on the couch. "Hey."

"Hi." He was the first person to speak since Trace and I had worked out our pseudo-plan in the bathroom. This was going to turn out to be much ado about nothing. I couldn't fathom being someone's mother. I knew next to nothing about babies and the five of them didn't seem like child people either.

He put his hand on my knee and squeezed. I leaned my head down on his shoulder. "You and I should talk about what happened."

"We should and will but first we have to make a conference call."

That seemed rather out of left field. "What kind of conference call?"

Kade strode over and sat on the other side of me. He placed his ever-present laptop down next to my coffee cup. "The kind that will re-establish order in the universe, so to speak, and set us up so that we're not in constant danger every day."

"This sounds like the stuff of fairytales, guys."

Trace nodded. "I could see why you'd think that. But when our grandfathers were in power, no one behaved like they have been. The old Council is gone. Alyssa and her background interference is over thanks to you, and it's time to return to that."

I sighed. "If you think you can make that happen, then go for it."

Warden and Derrick looked at each other. It was my W

who spoke. "We'll announce our intent to take leadership. Everyone wants a return to civility."

Derrick shook his head. "Everyone wants Warden to make the markets make sense again. They want Kade to secure their identities online. They want Trace to set direction for the agenda, for Judson to be a voice of reason."

Judson shrugged. "They want Derrick to be in control of the killers. They want us."

"Then do it." Sounded great to me. Then I just had to figure out how to make any of this work and what I was going to do with the rest of my life.

Kade nodded. "Connecting the call now. It's not so much a call as it's a speech. Judson will talk and then you will, Evy."

Wait. What? I turned toward him. "Why would I talk?"

"Well, you're going to lead the Alliance."

I put my hand on his arm. "Disconnect that now."

"It's not connected yet. I thought you might want clarification." He winked at me. Why did he have to be so adorable when he was being an asshat?

"Everly." Judson squeezed my knee again. "You are a natural leader. You brought us all together. You can do that for the Alliance. You make good plans, see things through many lenses. You're not afraid of violence, but it isn't your go-to solution. You are the one who pointed out to me that day that there were big problems in the world. Homeless who needed help, specifically. You can think about them. And then turn around and execute the fucker who betrays us. Or order it. Trust us, Everly, we didn't come to this lightly. You'll be good at this."

I ran my hand over my face. "They'll never accept it, and I disagree. I made terrible choices when it came to Alyssa. You guys could have been killed."

Trace continued. "But we weren't because Kade is smart. Because we trusted each other. Because he saved all of our lives. We did that because of you, because you told us we had to be loyal to each other, and we are all happy to listen to you." I didn't know that story and wanted to hear it sometime. "And we blasted our way out. We're not asking you to do this alone. There was no good way to handle Alyssa. Period. It was completely out of control. None of us saw that coming."

Judson rubbed his eyes. "My sister... listen, we can talk about that later. No one blames you and we all got out of there alive. We're taking that for a win. We need you, Everly. We can't do this without you, and I don't want to think of the world without us taking control. Things are rapidly spiraling down into hell. We can fix it." He squeezed my knee. "I know we can, and I trust you. You can trust you."

That was exactly what I needed to hear. I could trust me. When had I stopped doing that? Was it before or after Alyssa? Had I ever, really? I'd certainly faked confidence well enough the last years, acting like I was sure of myself. But they'd all seen through that a lot.

"I can't be allowed to make decisions that could hurt people."

Warden walked over and kneeled down in front of me. He placed his arms on my lap, which made Jud move his hand off my knee but Judson didn't indicate that he minded. "There are five people on the council. If it works appropriately, no one makes decisions alone. We're not mindless drones, we're not Alyssa and Ben's fucked up followers. We won't let you hurt people unless they need to be hurt."

This was all a moot point. "They'll never go for it."

Derrick winked at me. "They will. And it's time that they did."

"Wait a minute, you said five. There are six of us." Basic arithmetic was something I could do even if the rest of my mind had taken a hard left turn to confused-ville.

Derrick nodded. "I don't want a seat. Consider me the behind the scenes guy who has your back. That is part of what we'll do to ensure this. No one will fuck with us. Trust us, Everly. I know you can go that far. We trust you."

That was really what it came down to. Did I trust them to know what they were talking about? I did. This might blow up in our faces, but they'd clearly thought this through while I'd been in custody. That reminded me I needed to ask Kade a question. "The recordings of me shooting Alyssa?"

"Gone." He waved his hand. "Almost as soon as I got to a computer. Could probably have done that from my phone if I'd had it."

I tilted my head. "And Mercer?"

"Made bad choices." A muscle ticked in his jaw, so I was going to leave that alone, for now. He hit a button on the computer. "Connecting us now."

"We're doing this remotely?" I asked the question of anyone who wanted to answer me.

"For now." Warden kissed me before he spoke. "Going to put on a bit of a show. You'll know what to do. It's all audio. For now."

Kade nodded at Judson who sat forward. "This is Judson Smythe. Coming to you from our home in Montana. We're here because five of us are taking control of the Alliance unless another five would like to stand up and challenge for the right to do so."

Why had they bothered with in person meetings if this was possible? I chewed on my lip and answered my own question. The old Council had wanted them. There was no Council and no one else's rules of protocol to follow.

I stared at the screen. This was broadcasting to a thousand listeners. Was that how people were in the Alliance worldwide? And they wanted me to... lead them?

"Judson," an accented voice—maybe French?—answered him. "This is Luc Matisse."

Judson nodded. "Challenging, Luc?"

"Non," the answer came fast. "I am simply questioning the documents that have come across my desktop. Am I reading this correctly? You propose to have her sit with you on the Council? This is unheard of. We have a policy of no women in the Alliance."

It was Trace who answered. "Luc, this is Trace Hill. There is nothing in the documents anywhere excluding women. I've been through them with a fine tooth comb." He shook his head. He was lying? He hadn't done that? Why? Again, the answer dawned on me. We had those documents. These guys had gone into those lockers and taken things. They had been busy—ridiculously so—in the last two days. "Remember what year it is, brother. Time for us to get with the times. The Marrs have been in the family forever. They have deep Alliance roots and Everly has shown herself loyal time and again when there was no need for her to do so, considering we keep trying to kill her."

"Well, you don't keep trying to kill her." A voice I didn't know but clearly Warden did because he rolled his eyes at it. "My understanding is the five of you are sleeping with her. And where is Derrick Norris on this list? Aren't you some kind of unit now?"

"I don't want leadership, Klaus. Never did. But I will fight and kill for this council, including Everly. This is a done deal. It's not up for discussion. You can attack if you want or we can return to the civility of our grandfathers and get back to building our fortunes. Is anyone else sick of this bullshit? We want to let you live your lives."

"But a woman..." this Klaus person started until Derrick interrupted him again.

"Hell, man. Is your penis so small you can't stand the idea

that one woman will have a one-fifth vote on the Council? I mean... fuck."

"Okay," I interrupted before this continued. "We don't need this to degrade to that level right now. I am the afore-mentioned Everly. I think you've all heard of me before. Judson mentioned me quite a bit in the last speech he made." My J winced at that, and I squeezed his hand. "My family traces its Alliance roots back to the beginning. I know because I've seen the documents. I did that when I was in the vault earlier this week with Alyssa Smythe Norris. You guys don't know this, but you have been, for years now, taking your orders from a woman."

There was dead silence at my announcement. Kade turned to look at me, his brows lifted in question. I'd done this. I had to continue. "It seems ridiculous to me that things have to be done in secret within a secret society. Would you prefer to have me hidden, and your so-called leaders nothing but puppets and conmen or know that the people in charge are upfront with who they are and who they listen to? Yes, I am sleeping with all five of them. Yes, we are a unit. But I can tell you that we agree on very little and all have different agendas when it comes to the world. Your needs will be met. All you have to do is let your ego go and ask yourself if some of you would prefer your family legacy be continued on by your first-born daughter over some of your sons? I'd imagine some of you have very smart women in your family. Kind of annoying that you can't pass on to her what you built, isn't it?"

Silence met my query, which meant I was either reaching them or they'd all given up on listening to me because I was a woman.

"This isn't negotiable. I'm doing this. Derrick is not pursuing a spot on the Council, but make no mistake, he's here. And so are his assassins."

Judson spoke again. "Our goal is to return things to the

way they were and move us forward. With a yes vote today, Warden will stabilize the financial markets, and I will make sure our secrets go back to where they belong, underground. You have an hour to decide."

Kade turned off the connection.

All right... so that happened.

22

The votes came back eighty percent in favor of us. I ate the chocolate I'd decided was my new best friend in this era of one crazy thing after another and stared at the screen. "Is that a good number?"

"We needed more than fifty percent so, yes, a good one." Trace walked over to the computer and stared at the readout again. "The twenty percent that voted no will be watched, but they don't have even close to majority and I think they will back off as soon as the markets regulate. Warden?"

My W nodded and sat down at his own monitor. I'd seen Warden in concentration mode enough to know I wouldn't be hearing from him for hours until he came up for food or alcohol. I loved that I knew these sorts of things about him.

"I'm going to sit down and start going over the agenda people want for themselves. They're already coming in." Trace looked up at me. "You should get on this later. Take a breath and look later."

That was a good idea. I'd gone along with this, and now I had to figure out how to wade into these waters without drowning. Only time would tell how I did.

Judson rose. "Come with me for a second?"

I got off the couch and followed him from the room. Where were we going? We'd no sooner left the living room than he pressed me against the wall of the hallway.

He breathed hard, his intakes and exhales coming fast. I stayed still, loving the feel of his body against mine, the wall behind me, his gaze making me feel naked, exposed. "You okay?"

Judson shook his head. "Not even close to okay."

"I don't see how you could be." I ran my hands over his arms, feeling his muscles beneath my fingers. "Judson, I..."

He shook his head. "I can't fathom what happened, I can't begin to tell you how I..."

"Stop." He kissed my cheek, leaving his forehead pressed to mine. "I don't blame you."

"Judson, some day you will. There will come a time where you will suddenly feel that I'm just the woman who killed your sister."

He kissed me again. "Never."

JUDSON

I had to concentrate on breathing. Being pushed up against Everly helped. Any time I was near Everly she quieted my discomfort. That was a lot of pressure to put on another person so I wasn't going to tell her, but how I loved her went beyond reason for me. I needed her, I needed to make sure she was okay, that she had what she needed. And her presence quieted my demons, of which there was a much larger one present these days.

She thought there would come a time when I blamed her?

No. I should have been down on my knees begging her forgiveness for what my family had put her through.

I had to say something. She was waiting for me to tell her something, to explain any of my thoughts. "I think I'm going to pretend she stayed dead. Denial and delusions are okay when one is playing the it-didn't-happen game, right?"

Everly leaned her head to the side in the way that she sometimes did that showed off her long neck. I ran my finger down it, and she shuddered. "Jud, you can't do that. You know that."

"Honestly, it feels like losing her again. But worse in some ways because this tarnished all of my memories of her at the same time. Did I ever know her? Not since we were young. If even then. We were twins. Now, I have to lose her again but I hate her so it's... complicated."

She twisted her lips, pain evident in her gaze as she stared at me. "I love you, Judson. I'd not hurt you for anything in the universe."

I let out a breath I'd been holding. "You'll never know how much that helps. I love you, too. You... helped me be the person I always wanted to be. We'll remember that people need help, we'll remember that together."

She wrapped her arms around me and she held on. My Everly. She was home. We were all going to make it.

EVERLY

Weeks had passed since I'd slid into an Alliance role I'd never thought to have. My period was late, but I could hardly concentrate on it other than to ask Derrick to get me a pregnancy test from the store when he'd gone out. He had returned with one and it waited for me to go look at the results. It had been more than the few minutes I was supposed to wait to check.

My attention was actually on the scene in front of me. We were all on separate laptops. Kade was doing this from the back of the house where he'd set up his office and the rest of us were strewn around the living room.

A man I'd never met before spoke into his own monitor. The Alliance had modernized and not just because they had one woman out of a thousand now, but because the constant need for meetings was over. We could just take the call over the computer and we didn't have to get near them at all. If there was dirty work to be done, and so far there hadn't been, Derrick could either go handle it or send someone to do so.

I listened intently, although this was really more of Warden's purview. "So what you're saying is that you want Alliance help in acquiring the land?"

"I want them," the man from Texas on the video call said, "to eliminate our competition. I'll repay by putting a portion of the proceeds from the development, back into Alliance pockets. Maybe for Trace's next Mars project."

He technically didn't have one yet, but everyone we spoke to seemed pretty preoccupied with the idea that Trace would green light anything if someone said the word Mars. Despite this opinion, he didn't fall down every rabbit hole related to the word Mars.

"By eliminate, you mean what?" I sipped my water and waited for that response. "We aren't interested in killing non-Alliance people, if that is what you mean. Now, helping to turn their attention elsewhere might be something we could work on."

The man nodded fast. "I don't want anyone dead. I wouldn't have asked the old Council for that reason. But maybe you could help."

Judson nodded. I didn't think he really cared one way or

another. Warden was in favor of it. Trace would be intrigued on the turning attention part of this plan. Kade probably didn't care unless it was tech related. I tilted my head to consider this. "The town closest to the land? How is it doing economically?"

He opened and closed his mouth. "Not much to it. Population is mostly in agriculture, and it's failing."

"Well..." Now I had an angle here. "You are going to do something for them. Invest in the town. Let's see how you can take some of that know how you have to help some of those people. Come back with results in a month. I know time is of the importance. If you can prove the way you helped, you'll have a yes in a month which should give you six months of time for us to help you."

He rapidly blinked. I hoped he wasn't about to have an aneurysm. "Okay. I'll do that."

"Great. See you then."

Our connection died, Kade obviously turning it off. Judson laughed. It was a sudden sound and not one he made very often, considering he was in mourning and also disbelief at the same time, a problematic combination.

"He just shit himself. Well done." Judson got up. "I don't think we'll have to kill anyone over this."

We ended every Alliance conversation this way. Did we have to kill anyone? So far it was no, but I knew better than to think that was permanent.

The guys were figuring out their place in life. Derrick spent his days designing how he was going to improve and expand the house. There was going to be a second one with even more bedrooms and bathrooms.

Kade was still working on his hide-from-the-satellite device, and he'd reopened his tech consulting company. No one knew it was Kade's. There were a million steps between him and the client, but it was his. Warden was busy. He'd opened a new fund and was getting things straightened in the world economy. The news talked a lot about natural correction, and in a way it was. Warden was naturally meant to be doing this. Trace had Mars ahead of him. With a list of ten investors, he was less interested in making them a mark as he was in selling others to the idea. If he wanted to go back to teaching, he'd not said that yet.

Judson went out looking for real estate. He was going to open a clinic, one where patients would travel for plastic surgery and stay during recovery. It would be luxury with nothing else around it. I was glad he had something to think about other than the things that made him preoccupied.

As for me, I didn't have the slightest idea what I'd do with my life. I sighed. Much of it had to do with whatever was going to happen when I looked in the bathroom and saw the lines on the pregnancy test.

I rose, and Judson grabbed my arm. "I finally have your college graduation present."

I blinked. "What?"

"Your college present. Everyone has gotten you something but me."

I had completely forgotten. Yes, I owned a car, a yacht, and a house. And diamonds I was afraid to wear but I'd put on some time for Derrick because he really did want to see me naked with just them around my neck.

"I told you, Jud. I didn't... Oh, you've already done it. What did you get me?"

He wrapped his arms around my waist. "No more basements."

Now that didn't make any sense. "There are always going to be..."

"No." He held me close. "No more of our people holding people hostage. It's illegal. I made it a directive and everyone, as far as I can tell, has released their prisoners. I can't promise it'll never happen again, but right now at this second, everyone is free. No more basements."

I didn't expect the tears, but they came, hot and streaming, from my eyes. He'd done this. Hell, there was no way he'd done it alone. I looked around the room. They were all there. Each of them would have had to have played a role in Judson's gift.

I couldn't form words, but I held him tightly in my arms as I shook. That was a beautiful legacy. "Thank you."

He kissed my lips. "The guys helped me. I needed info only they could give me, although it was my idea. These are good tears, right?"

I sucked in a breath. "Yes. Good tears."

"Great." He gave me a wobbly smile.

Judson passed me on to Derrick who kissed my forehead and then my nose. "This really was all Judson. We just got in touch with people. It was Judson who thought to have Kade tap into Mercer's old programs to find out who had who where."

They were all so much smarter than I was. I turned toward Kade who embraced me hard. "Judson remembered how much you wanted this, and I was happy to help."

Trace laughed, and I let go of my K to kiss him on the mouth. "I didn't personally want to empty the basement. You know me. I'm so fine with torture."

I pinched him, and he laughed, which just left Warden. He pushed my tears away with his thumbs. "Why the tears?"

"I finally feel like we might be okay. If there are moments when we can personally make it so there aren't people locked in the basement for the Alliance, then maybe there is hope after all."

And there had to be. Because that pregnancy test in the bathroom? It had two pink lines.

TWELVE YEARS LATER.

I wasn't really listening to what the idiot on the other side of the room blathered on about. I didn't need to. I already knew what he'd say. We had the proof he'd been stealing from the Alliance for over a year to the amount of four million dollars. Warden was pissed. There was nothing he disliked more than when an accounting ledger didn't add up.

And to have it be one of his own people? That was awful.

We were in a safe house—Warden, Derrick, and me—going through the motions of listening to this man. It really was ridiculous. He didn't seem to have an excuse. He just wanted it.

My mind drifted. It was the middle of February and even though the weather in Montana was cold, I'd much rather have been home with our family than here with this idiot.

We'd only been gone a matter of hours, and soon this would be over and I'd be back home with them again, even if we lived in a perpetual state of chaos brought onto us by the constant noise our five daughters between the ages of three and eleven caused.

I wouldn't change a thing.

I'd had enough. Thinking about the girls meant I wanted to be home with them.

"Mr. DayHarb, did you or didn't you steal from the Alliance? Taking money that was set up for the use of our members in pursuit of their families' empires for your own good without permission?"

He stuttered. I guessed I was scarier than Warden. "I d-did."

I pulled out my gun. "That was a very poor decision. I tell my kids all the time, it's important to make good choices and this? This was a terrible one. Decisions and choices have repercussions and yours is that you are going to die. I'm not sorry. The good news that you can carry to the great beyond is that we won't take this out on your offspring. Your son will inherit his rightful spot in about forty-five seconds."

"They never should have let women into the Alliance. It's a disgrace."

Oh, that old chestnut. Misogyny died hard. But Jim DayHarb did not.

I raised my gun.

The sounds of little girls screaming greeted us as we stepped from the cold wind blowing outside into our warm, light filled home.

"Mommy!" Monica stormed through the door. At eleven and the oldest she was rather sure of her place in the world. It probably didn't hurt that her first two years in life she'd only been set down when she wanted to be and had otherwise ruled over all of us like she'd been born to do so.

She looked like Trace, even if he insisted she looked like me.

I ran my hand through her hair. We hadn't cut it in a year. She was overdue, but she didn't want it and Monica did tend to get what she wanted. But then again so did all the girls.

"Mommy," she tried again. "Alexandra took my brush, and she hid it. I know she did and she won't confess."

She probably had. Judson's daughter was nothing if not sneaky and almost from birth had set out to drive her big sister crazy. If only Monica understood that all Alex wanted was her adoration and attention.

I shook my head. "I'll talk to her."

Monica sighed dramatically. "She's so *annoying*."

Alexandra sat on the counter across the house. When she saw me, she grinned, showing teeth. Yes, she'd taken the brush. I'd get it back, but I'd probably have to negotiate with her for it.

"Hey..." Her father walked up, kissing me on the lips. "Go ahead."

"The transaction is handled." Warden kissed me on the cheek, stepping by. "Everly was very helpful and Derrick wasn't going to let anything bad happen."

My D shrugged. "You never do know."

That was true. We'd learned that over the years. Better safe than sorry. His daughter, Reese, spun in a circle, singing to herself in the middle of the living room. She was always happy, and it was beautiful to witness. Derrick kissed Monica on the head before he scooped up Reese and went to see the others.

Where were the littles? As if on cue, the youngest two, Warden's daughter, Deborah, and the baby Aria, who was Kade's, rushed into the living room. They were five and three, both of them dressed in unicorn costumes.

I stood there and watched. This was *mine*. If Ben hadn't taken me under Alyssa's direction, I'd never have had this. We would have all broken up. Or maybe I'd have seen one or two of them until it fell apart. I couldn't have been the person who had this if I hadn't lived through Ben's basement.

My five Letters gathered in the middle. They were talking about their days. I listened, but it was more like I watched them. We'd spent over a decade together and there were still times I couldn't believe I got to have this. That the pitfalls and near misses and the pain ended with this.

Oh, I wouldn't recommend how we'd met to anyone as a dating strategy. But these were my Letters. Derrick. Judson. Kade. Trace. Warden. My forever loves. And our family. We'd fight to keep it, run the Alliance until we could pass it off safely, if ever, and protect each other until our dying breaths. I'd never imagined leading a secret organization older than time but there it was, also mine.

My loves. My daughters. My secrets to keep. All mine.

I was Everly Marrs. I'd fought to be the woman I'd become. Lover. Mother. Killer. Leader. I could wield a gun, ending betrayers, and then come home to help with math homework and assist in cooking dinner. I knew how to blackmail, to coerce, to protect, to destroy, and to build better futures. I was all those things. I stepped forward into the crowd that was my family.

This might not have been everyone's happy ending, but I loved it—messy and dirty like it was. This was beautiful.

"What are we doing tonight? Anyone want to order pizza?"

AFTERWORD

Thank you so much for reading the Kiss Her Goodbye series. I was sad to say goodbye to Everly but I loved writing her and I hope you agree I gave her a happy ending through the darkness, even if its still not all flowers and light in her world. How could it ever be?

I hope you'll come and check out some of my other works! Have you read...

My completed contemporary RH series, called Reverse Harem Story? https://amzn.to/2HYbnWL

My completed paranormal RH series called Last Hope? https://amzn.to/2HJtyjL

My almost done Science Fiction romance series called Wings of Artemis? https://amzn.to/2HK4OYP

My completed male/female shifter series called Westervelt Wolves? https://amzn.to/2Un6MnW

My ongoing werewolf series called Fallen Alpha? https://amzn.to/2HMu7JI

My completed young adult series called The Warrior? https://amzn.to/2UgJRdz

I've been writing for ten years and I have over 80 books published, having written for a decade. I'd love for you to check out the rest of my work. And to come join my readers' group: https://www.facebook.com/groups/rebeccasrandomness

Please turn the page for a complete list of my books. –RR

ABOUT THE AUTHOR

As a teenager, I would hide in my room to read my favorite romance novels when I was supposed to be doing my homework.

I am the mother of three adorable boys and I am fortunate to be married to my best friend. I live in Austin Texas where I am determined to eat all the barbecue in town.

I am in love with science fiction, fantasy, and the paranormal and try to use all of these elements in my writing. I've been told I'm a little bloodthirsty so I hope that when you read my work you'll enjoy the action packed ride that always ends in romance. I love to write series because I love to see characters develop over time and it always makes me happy to see my favorite characters make guest appearances in other books.

In my world anything is possible, anything can happen, and you should suspect that it will.

I'd love to hear from you! Please visit my website at www.rebeccaroyce.com to sign up for my newsletter and learn about my books!

Here's where you can find me online:

Rebecca's Randomness Reading Group https://www.facebook.com/groups/RebeccasRandomness/

https://www.rebeccaroyce.com

https://www.facebook.com/authorrebeccaroyce/

www.twitter.com/rebeccaroyce

Instagram: rebeccaroyce79

MeWe: RebeccaRoyce
Cheers!!
Rebecca

Eternal

Always

Evermore

Endless

Wards and Wands

Hexed and Vexed

Curse Reversed

Meow, Baby (novella, co-written with Ripley Proserpina)

Tragic Magic (Coming Soon)

Safe Haven

Everywhere and Nowhere

Dimension X (coming soon)

More coming soon....

Soul Bound

Prisoner of the Dragons

More coming soon....

Shadow Promised

Strange Days

Weird Nights

Bizarre Years

More coming soon...

The Warrior (completed series)

Initiation

Driven

Subversive

Redemption

Justice

Warrior World (spin off of The Warrior, completed series)

Deacon

Micah

Jason

The Westervelt Wolves (completed series)

Her Wolf

Summer's Wolf

Wolf Reborn

Wolf's Valentine

Wolf's Magic

Alpha Wolf

Angel's Wolf

Darkest Wolf

Lone Wolf

Fallen Alpha

Alpha Rising

Alpha's Strength

Alpha's Sacrifice

Alpha's Truth

Alpha Enticing

Hidden Alpha (coming soon)

The Capes (completed series)

Seductive Powers

Adrenaline Rush

Last Ascension

The Conditioned

Eye Contact

Embraced

Unlawful (coming soon...)

The Outsiders

Love Beyond Time

Love Beyond Sanity

Love Beyond Loyalty

Love Beyond Sight

Love Beyond Expectations

Love Beyond Oceans

Love Beyond Flames

Love Beyond Lies (coming soon)

Cascade (completed series)

Haunted Redemption

Phoenix Everlasting

Fragility Unearthed

Persuasion Enraptured

Reverse Harem Story (completed series)

Unconventional

Unexpected

Undeniable

Kiss Her Goodbye

Hard Truths

Dark Truths

Deadly Truths

Shifter World

Planet Bear

Planet Wolf (coming soon)

Stand Alone Titles

Under The Lights

No Quitting Allowed

Mr. Wrong

Bite Marks

Bitten Surrender

The Vampire and The Virgin

Demon Within

Crimson Lust

Call Me Crazy

The Storm (writing with Ripley Proserpina**)**

Lightning Strikes

Thunder Rolling

The Deluge (coming soon)